River Current

River Current

M. Lee Martin

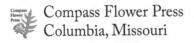 Compass Flower Press
Columbia, Missouri

Cover art by Aubrey Bildner

Published by
Compass Flower Press
Columbia, Missouri

Library of Congress Control Number: 2021901971
ISBN: 978-1-951960-14-8 Trade Paperback
ISBN: 978-1-951960-15-5 Ebook

Dedicated to my mother, Ramona, the "Phyllis" of my heart.

Chapter 1

The Current River runs clear and inviting, dark and mysterious deep in the hills of southern Missouri. The river is spring fed and watercress billows bright green against colorful river rock under its crystal current where the waters run shallow. In the deep parts, dark green and bone-chilling, the water swirls in bewildering undercurrents, confusing anyone unlucky enough to find themselves amongst its rocky depths after a jump from the tall cliffs that border the river.

River Leap is one such place along the river, a few miles west of the small town of Westfall, Missouri. It is a park on the river bank where families picnic, roasting hotdogs and eating watermelon and enjoying the coolness of the river during hot summer days. Here the river park ascends to a high rocky bluff—an exhilaration of height where teenage boys, having taken leave of their senses, dare each other to jump from the highest rock. The rocks at this part of River Leap are a jumbled mass of tall boulders—some rounded, some jagged, a few flat and slippery, providing perfect ledges from which to jump or be pushed. Tommy O'Rourke found himself one of the unlucky ones when, amid foolhardy whoops from his friends, he ran off the highest ledge, slipping and losing his balance at the last second and careening down into the river, hitting his head on a low rock hazardously projecting out from the others. The yells suddenly silenced as the boys leaned out from the rock ledge and anxiously looked down at the water rippling out from where Tommy had gone in. After a few moments he didn't appear, and several boys clambered down to the water. There were shouts and dives and minutes passed and still no Tommy surfaced. The commotion began to attract the attention of the adults who were sunning in a safer part of the park, where the river bank stretched wide and flat and the current slowed as it ran over river stones in the shallows.

It was Herbert Williams, the high school history teacher, who dove in and finally found Tommy. His body had been wedged between two boulders deep down in the shadowed green river waters. Herbert might not have found him at all had it not been for the tendril of blood sending out an inky trail in the water. Herbert pulled but couldn't get Tommy free. He swam to the surface gasping for breath, yelled "I found him," then dove down again, followed by two other boys. After much tugging on Tommy's pale limp arms, amid shouts to one another that were muffled beneath the water and bubbled up unanswered, Tommy was freed and his bleeding body was hauled up to the surface. He was carried over to the river bank across the stones and laid down on the grass. Mr. Jenkins, owner of Jenkins Shoes and Leather Goods down on Main Street, began pushing on his chest. Tommy's lips were blue and his face and chest were smeared in river water mixed with blood from a gash in his head. Some of the children began to whimper; his friends stood in shock. Mrs. Stultz ran to her car and drove into town to get help.

Tommy was declared dead, and Tommy's mother yelled and cried at city hall to do something about that place up at River Leap Park to keep crazy teenage boys from jumping off those dangerous rocks. A "Keep Off the Rocks" sign was posted at the top, but it was soon stolen. A fence was tried but was eventually pulled down. Parents read the riot act to their sons, insisting they stay off the rocks. Some did, some disobeyed. That was in 1946, and soon time passed and the memory of Tommy O'Rourke was only a ghost story whispered at sleepovers and camp outs. The tale stretched to include other untimely and gruesome deaths at that particular rock outcropping—some maybe true, some maybe not.

Time moved on. Teenage boys didn't really get any smarter, but maybe there was something in the way of caution handed down to younger children, because by 1956, which is when this story begins, though boys still jumped off the rocks now and then, there hadn't been another jumping-off-the-rocks-and-dying incident that anyone could truly recall for a while. Maybe it was only a matter of time.

To this day, the large rocks and ledges for which River Leap Park got its name remain, the river still runs cold and dark and deep at that point of the outcroppings, and the current continues to swirl green and ghostly, no doubt hiding all manner of secrets.

Chapter 2

1975

Ray Bellamy pondered the letter he held in his hand along with the sad and interesting fact of how life seemed to circle around and kick you in the ass when you least expected it. Mrs. Viola Meeks, dearly beloved benefactor and guardian angel from Ray's childhood, had died. Her son Jackson had called him the night before to tell him the news, and Ray had sat alone in his large front room most of the night, missing and mourning this lovely woman.

The letter had arrived this morning, special delivery from the estate lawyer, and it explained that Viola had left him her house. A fine thing except for the fact that the house was located in the small Missouri town of Westfall, where all manner of bad things had happened in Ray's childhood—deserting mother, alcoholic father, cheating girlfriend, best-friend betrayal, and a bullying local deputy who had Barney Fife syndrome. That was back in 1957, some eighteen years ago. Common sense allowed for the obvious deduction that visiting the town to claim Mrs. Meeks's sweet but unassuming house might not be altogether worth it.

The only part of the whole town that really meant anything to Ray was Mrs. Meeks herself and her prized imported hydrangeas, planted and tended by both himself and Viola at a time when her motherly care toward him was a rare and precious thing. That was just about the only sweet memory he cared to conjure up when he thought of Westfall or its inhabitants or their houses.

And the river, he thought. Contrary to the people of the town, the river was a steady force of nature to be both enjoyed and respected. Its consistent dependability, its power and beauty were the reasons Ray loved the river so much.

Ray looked out the window that made up an entire wall of his beautiful home and took in the picturesque view of Kentucky Lake; he was pleased with the rich lushness that surrounded him. Here and now in 1975, he was doing very well thanks to those prize imported hydrangeas and Viola's love and guidance. Eighteen years and hundreds of miles had served well to put time and distance between Ray and the town and its dysfunctional players.

And yet . . . he was curious. *Maybe some of the folks had changed?* Ray pondered this intrigue with uncertainty. He didn't know for sure because he had left them all behind, but he was pretty certain that, except for Mrs. Meeks, none of them had improved upon their sorry states in life. He rubbed across a scar on his forearm left from an altercation with that loathsome Deputy Westley Culpepper to prove his point.

But still . . . he did this sometimes. Wondered. How were they doing? Would they remember him? Would they care? They had cared at one time. At least some of them. Lydia Campbell and Shane Cooper and Shane's little brother Sam had all been his friends once. They had all loved each other once. Someone had once told him he had a propensity to romanticize the past. A bad habit that kept you hoping.

Ray tossed the letter onto the counter. *Fuck romance. And fuck Westfall too.* The town had never done right by him. Life was hard and people betrayed you. No need to start thinking that people could really and honestly love you. However . . . a sweet old lady with skin the color of coffee who had long ago showed him some tenderness and how to grow pink and purple flowers had once made him think so. He sighed and shook his head. He was only fooling himself.

Walking down the sleek hardwood floors in the hall, he reached up to the top shelf in the closet and pulled down a box and brought it to the granite counter in the large and airy kitchen. Letters from Mrs. Meeks. She had been good at sending him letters with news of the comings and goings of Westfall throughout the years, although he would have sworn to anybody he didn't give a damn. He thumbed through the envelopes, seeing Mrs. Meeks's lacy handwriting, and found the one he was looking for, dated several years back. Then it hit him. Viola was gone. Viola was dead. He pulled the envelope out of the box and held it up, and his eyes began to sting with tears and memories of long ago. He cradled the letter to his cheek, his face wrinkling in sadness, and the tears began to fall.

He'd had Viola and her son Jackson and his wife and their kids out to his place twice since it was built. He loved showing it off and thanked Viola a million times over for her being the reason that he was so successful. He hadn't seen Mrs. Meeks in over three years. That was when they'd met at Cape Girardeau. She'd written to say she'd be there for a family reunion in April. Ray would be in town at the same time for the Mid-America Growers Association conference, so they met for breakfast. She had looked good and it felt good to have her hug him. It felt good to hug her back. He hadn't known then that it would be the last time he'd see her. Time had just gotten away from him. How had he let that happen?

He drew a sad breath, sniffed, and lowered the envelope from his face. He pulled the letter from the envelope, dated November 9, 1966, and flipped to the second page, second paragraph. He knew exactly what he was looking for, the exact line; he'd read it some two or three hundred times by now. He'd almost torn up the letter after reading that line, but he'd kept it. Maybe he enjoyed being punished.

As you may have heard, Lydia married the Cooper boy.

One line. At the time he'd read it, it had struck him like a hammer slamming into his chest. His breath had actually stopped and stuck. His lungs, the muscles in his chest and throat, froze. Then something clicked, and instead of freezing up, everything started rushing at him at a hundred miles an hour. His heart began to race; the room swirled. Maybe he had hoped he'd been wrong about his once-girlfriend Lydia Campbell and once-best friend Shane Cooper. Maybe he'd questioned his abrupt leaving those many years back. But there, in black and white, was sure and certain evidence of betrayal. Lydia and Shane waited just long enough after he had left town to make it look respectable.

Now he wiped at his tears and blew out his breath. He laid the old, crinkly letter on the counter next to the new letter from Mrs. Meeks's lawyer and studied them. Then he shook his head and went over to his liquor cabinet and studied the bottles of fine wines, brandies, and bourbons, all favorites and freely flowing for visiting friends, a string of girlfriends that never lasted, deck parties, and holidays. He pulled out a bottle of whiskey and poured a splash of amber liquor into a lead crystal glass and studied it. The rainbow twinkling from the glass's many facets was proof that he had made it. He had risen above all that small-town nonsense. He was wealthy—in friends, social life, travels, and finances. Ray Bellamy had done well, and he liked his life.

And yet, there was something to be said about going back to your roots, letting everyone see what a success you'd turned out to be, all despite the poor and misguided upbringing from a drunken father, all despite the betrayal of his friends. That rotten deputy was no longer around, which made Ray smile a slow, wicked smile. With that son of a bitch Westley Culpepper no longer around, it made going back a tad more likely. He took a deep breath. Maybe he'd stayed away long enough. He held the glass up—to Viola Meeks—then tipped it back and drank. He knew he would go back.

Chapter 3

1975

Lydia Cooper reached down and scratched at her white pantyhose as she sat at the nurses' station at the Riley County Hospital in the small river town of Westfall, Missouri. She and Bonita were the nurses on duty. Dr. Scott had left for the night about an hour ago with orders to call him if needed. Only one of the five rooms in the small hospital had a patient. Room 3, at the end of the left hall, held Mrs. Teegarten, an overweight diabetic sent up from the Riley County Nursing Home for breathing problems. Mrs. Teegarten had been Lydia's social studies teacher back in her high school senior year, which was eighteen years ago, and Mrs. Teegarten had been old then. Lydia pressed her eyes closed, not wanting to think about high school or anything that had happened that year of 1957.

Times had changed and things had moved on. She was now head nurse at the hospital in Westfall. Just seven years old, and constructed from private donations from the community and a bond issue she had worked hard to get passed, the little hospital sat atop a rise in the middle of the town and provided health care for people of Riley County, saving them the thirty-minute drive up the road to the hospital in Poplar Bluff.

Lydia had gotten her nursing degree at Southeast Missouri State at Cape Girardeau and had planned to never come back to Westfall ever again. The town was too small and held too many bad memories, but life had a way of changing in ways you'd never dream, and with no uncertain amount of dismay she found herself right back in the town she had been so determined to leave behind. It had not been all bad, she now thought with a smile. The heart could heal and love again, and that was just what had happened. She was now married and the proud mother of a beautiful blonde six-year-old boy, Cody Cooper, the treasure of her life.

The fluorescent light above the desk buzzed annoyingly and was giving Lydia a headache. She rubbed her temple, then tucked a strand of blonde hair up under her white nurse's cap. Bonita sat at the back of the counter, wiping down specimen jars with alcohol, the harsh smell wafting through the air, mixing with the permanent Pine-Sol aroma of the hospital. She was talking on and on about a movie she'd just seen with her friends about a big shark called *Jaws*. Bonita's droll voice was not helping Lydia's headache. She took another potato chip from the bag of Cooper's Chips lying on her desk, hoping it would help make her feel better.

She could see Zeb, orderly slash ambulance driver slash all-around hospital handyman sitting in the breakroom, his legs kicked up on the edge of the table as he leaned back in his chair yelling at the little black-and-white TV as it reported about some scandal that was happening in politics. Lydia didn't have much stomach for politics, especially after all the Nixon I-am-not-a-crook resignation mess. Although the *Roe v. Wade* case a few years ago had certainly been intriguing for her. Women's reproductive rights were good. Forced birth was not. That was the kind of politics she could get behind. She gave her head a shake and sighed. It was going to be a long, slow night.

She bent her head to the report she was writing. She was concentrating so hard on completing the details of Mrs. Teegarten's admittance paperwork that she hadn't heard the front entrance door open. She sensed more than saw that a man was now standing in front of the counter. She raised her head and looked up at him—tall and lean, pale and bleeding from the shoulder. He held a cloth to his nose, which was also covered in blood. She thought she heard him mumble "Ollie shot me." He swayed a bit, then dropped like a sack of flour to the floor, totally disappearing from her view. She blinked at the empty air in front of her. Had she really just seen what she thought she had seen?

With the sound of Zeb's TV singing the Alka-Seltzer jingle in the background—"Plop, plop, fizz, fizz, oh what a relief it is"—Lydia leaned over the counter. There he was. Her mind hadn't been playing tricks on her. Bonita had stopped her movie critique and was getting up from her chair, and then their "professional" adrenaline finally kicked in, and they quickly circled the counter and bent down on the floor next to the wounded man.

There was now a lot of blood, both on the man and the floor. Lydia reached out to test his forehead. He was cold and clammy and his color was quickly turning from pale to gray.

"Zeb!" she yelled as she grabbed the man's wrist and felt for a pulse.

Her scream was so loud and so sudden that Zeb startled, causing his chair to tip backward at a precarious angle. His legs flew up and his arms flung out crazily, turning windmills in mid-air to keep the chair from falling back. Gravity decided in his favor, and the chair landed back down on all four legs. He scrambled out to the lobby.

The three of them quickly got the man on a gurney and rolled him down to Room 4, where they got him into bed. Lydia did her best to stop the bleeding and started an IV. Bonita ran back and forth with gauze and pads, then she had a moment to call Dr. Scott.

Things were in quite a flurry as the three of them worked to stabilize the man. When they finally began to get the situation under control, Lydia sent Bonita back up the hall to help Zeb. They cleaned up the blood on the floor in front of the reception desk and the drips tracked in from the front door.

"I never seen him come in," Bonita said. "Just appeared like a ghost. Never heard a thing."

They looked up to see Dr. Scott walk in.

"Room 4," Bonita said, pointing down the hall.

Dr. Scott washed up, then set about examining the patient, which confirmed the need to remove a bullet from the man's shoulder. Lydia stayed close and provided assistance as Dr. Scott cleaned the wound and stitched up muscle and skin with a pronouncement that his handiwork wasn't pretty, but that the shoulder should heal all right. The man had been barely conscious ever since he'd fainted on the hospital reception floor, and with the painkiller Dr. Scott had administered, he would most likely be in twilight for several hours. With the assurance that he was resting quietly, Dr. Scott and Lydia walked back up to the reception area.

"Well, you all sure had some excitement here tonight," Dr. Scott said. "Hell of a night. How's Mrs. Teegarten?"

"Resting," Bonita said. "Vitals are all good."

"Good. Well, maybe that's the end of our fun for a while, but you never know. I hear the Jamesons are in town having their reunion up at their river cabin. There's usually a broken bone or a busted nose when that gang gets together. I'm going to head back home after I clean up and try to get some sleep. Clinic opens at eight." Then he turned, but before he walked into his office, said, "And oh yes, call the sheriff. Let him know we got a gunshot victim up here."

That will be a fun phone call, Lydia thought. The commotion having passed, her knees began to shake, and she lowered herself into a chair before her legs gave out. She looked down the hall to where the man lay. She knew him. Shivers had gone straight up her spine to the roots of her hair when she had suddenly recognized him as he had lain bloodied on the floor. The man was Ray Bellamy. Her high school sweetheart. They had loved each other. Or so she had thought. He had left her. Eighteen years ago. She had never heard from him since.

Lydia knew that Sheriff Kinley was out of town visiting his sick mother over in Paducah, so Shane, Westfall's deputy sheriff, was the one who'd have to come down and make the report. Shane Cooper was Ray's high school buddy. Best friend actually. When Ray left town, he left Shane too, not just Lydia. They had all been friends, and they had all been stunned when he left. No word. Eighteen years. And now he was back.

She reached for the phone to call Shane, but she couldn't do it. "Bonita, could you call Shane. He'll be down at the station. Tell him the gunshot victim is Ray Bellamy." She stood up and headed down the hall to check on Ray, and then she turned back. "And, Bonita, he'll ask you to repeat the name. Do it. Twice if you have to."

Chapter 4

Deputy Shane Cooper wasn't able to get to the hospital until close to one o'clock in the morning. Right before Bonita called, a pickup truck had squealed into the station parking lot and two Jameson cousins got out. They began carrying on about how there was a fight at the family cabin. Merle and Wanetta Jameson were up at the cabin yelling and threatening each other, and sides were being picked and all hell was breaking loose. There was no phone line up at the Jameson river cabin, and it took twenty minutes for Shane to drive up there. It took another hour to sort things through, and Shane did a lot of yelling himself about making arrests if everybody didn't simmer their asses down. A few forced apologies, a few awkward handshakes later, Shane felt it was okay to leave. Callie Jameson asked to hitch a ride back into town with him as she wasn't staying up there with her crazy cousins one second longer, so Shane had to drop her off at her grandma's house. Then he circled around to the hospital. With the sheriff out of town, and only one deputy, things got taken care of as soon as they could, which sometimes meant a slower, slightly backwoods river-town rhythm.

In addition to the small hospital, Westfall had one slightly dilapidated roadside motel, the First National Bank, a Ben Franklin Five and Dime, Jenkins Shoe Store, Lee's Grocery Store, a Rexall Drugs, Miller's Auto Sales, the Catfish Grill, and various other establishments. With a population of 1,607 and the Current River a large draw for recreation, the town would wax and wane between droll monotony and all manner of nonsense depending on the season and the number of misguided tourists out on the river. On this particular night, when Sheriff Kinley was away, the town would of course decide to go berserk all at once.

Rolling his shoulders to ease the tension and prepare himself for seeing a man who had once been a good friend—or so he'd thought—and who had seemingly dropped off the face of the earth when he left town, Shane walked in to see Bonita sitting at the reception desk. "Where's Lydia?" he asked.

"She went home about an hour ago. Said she had a headache. Gunshot patient is down in Room 4."

Shane looked down the hall and let out a heavy sigh. *I just bet she has a headache*, he thought. This whole sudden-appearance-of-Ray-Bellamy thing was causing him to have one too, although some of it could certainly be remnants from the Jameson fracas. His best friend lay down there in a hospital bed. A long-lost best friend. A friend that he had mourned and missed for eighteen years and wondered if he'd ever see again. And a man that Lydia had no doubt mourned and missed too, despite her attempts to insist otherwise. Obviously seeing him had been hard on her.

Part of Shane wanted to run down the hall and shake Ray and wake him up and ask him a thousand questions. Part of him wanted to turn around and pretend that Ray had never come back to town because, despite missing him, their lives had gone on okay without him, and Ray being here would no doubt cause a fair share of emotional upheaval. Shane had to complete the report though, so he ran a hand down his face and resolutely headed down the hall.

When he'd first gotten the call, and he had asked Bonita to repeat the name just like Lydia said he would, it wouldn't register. For the first few seconds as his brain tried to wrap itself around the information, he wondered if it might be an unlikely coincidence—that it was some other man by the same name as his childhood friend. But then Bonita told him the man had said "Ollie shot me," and he remembered hearing earlier that day that Ollie Bellamy, Ray's dad, had come storming into Scooter's Catfish Grill, waving a gun around and yelling some rubbish about having to protect himself against robbers. Most of the folks at first didn't pay much attention to him, because if Ollie didn't have something to be irritated about, he would make something up, and this hullabaloo seemed par for the course. But he'd kept waving the gun around, and it seemed like only a matter of time before Ollie took his exasperation out on some unlucky patron. Scooter realized this was not good for business, so he managed to wrestle the gun from Ollie and told him to simmer down.

Shane contemplated all this information for a moment, and it didn't take a great mathematician to put two and two together. Ray and his father fought like cats and dogs when Ray was young, and that had undoubtedly not changed. He'd definitely be dealing with Ollie, but if Shane knew Ollie, he was probably drunker than a skunk by now, and despite his uneven temper and owning a gun, which was now no longer in his possession thanks to Scooter, Shane was pretty sure that Ollie was not an immediate danger to society.

Shane walked down the hall and turned into Room 4, where it was hushed and dark save for a red light on the nurse's call button and a small lamp glowing amber on the bedside table. Ray lay asleep, half propped up on several pillows, shirtless, a sheet pulled up to his waist, his shoulder wrapped in a bandage, his arm wrapped in a sling.

Shane blinked to get accustomed to the dim lighting, but also to determine that he was indeed looking at a thirty-six-year-old Ray. In the past eighteen years, Shane had acquired a bit of a paunch and his hair had slightly thinned. In stunning contrast, Ray lay there looking like he'd just stepped back from his glory days, as if he had just finished lifting weights in the school gym or been swimming out at the river and jumping off the rocks at River Leap. Ray's dark-blonde hair was still thick, his biceps and chest well-defined, his jaw strong. The only thing missing was the cocky grin. Just as in high school, and even lying there asleep, Ray still projected a sense of effortless charm and self-assuredness.

Shane stood there for several minutes. Scenes from his high school days lit up the quiet, dark hospital room. Shouts of "Go faster" echoed in the dimness of the room, and Shane could feel the wind rushing by as he and Ray, Shane's little brother Sam, and Lydia rode around in a car that Ray had fixed up, all of them whooping and laughing and having the time of their life. There was Shane and Ray and Sam skipping stones from the riverbank; now they were swimming and splashing in the river. Shane could feel the hot summer sun on his back and the shocking cold of the spring-fed river as he splashed into the water. There was Shane and Ray digging a flower garden for Mrs. Meeks so she could plant her prized imported hydrangeas, both of them hot and dirty but feeling good about helping a sweet old woman. Now they were sitting at the table with Sam and Shane's mom and dad, eating pork chops, laughing about some crazy story Ray was telling. There was Ray and Lydia dancing at prom in the high school gym to Elvis's "All Shook Up" while Shane and probably every other boy in the gym looked on and envied Ray because he had the prettiest girl in town. Then the scenes faded. The room turned dark again.

Shane blinked back what he would insist were not tears. Seeing that Ray was going to be out for a while, he used that as an excuse to get out of the room fast; he turned and walked back to Bonita at the reception desk.

"What's his, what do you call it, prognosis?"

"Doc Scott took a bullet out of his shoulder. His report here says the bullet was lodged within four centimeters of a main artery. That's pretty close. He was bleeding pretty bad when he came in. He'll need to rest and his arm will be a mite sore, but he should be okay. And it looks like he got punched in the nose too, so that'll be sore. Guess he's pretty lucky."

Shane nodded at this information, feeling a sliver of anxiety snaking up his spine. What a crazy set of events if Ray had come back after all this time only to be killed the same day. Goddammit, Ollie. "How long you think he'll be out?"

"Most likely another hour or two, at least."

"All right, well, I'm going to go find Ollie Bellamy and then I'll be down at the station. If he wakes up, call down there. If I'm not there tell Brenda to find me and let me know."

Shane drove over to Miss Lipperton's Victorian house where Ollie stayed, but he wasn't there. He drove around town, the houses quiet and dark this time of night. It was a hot night, and he drove with his car window down. The smell of the river, like a spring-fed woodland thicket, came in on the warm breeze. Tree frogs called out their nightly tune; his car radio, turned low, played "Love Will Keep Us Together" by Captain and Tennille. He drove slowly, and after a few turns around several blocks, he found the scrawny little man walking in the middle of the road down by the town square. Ollie was known for keeping crazy hours, walking around town, and often proselytizing about some crazy government conspiracy or the latest research about something. He was usually drunk or looking for a drink. Shane pulled the cruiser up beside him and slowed to match Ollie's pace.

"Evenin' Ollie. A little late for you to be out, don't you think?"

Ollie didn't look at him but kept walking. Ollie didn't much like law enforcement. "Takin' a walk ain't breakin' no laws," Ollie huffed.

Shane reached over to turn off his radio. "I hear tell there was a ruckus earlier today down at Scooter's and you were involved."

"Don't know nothin' 'bout it."

"Well, let me fill you in. Right now, Ray's down at the hospital with a gunshot wound to his shoulder. Doctor's report says a bullet missed a main artery by a smidgen. He came close to being killed. Now what kind of a homecoming is that?"

Ollie kept walking.

"Did you shoot your son, Ollie?"

"Don't have a son. Not for a good eighteen years or so. Little bastard up and left."

"Did you shoot Ray Bellamy?"

Ollie turned to the car. "Am I under arrest?"

"You just might be if you don't answer my questions. Now I got witnesses, Ollie. And I want some answers."

Ollie stared for a second longer then turned and continued walking.

"I can follow you in this car all night if I have to."

"Suit yourself."

"Goddamn it, Ollie. Get in the car. I need to get some information." Shane was quickly losing patience.

Ollie kept walking.

Shane sighed. He could strong-arm the little man into the car, but he knew Ollie would set up a caterwaulin' and likely wake the neighbors, and Shane had no mind to call any attention. He rubbed his forehead and offered Ollie the one thing that, while he knew wasn't proper, would get him into the car without a fuss. "I'll get you a beer."

Ollie stopped and turned with hopeful expectation. Then with a sloppy, lopsided grin, he circled the car and got in. Shane quickly locked the doors and headed to the jail.

At the station, Brenda sat filing her nails and listening to her little transistor radio, tuned to KJAC 95.3 on your radio dial and Charlie Rich singing about the most beautiful girl in the world. Shane came in leading Ollie by the arm and tossed his hat on his desk. Keeping a hold on Ollie, with Ollie complaining that he was hurting him and Shane not caring, he got a beer from the breakroom fridge, grabbed a pad of incident report forms, then led Ollie into their meeting room that also stood in for an interrogation room, not that there were a lot of interrogations.

"Okay," Shane said, pushing Ollie down into a chair. He popped the top on the beer bottle and put it in front of Ollie, and then started writing on the incident pad.

"Name."

Ollie took a nice long pull on the beer. "Ollis Leroy Bellamy."

Shane wrote, thinking he'd never known Ollie's middle name before, not that it mattered.

God could not have had that big of a sense of humor to give the world more than one Ollis Bellamy, so it was doubtful there was more than one, both physically and metaphorically, in the entire state of Missouri.

"Date of birth."

Ollie scratched arthritic fingers through his gray mop of thick and oily hair. "Now let me see. March 8 . . ." Then he stuck out his chin and scratched his skinny neck. "1918? I used to know."

Shane sighed and wrote down 1918. Close enough.

"So, tell me what happened."

Ollie took another drink then lowered the bottle. "When?"

"You tell me. When'd you shoot Ray?"

"I never shot no one."

Shane slapped the table, causing Ollie to jump, the beer in the bottle sloshing up and splashing on the table.

"Goddammit!" Ollie yelled. "Now you gone and caused me to spill my beer." He licked at the beer dripping off his hand.

Shane glared at him, calling on what little patience he had left. He truly wanted to be an honorable officer of the law, but sometimes this little town just couldn't move past being a poor excuse for Mayberry R.F.D. It didn't help that Ray sat up in the hospital and Lydia was home with a headache and Shane's emotions about that were all over the map and Ollie was nothing but a poor excuse for a human.

"What! Time! Was It! When you shot Ray!"

Ollie started to take another drink of beer, but then started coughing. It was a mean cough, coming from years of smoking and drinking and hard living. When he'd finished his hacking, he placed his skinny hand on his skinny chest. "Land o' livin', that was a bad one. They're gettin' worse. I think I might need to see a doc." He coughed again and Shane sat silently watching the show, impervious to the performance and hating every bone is this annoying little man's body.

Ollie took a few deep breaths and dramatically blew out air, then swirled his head and neck as if this sorry maneuver would undo years of what so much rotten living had done to his poor decrepit body. "You know, a cigarette always makes me feel better."

Shane gave him a squinty-eyed look of disdain and, resisting the urge to punch him in the face, he took a deep breath, stood up, and gruffly walked out of the room. He found a pack of cigarettes and a lighter on Sheriff Kinley's desk, brought a cigarette back, and lit it for him. Ollie took a nice long puff and leaned back in his chair, blowing the smoke toward the ceiling.

"Now that's what I'm talkin' bout." He gave a small cough and pointed the lit cigarette at Shane. "Just out walkin' by my lonesome and a real nice feller drives up and next thing ya know, I'm enjoying a beer and a smoke. Ain't America great."

Shane held up his pen and pointed to the report. "Time of the shooting!"

"I could use another beer."

Shane dropped the pen, shot up from the table, and drug Ollie by his collar into the hallway. Brenda jumped in her seat from the commotion and watched with wide eyes. Boy, was she going to have a story to tell the gals down at the Cut 'N' Curl about how handsome Deputy Cooper had his hands full with that no-good town drunk Ollie Bellamy.

Shane drug him over to cell number one and threw open the cell door, causing it to clang back against the bars. The whole time Ollie was howling like a cat, the beer and cigarette having been lost in the scuffle. Shane threw him onto the cell floor then backed out and slammed the cell door shut.

"What in tarnation! Goddammit, I lost my cigarette!" Ollie held himself up on all fours, searching hopefully around on the floor to see if the cigarette had made it into the cell with him. "You know Shane, I knew you when you was a little punk kid. You little good-for-nuthin' upstart. You and my boy runnin' all over town causin' Deputy Culpepper all kinds of trouble. You think you're so big and tough now!" He stopped to cough. He pulled himself up on the cell bench. Bent against the coughs, his back and shoulders showed thin and bony underneath his dirty shirt. "Little bastard." He coughed some more. "Let me out!"

"You can get out when you're ready to talk. In the meantime I'm holding you for shooting with intent to kill, public drunkenness, and obstructing an investigation. And if I think of any more charges, I'll add them on!"

Shane reached over and grabbed the key ring and locked the cell door. He placed his hands on the cell door bars and violently shook them to ensure as well as to demonstrate that the door was locked tight.

Ollie stood up and took hold of the bars as well. "You're so danged full of yourself, walking around all big and important with that badge. We all know you turned down that scholarship to college. You were dumb. And you were chicken. You knew you couldn't deliver the goods. You also didn't want to leave Lydia, did ya? With Ray gone you thinkin' you had a fair shot at her. A big toad in a little pond."

Shane shook his head at him. "Wanna bring up history, old man? How about what a sorry excuse for a father you were to Ray. Beating up on a little kid. I saw the bruises! You not only abused him, you neglected him, never fed him. He probably would have starved if it hadn't been for Mrs. Meeks and my mom. And now he comes back to town and the first thing you do is shoot him? Now, I'm trying my darndest to be a better deputy than the likes we've had around here before, but your sorry lot is sure making it hard."

He turned to Brenda and dropped the key ring on her desk. "Give him his obligatory Dixie cup of water every hour, but other than that, pretend he doesn't exist."

Brenda looked from Shane to Ollie and back to Shane and nodded.

Shane turned back to the cell. "And if I ever see you waving a gun around in one of the establishments here in town, I'll throw you and the gun in the river and pray your sorry stinkin' ass sinks to the bottom."

Just then the phone rang and Brenda answered it. She nodded, said yes a couple of times, then said "Okay, I'll tell him," and hung up.

"That was the hospital. Said to tell you Ray's comin' to."

Shane turned his head slowly to cast an incriminating glare at Ollie, who released his hands from the bars, backed up, and sat silently on the cell bench.

"Guess now we're going to find out what happened." Shane nodded to Brenda, put on his officer's hat, and headed out to the hospital.

Lydia had not been lying when she told Bonita she had a headache. Assisting Dr. Scott and being that close to Ray after all these years had pulled every nerve in her body tighter than a banjo string. When Dr. Scott was done, and as soon as she was assured that Ray would be okay, she just had to get out of there, so she headed home, telling Bonita to call in Maybelline if things got busy. Walking into the hushed house, she went straight to the guest bedroom, opened the bottom drawer of the dresser, and pulled out her old high school yearbook. She sat in the wingback chair, holding the book in her lap. She turned on the small lamp on the dresser and traced her finger along the raised lettering on the front of the book—*Westfall Warriors, Class of 1957.* Then she opened the book, the smell of the musty pages—along with the old perfume of a pressed carnation from the prom, car engines, and county fair cotton candy—sending her back in time.

She picked up a black-and-white photo lying among other loose-leaf notes and pictures in the front of the book. The photo was of her standing next to Ray, a bright smile on her face and her head tipping against him. Ray leaned back against an old car, tall and cocky, his arm draped over Lydia's shoulder, his long legs crossed at the ankles of his boots. Shane stood on the other side of her, his hair gleaming in the sun, and Sam crouched in front, making a goofy face and flexing laughingly skinny biceps. She remembered they had been up at River Leap Park when the photo was taken. She could see the Current River flowing behind them in the picture. They had so many good memories on that river. They were standing in front of one of several cars that Ray managed to buy for a few dollars and fix up. She remembered this one was the two-toned teal Chevrolet. The seats had been torn and the engine smoked, but they all had a blast as Ray drove them around, up to River Leap, out around the county roads, often being chased by Deputy Culpepper. That car had lasted about a month or so until it gave out, and Ray went on to fix up another one.

She traced her finger across Ray's face in the photo, then across Shane's, then lower in the picture across Sam's. She laid it down, shoved aside a flyer to the 1957 Riley County Fair, and picked up a photo of Ray standing next to Mrs. Meeks. Ray was holding a pot of prize imported hydrangeas, and Mrs. Meeks was proudly holding up a ribbon for first place in the horticulture submission category, her smile wide and proud against her dark skin.

Lydia realized of course why Ray was back in town. Three days ago, Mrs. Meeks had died. Her funeral was tomorrow, or rather today now that it was past midnight. She put her fingers to her lips and realized the sadness of it all. Of a time gone by. Of her first love. Of innocence lost. And that Ray had not come back to see her like she had once hoped so long ago. He had come back for Mrs. Meeks.

Chapter 5

1956

Ollis Bellamy, better known as Ollie to his very few and far between friends, was a squirrely man given to binges of nasty drunkenness and high dramatics in between episodes of proselytizing about subjects as varied as religion, how to manage your money, what the damn politicians in Washington D.C. should be doing, and how to catch a bigger catfish. His sermons could occasionally intrigue you, but most of the time they drove you batty. It was with some interest then when the town folk learned that Ollie had managed to cajole the wayward yet beautiful Merleen Avis into marrying him. The interest soon dissolved when they realized beauty was about the only thing Merleen had going for her—she was two parts stupid as a stump, and one part thick into worshiping idols. Ollie was not of idol material, although he had Merleen thinking so, which was the sole mainstay of their marriage.

The town heaved a disgruntled sigh when they learned Merleen was pregnant. Good God, they were procreating. Everybody worried for the baby as the combining of Ollie's and Merleen's genes could not be a good thing. But mother nature had a way of sometimes making the best out of something that clearly had no best in it. The baby was as handsome as his mother was pretty, and as smart as his father could sometimes be in his rare lucid and sober moments. To everyone's dismay, Ray got the lucky end of the stick and came out altogether normal despite the odds.

However, the town still worried as Merleen showed little aptitude for mothering. Ray was still a baby when she took to staying out at night, usually heading to Pocahontas, Arkansas, to frequent different liquor establishments down that way. The nights turned into several nights, then into weeks and then several weeks, until finally, when Ray was about four years old, Merleen never came back. To this day nobody is quite sure where she ended up or how Ollie managed with the little one. He was known to have a short temper and it was obvious that the back side of his hand often found any side of Ray's face, back, butt, arms, legs, or whatever body part seemed to be the most handy, but we can at least say that he did one better than Merleen by not abandoning the child.

Nature sometimes has a way of turning things into the opposite of their environment and construction. In spite of his mother's absence, his father's alcoholism, the beatings and misguidance, Ray grew into a handsome, smart, and well-mannered young man with a smattering of cockiness. He was blessed with a healthy and strong body, a penchant for being a daredevil, spunk and pluck, natural good sense, and the ability to roll with it and rise above it all. Put it all together, and the boy could charm everyone from the very strict Miss Lipperton, the town librarian, who looked the other way when Ray snuck library books out without a library card because she knew the boy's father wouldn't sign for a card for him and besides, the boy always brought the books back; to Fred McIntosh when Ray stole fish off his bass line because he knew the boy was hungry because the boy's father never fed him; to Earl Granger up at the North End filling station who gave him a job not only because the boy needed the money but also because the boy was good with cars.

By his junior year in high school, Ray's life consisted of hanging with his friends Shane and Sam, working on cars, and keeping out of beating distance from his father and Deputy Culpepper. Maybe it was survival, maybe it was a true inclination toward the comical, but Ray found fun and laughter in almost anything. After Ollie would sock him upside the face, Ray would rub his jaw and laugh at him, then slam out of the screen door of their sorry little tar-paper shack and run for the hills. After he and Shane and Sam accidentally popped the clutch, letting that rusted '47 Chevy truck roll back into the river, Ray started laughing himself silly as the three of them scrambled as fast as they could out of the truck before it was totally submerged. They eventually talked Earl into bringing his wrecker up there and hauling the sorry vehicle back out of the river.

He was known for pressing his luck while trying any number of far-fetched tricks. He laughed when he entered the school talent show and sang a made-up rendition of "Take Me Out to the Ball Game":

Take me out to the river, take me out to the park
I'll get a fishing pole, you get the bait
We'll get some beer, I can hardly wait
Hope there'll be girls in bikinis
Hope I'm the one that they pi-i-i-i-ck
I'll take 1, 2, 3 lovely girls
They can all sit on my . . .

(long pause here for effect and a brilliant smile to finish it off)

knee!

Principal Buhlig shooed him off the gym stage as soon as he figured out what was happening, but the song had been sung and all of the students in the gym were hooting and hollering with great delight. Ray laughed practically the whole time he spent in detention for it too. He laughed when Morgan Kingsley told him they had to break up because her father wouldn't allow it. He kissed her and sent her on her way with nothing but good and loving thoughts because, truth be told, he knew anything with Morgan and her rich and uppity daddy was never going to last anyway.

The only time Ray didn't laugh his way through something was when he and Shane and Sam got the lame-brained idea of tearing up Mrs. Meeks's hydrangeas when he was about fourteen years old. Being bored teenage boys in the middle of a dull and hot summer night, it had seemed like a good idea at the time to sneak up through the yard, army crawling the whole way and snickering about how they'd fix old Mrs. Meeks, who was always bragging about her prize hydrangeas. Under a summer moon casting a silvery light, they first pulled off the petals all delicate-like but soon got caught up in the game and started flapping flower heads like bayonets and sending the blossoms raining down like confetti across Mrs. Meeks's yard. It was a sight to see, and when they were finished, her yard looked like it was covered in snow. They kicked and skipped through it and were quite the jolly little fellows.

Their shenanigans were brought to an abrupt stop by the portentous squeak of Mrs. Meeks's screen door as she came out to check what in the sam hill blazes was going on. The boys made a run for it, but it looked like a cavalry of drunken clowns as they turned and tripped over one another in the dark night. Somehow Sam fell into a wheelbarrow and Ray bounced off Shane, who fell onto a board supporting the wheelbarrow. This created enough heft to launch Sam into the air, sending him in a low arc across the yard to land unceremoniously in a mound of soft but decidedly stinky mulch.

If Mrs. Meeks was perplexed as to why a young white boy was flying over her yard, legs and arms flailing in the moonlit sky, she decided that it was probably not the time to investigate. She wouldn't have been fast enough anyway. Ray and Shane, having held their breath as their heads turned in unison to watch Sam's path across the night sky, were momentarily petrified over this alarming development in their late-night tomfoolery. But they quickly took action, both of them grabbing Sam under each arm and dragging him off into the dark of the night. Viola frowned and turned her ear to the sound of a young boy moaning accompanied by two other boys shushing him to keep quiet. Eventually the tree frogs and crickets, temporarily silenced by the raucous outburst, recommenced their mating calls. Mrs. Meeks squinted out into the dark. It had happened so fast that she questioned for a moment if she had actually seen what she thought she had just seen.

Now Viola Ruth Meeks had lived a good life, as good as a black woman in south Missouri could live during that time. Viola had married Sullivan Meeks when she was nineteen, and the two raised a small vegetable farm in New Madrid County in the bootheel of Missouri. She and Sully had one son, Jackson, who grew to be a fine boy. They brought him up right, and he went away to Lincoln University in Jefferson City and got degrees in history and education and moved to St. Louis where he became a high school teacher. Sully died of a heart attack when he was fifty-nine, far too young as far as the broken-hearted Viola was concerned. She sold the farm and moved to Westfall where two of her older sisters lived. Viola bought a house at the edge of town where other black folks lived, out west off the road that headed to the river.

It was a nice enough neighborhood, but Viola's yard was the prize of the block. She grew beautiful flowers—roses, tulips, lilies, irises, daisies, zinnias, portulaca, cockscomb, lilacs, and azaleas.

She also had redbud trees, dogwood trees, forsythia bushes, and flowering crabapple trees. Her yard was a veritable explosion of color in the spring and a wondrous kaleidoscope all through the summer and into the fall. She kept the local florist supplied, and it helped add to her income in addition to bringing her great joy and contentment.

Of all the beautiful delights she brought forth from the earth, Viola was most famous for her hydrangeas. They were imported from New Orleans, and she pampered those bushes like newborn babies. The soil had to be mixed with the right combination of lime and potassium. They had to have just the right amount of watering, just the right amount of sunlight. The flowers bloomed fat and velvety in delicious shades of cotton-candy pink and baby blue. They always won the blue ribbon at the county and state fairs—locals gave up trying to compete against her—and they were always requested in the floral arrangements down at Cindy's Floral and Bouquet on Main Street. The boys had done a hellacious thing indeed—the harebrained destruction of these hydrangeas was a great loss for Viola as well as the whole town.

It was the day after the hydrangea beheadings when Sheriff Tyler picked up Ray, Shane, and Sam, and several other neighborhood boys, and brought them down to the courthouse. He lined them up out front on the sidewalk where nice Mrs. Meeks stood holding what was left of her poor hydrangeas. Her face was sad and you could tell that she had been crying. Sheriff Tyler informed the boys that Mrs. Meeks's prized imported hydrangeas had been ransacked last night, and that, according to Mrs. Meeks's recap of the events, they were fairly certain that the floral massacre was at the hands of one or more teenage white boys, and the person or persons who were responsible needed to step forward that instant and face the consequences.

Deputy Culpepper, tall and imposing, with a large forehead and strong jaw offset by doughy cheeks and small, deep-set eyes, was also standing guard and harrumphed a most disgusted harrumph. He postured with dramatic self-righteousness and waited with bated breath to exercise his civic duty by handing down an appropriate punishment.

The boys looked on wide-eyed, not knowing what the punishment might be. But if Sheriff Tyler—the wise and elderly beacon of law-abiding and god-fearing town leadership—had anything to do with it, it would most likely involve several hundred push-ups, a turn at raking through the town garbage dump, helping tar Second Street, painting the south side of the courthouse, and all number of torturous penances. Not one boy stepped forward.

But it was Ray who saw the sadness on the old lady's face. He'd heard she was a widow and missed her son, who lived in St. Louis, and also that she was a real nice lady who had quite the touch with flowers; now that he thought about it, what he had done was downright shameful. Ray felt just terrible. With no thought toward any discipline that was surely to come, Ray could only think of how he had sorely wronged her, and so he stepped forward. Shane and Sam's heads whipped in his direction, but Ray raised up his hand before anybody else could say anything.

"I did it," he firmly said. "I thought it would be funny, but I see now it's not. I'm very sorry Mrs. Meeks."

Deputy Culpepper was in front of Ray quicker than a duck on a june bug and stuck a finger in front of his face. "I knew it was you, you good-for-nothing little scoundrel. You're nothing but trouble. Now see here, being as you saw fit to tear up this poor lady's garden, we got several—"

"Wait." The voice came from Mrs. Meeks, quiet yet strong. "As I see it, tearing up the flowers isn't breaking the law, so I'd like to be the one who hands down the punishment."

"Oh, it is breaking the law, Mrs. Meeks. Several, actually. Trespassing, theft—" Deputy Culpepper held out his hand palm up as he began to tick off the offenses on his fingers.

Mrs. Meeks held up her own hand. "I don't want to press charges. I will deal with this in my own way. Thank you, Sheriff and Deputy, for helping with this. At this time, I would like to talk to the boy."

Culpepper blustered about, clearly not satisfied. "Well, well, well now . . . just what are you going to do? We can certainly hand down punishment to fit the crime, Mrs. Meeks. The boy is responsible for grave damage and disrepair to your yard, and we can—"

Mrs. Meeks again held up her hand. "I said what I said."

"Culpepper," Sheriff Tyler said sternly. "You heard the lady." He turned to Mrs. Meeks. "Ma'am, if it's okay, can we ask what you have in mind? You see, we don't want other boys thinking they can get away with this kind of thing, so a strong punishment will certainly go a long way in deterring other young fellows from doing anything like this again."

"Oh, you can rest assured, Sheriff Tyler, that it won't happen again. I've got me a watchdog now. And what I have in mind for young Ray here is that he will be replanting my garden, tilling and tending it throughout the year. He'll be hauling soil and getting fertilizer from Mr. Featherston's chicken coop. And he'll be presenting next year's prize hydrangeas at the county and state fairs." This brought snickers from the lined-up boys, who knew no self-respectful teenage boy would be caught dead inside the horticulture tent.

"Quiet!" Culpepper yelled, but he looked pleased that Ray was the butt of embarrassment. "Mrs. Meeks," he said as he puffed in Ray's direction, "you let us know if Ray doesn't fulfill his gardening duties. We will certainly be on him ready to exact further punishment; you just say the word. You better straighten up and fly right, you hear me, kid!"

"Oh, he'll fly right," Mrs. Meeks said. "He's going to have to get up at five in the morning every day to help me work. He's going to have to do that before his school. He'll be too tired to cause any more tomfoolery."

And that's how the relationship between Ray and Mrs. Meeks began.

It would not be too ostentatious of a statement to say that tearing up Mrs. Meeks's hydrangeas and fulfilling the punishment for it was the best thing that ever happened to Ray. He started working with Mrs. Meeks the very next morning with the backbreaking duties of digging up a new flower bed, shoveling dirt into a wheelbarrow (the very one from which Sam went flying), and hauling that wheelbarrow to the other side of the yard and dumping and digging and planting and bending and sweating and scratching and slapping at flies who seemed to be having a heyday biting him on the back of his neck the entire day. He drew the attention of curious neighbors whose skin was much darker than his, and they sat on their porches and fanned themselves while they observed the comings and goings of a white man doing the bidding of a black woman, the likes of which one could only be ascertained by explanation that the world had surely flipped upside down.

At first he paid them no mind, but Ray being Ray, he decided to give his spectators a show. He held the shovel handle like a microphone and sang an Everly Brothers rendition of "Bye Bye Love." He danced a jig and then laughed, which would get them to laughing. Pretty soon Mrs. Meeks, who was working right along beside him and couldn't help laughing herself, broke into Georgia Gibbs's song "Dance with Me, Henry," and then the whole neighborhood was dancing and singing, clapping and skipping out in the road. It was true that Ray was certainly the charmer, and he soon became a true friend to the little neighborhood outside of town on Route K, but it was also true that Viola Meeks would soon become the most important woman in his life.

Through Viola, Ray learned about soil and lime and potash and weather, and not only flowers but vegetables and fruits. He also learned how good, hard, backbreaking work could produce the finest that nature had to bestow. And most importantly, he would learn of the patience and love of an old woman who no longer had a husband and was willing to spread a protective arm over the boy who no longer had a mother. The two made a paradoxical pair as they worked together in the garden, went to farmers' markets, and drove to Poplar Bluff or Pocahontas to buy plants and herbs and seeds. Others looked rather dubiously on this unlikely partnership.

True to Viola's word, Ray presented the hydrangeas at the Riley County Fair the next year; however, not with humiliation but with humility and pride. They of course won the blue ribbon. Ray's pluck and charm and grand gardening storytelling throughout the past year had cast such a provocative light on the whole production that nobody wanted to miss the unveiling of Ray's and Mrs. Meeks's hard work. All of Ray's friends were there to see it and cheer him on, and the county fair horticulture tent was now the most popular and entertaining place to be. It was only Westley Culpepper who gritted his teeth and begrudged the whole darn thing as he couldn't for the life of him figure out how this scalawag of a kid had turned a punishment into a ceremony.

Chapter 6

1956

Lydia Campbell and her mother Phyllis lived in Paducah, Kentucky, and might never have moved to Westfall had they not been neighbors to Suzanne Culpepper Holmes. Suzanne had moved down to Paducah with her husband some several years before, leaving behind her parents and two brothers—Russell, the good brother, and Westley, the bad brother.

It had all started when Suzanne introduced Russell, who would drive down to Paducah to visit his sister every other month or so, to Phyllis. It became very obvious as they sat on Suzanne's porch eating blueberry pie that Russell was quite taken with Phyllis Campbell. The attraction became mutual when Phyllis saw Russell's playful charm when he asked her during one of the earlier visits if she was married.

Phyllis had replied, "Well, my husband took off several years ago, and right now I'm in the middle of divorce proceedings. So I'm not quite sure what that makes me."

"Better off?" Russell had offered with a shy grin.

After that, Russell's visits started happening every other week.

Fifteen months later, Phyllis was now Phyllis Culpepper and Lydia had a new stepfather.

Lydia wasn't quite sure what all her mother saw in Mr. Culpepper. He was quiet and actually a bit boring as far as she could tell. But she was old enough to see that Russell offered stability and presence—two things Phyllis had been craving for quite a while since Lydia's dad had left to find work in Beaumont, Texas, some seven years ago, sending money home the first few months and then seemingly dropping off the face of the earth. It also didn't hurt that Russell owned the Culpepper Clothing Store in Westfall, which provided for a nice income and well-established relations in town. Phyllis saw this as a step up in society, and even if it was the good river folk of plain and certainly not pretentious Westfall type of society, it would do. It was a far better rung on the ladder than being abandoned by her husband, a single mother working at the Paducah Natural Gas company as the front office clerk.

Phyllis had attracted a few likely suitors in the past, but she had still been married and had held out hope that the roving Mr. Campbell would return to his wife and daughter. Phyllis had spent several of her peak years pining for that good-for-nothing husband, but she finally divorced him.

Some people did not look kindly on a single mother, as was so disdainfully articulated to her one day by a well-to-do Paducah socialite when she patted at her perfect coiffure and commented on Phyllis's state of affairs, "You should be ashamed of yourself. I will pray hard for your redemption."

This had upset Phyllis, but she held her head high and calmly but firmly told the snobby-nosed lady, "I will pay for my sin, but I will not pay for my errant husband's." Now, thanks to Russell's wonderful timing and attentiveness, those judgmental socialites would no longer have to pray over Phyllis's wayward soul.

Overly friendly, red-haired, talkative, perky, and a good dancer, Phyllis probably could have landed a man with more personality, but by the time she was thirty-seven, she saw in Russell a man who had two perfectly wonderful features: one, the lack of gumption to run off to Texas and leave her; and two, the loving willingness to listen for hours as she talked about the latest news, philosophies about some such or another, town gossip, whatever was going on in Hollywood or England's royal circle, or the latest book on the bestseller list. Russell was quite satisfied to listen to Phyllis, because she was the most interesting woman he'd ever met.

At forty-six, he figured it had been preordained that he would live a life of confirmed bachelorhood as the pickings left in Westfall were pretty slim. He never dreamed that he could attract a pretty and smart lady such as Phyllis Campbell, but he thanked the gods every morning when he rolled over in bed and saw the luscious rump and bright-red hair of his bride lying next to him. He might be a quiet, mild-mannered man, but he enjoyed a good tussle in bed, and Phyllis, being of a fiery personality, was always more than willing to accommodate him. At this advancing stage of his life, Russell was very thankful for good timing and his sister's close proximity to single and ready-to-be-married Phyllis Campbell.

Lydia wasn't nearly as happy as the bride and groom, but love for her mother bid her to accept what she had been given and, to tell the truth, things had been worse than what she was being given now. She dutifully moved her things into the tiny upstairs bedroom of Russell's house. It wasn't bad, but she had to be careful to duck when she got close to the wall so she wouldn't hit her head on the sharp angle of the ceiling, and it was hot as blazes since there wasn't any air conditioning. Russell had bought her a fan that afternoon and plugged it in, apologizing for not thinking of it sooner and then commencing to repair the screen on the window so the bugs wouldn't get in.

She could see that her mom was finally, thankfully happy, and that was important. Lydia had lived through too many nights with her mother sobbing into a beer bottle, wailing about the shortsightedness and unreliability of men. Lydia had at different times tried to comfort her, or avoid her, depending on the level of drama and drunkenness. Those nights were always followed by Phyllis coming to her bed the next morning with beer-soured breath, crawling up next to her and hugging her and apologizing and promising that things would get better. Well, now things did seem to be better, at least for her mother, and Lydia was hopeful they would be for her as well. Lydia just needed to get used to living in a new town, with new people and all their small-town quirks.

The town mailman, nicknamed Beaver because of an atrocious overbite, had welcomed them with a much too energetic overture, which caused Lydia to have to suppress her improper laughter. Phyllis simply handed him a glass of fresh-squeezed lemonade and smiled her most appealing smile while casting a sideways warning glance at her daughter. Mrs. Crabtree, Russell's cashier at the clothing store, with her hair teased big enough to keep her pencils stored there, had hugged Lydia to her large breasts and proclaimed that she was so happy to see Russell's new family. The butcher at the grocery store, a young man named Skip with dark, slicked-back hair and his cigarettes rolled up in his T-shirt sleeve, handed Phyllis her package of pork steaks with an animated nod of his head and an overly dramatic wink at Lydia. Everybody in the town was curious, but Lydia wondered what stories were being spun about them in this season's town gossip.

Phyllis loved it. Having had no formal education past high school, she was still whip smart, shrewd, funny, outgoing, and so full of self-confidence that she was of a mind to occasionally tell God how to manage his affairs. She saw the town, with its cliques and quirks, not as a hindrance but as a challenge. She, of course, would overcome. Anyone else might have politely waited their turn to be welcomed into town society, but Phyllis, being Phyllis, did no such thing. Her style was more to take the town by the horns, and instead of getting to know the town, she made sure the town got to know her.

Lydia would have preferred her mother had more of a filter, but on the other side of that coin, it made for entertaining times, as well as influencing a daughter who was also whip smart, fun, and eventually confident too. It was normal for Phyllis to have a party and invite Westfall folks in instead of waiting for someone else to have the welcoming party first. It was normal for Phyllis to argue with Principal Buhlig at the Westfall High School that Lydia, a junior, be allowed to take senior biology because her daughter could handle the subject matter. And it was normal to walk into the First Baptist Church service that first Sunday in town with Phyllis looking around with a keen eye and proclaiming to her daughter with a self-assured smile, "Chin up, dear, we're going to be okay. We're the best-looking ones here." And Lydia did raise her chin, and Lydia believed every word her mother said.

It's one thing to have your mother's undying love and support, but Lydia still hoped to meet a few friends her own age. Thankfully, she didn't have to wait too long and was pleasantly surprised when on the third week after they'd moved in, Russell's next-door neighbor, Mrs. Winterowd, and her two teenage granddaughters came over to say hi. The girls explained they lived in Rolla and visited their grandma for several weeks in the summer, and if Lydia was up to it, they'd take her to River Leap that afternoon. The hot attic bedroom had become a bit stifling even with the fan, and the opportunity to hang out with new friends at the cold river sounded perfect. It turned out Lydia had no idea just how perfect it would be. At River Leap, she would meet the boy of her dreams.

Betsy, the older sister who could drive, drove her grandmother's old Buick into the River Leap parking lot and they all got out, grabbing their beach towels and sunglasses. If Betsy had said once, she'd said two dozen times how pretty Lydia's red-and-white-striped bathing suit was. And Marjorie, the other sister, had gone on and on about Lydia's blonde hair. Lydia had been embarrassed at first, then Marjorie said, "Tell me something you like about me."

Lydia stalled, trying to think quickly. "Um . . . I like your bathing suit too. Blue's a great color on you."

"Do me!" Betsy demanded.

"I like your car," Lydia said with a mischievous grin.

Betsy made a face. "That's not about me. And it's not even my car." All three girls laughed.

"Afternoon, ladies." They turned to see Deputy Westley Culpepper, Lydia's newly acquired step-uncle, walking up to them. "Why, hello Lydia. I'd heard my brother's got you and your mom all moved to town. Y'all gettin' settled in?"

Lydia nodded. "Yes." It was all she could think to say as she wasn't sure whether to call him Uncle Wes, Westley, or Deputy Culpepper.

Wes gave a self-important tip of his hat at the girls and shifted up his pants. "Afternoon, girls. I see you're in town visiting your grandma Winterowd." He puffed up quite proudly to demonstrate his knowledge of the town's comings and goings. "As deputy, I don't miss much, ya know." He flashed a white-toothed smile to the girls, then pointed a finger at Lydia and winked. "Melva Dean and I'll have to have you out for dinner, Lydia. You might remember our two boys at your mom's wedding. They would love having you over. We can grill us some burgers. If I do say so myself, I'm the best griller in the county."

Wes smiled at the girls, and in the haze of his delusional belief that he was God's gift to women, assumed that their silence was because they were too overtaken by their awe of him.

Lydia thought him an irksome boor, but nonetheless felt obliged to acknowledge her step-uncle's invitation. "That would be nice," she said, thinking the exact opposite, then looked at the other girls for a way out of this awkward exchange.

Betsy gestured toward the river, beach towel slung over her arm. "River's a-calling."

"Yes, well, you girls best be gettin' down to the water. You're missing your fun. Now let me know if you need anything, you hear, Lydia. We're family. And that goes for all y'all too, Betsy and Marjorie. Always here to help." Westley flashed his toothy grin again. The girls each gave a dutiful smile then backed away and headed toward the long flight of concrete steps that led down the hill from the parking lot toward the river.

"He gives me the creeps," Betsy said when she was sure they were out of earshot. "Sorry he's your uncle. At least he's not a blood relation."

Lydia chuckled. "I met him at Mom and Russell's wedding. He acted like he was quite the thing out on the dance floor, but I thought he looked like a duck in heat. I can't seem to look at him without remembering that god-awful dancing." This sent the other two girls doubling over in laughter.

Then Marjorie snorted and pretended to hike up her pants. Using a lower voice, she said, "Ya'll girls let me know if you need anything. And as soon as I quit duck dancing, I'll come to your rescue."

They laughed again and walked down past the picnic tables where several families were grilling pork steaks and hotdogs and drinking lemonade. Several different groups of people played and splashed in the river. Lydia followed her new friends to the upper part of the bank where it was grassy, and they spread out their towels. She stretched her arms to the heavens and breathed the summer air, cocked her head back, and, for the first time, was thankful for Russell Culpepper coming into their lives.

Lying back on their elbows on their towels, Betsy gestured to an outcropping of large rocks, some of them big boulders that jutted out over the river. Several young boys in cutoffs were jumping, diving, and pushing each other off the rocks. They were coming precariously close to the rocks below, which looked sharp and dangerous. "That there is where the park gets its name—River Leap."

"Good gosh, some of those boys might get hurt."

"Oh, they have," Marjorie said, removing her sandals. "Some seven or eight years ago they used to jump off that highest point." Lydia looked up in the direction where Marjorie pointed. Trees and bushes grew at the top, and most of the rock outcroppings were in the shade. It was actually very pretty. "One time, Johnnie Walker jumped off but didn't hit the water clear. He went way down. It's pretty deep right up close to the edge of the rocks there. You can tell because the water is that deep-green color. Out there," she gestured where other people were standing around in waist-deep water, "the water runs shallow and clear, but up next to them rocks, it's really deep. Anyway, Johnny hit his head, cracked it wide open. The water turned all bloody."

Lydia blinked at Marjorie. "His name was Johnnie Walker? Like the whiskey?"

The girls suddenly laughed at the idiocy of her question. "Dang it, Lydia. This is serious. People have drowned in that part. It's dangerous. After finally there'd been too many drowned, they set up an ordinance or something, and you can't go up to the very top and jump anymore."

The girls were silent as they looked up at the top of the rocks. "Wait. They really named him Johnnie Walker?" Lydia asked again, and Betsy threw her sandal at her and they laughed again.

Then a beach ball came sailing up toward them. It landed at Lydia's feet and she looked at a group of guys standing in the water with their hands up. "A little help!" called one of them. Lydia stretched her leg out and deftly lifted the ball with her toes then kicked it back out toward the boys.

"Oh boy," Betsy said, sliding her sunglasses down her nose and peering out at the boys. "That is the most delicious Ray Bellamy walking up toward us, ladies. Smile your most enchanting smile."

Ray walked up and stood there, in all his handsome teenage glory. Water dripped from his dark blonde hair and his well-defined naked chest. A nicely tanned arm held the beach ball to his hip, and he nodded. "Betsy, Marjorie. When'd y'all get into town?"

"Yesterday," Marjorie managed to squeak out.

"And how long y'all staying?"

"Two weeks."

"Great. So who's your new friend here?"

Calling upon a daring nerve she didn't realize she had—the attention of a good-looking red-blooded boy when you're a good-looking red-blooded girl can make you do all kinds of things you didn't realize you were capable of—Lydia stood up and held out her hand. "I'm Lydia Campbell. My mom and I just moved to town. Mamma married Mr. Culpepper."

Ray's eyebrows went up as he took her hand and shook it. "Lord o' mercy, please tell me your mamma didn't marry Wes Culpepper."

Now Betsy stood up. "Well, since Wes is married to Melva Dean and has two sons, that would seem a mite unlikely, wouldn't it?"

Ray and Lydia stood there looking at each other, their hands slowly unattaching from their handshake. They had heard Betsy, but as their gazes and senses were fixed on each other, they didn't acknowledge her.

"Mamma married the other Culpepper—Russell."

"Hey, Ray! The ball!" his friends called from the water. Ray stared at Lydia for a second longer, then another second and another second, and then he just decided to keep looking at her. He lifted the ball and heaved it backward over his shoulder while still looking at her. He noticed this caused a slow appreciative smile to appear on Lydia's face, and he smiled back. But now the guys, also being red-blooded teenage boys, had forgotten about the ball and were making their way out of the river and up to where the girls were. Pretty soon they were all sitting around talking and flirting. Introductions were made, and Lydia found herself sitting with new friends and deciding she rather liked the town after all.

Chapter 7

1956

Growing up, Shane Cooper didn't need a lot to be happy. He was satisfied hanging with his best friend Ray, riding their bikes, or later, driving in a fast car, playing baseball, swimming in the Current River, and engaging in all manner of horsing around that would occasionally create the necessity of avoiding Deputy Culpepper. There wasn't much Shane did that didn't include Ray. They pretty much did everything together. They even loved the same girl.

Lydia Campbell, the new girl. Blonde hair, blue eyes, long legs. The perfect package and every boy's fantasy. And while Lydia's physical beauty certainly fed his dreams, there was no denying that after he got to know Lydia, her quick wit and ability to easily laugh made her even more desirable. Thoughts of pulling her close and kissing her and finding out what was underneath that red bathing suit were about the only things he could think about for a full month, no—maybe a full three, maybe ten full months after first seeing her. Shane wanted her. Like he'd never wanted anything else.

It didn't surprise him of course that Lydia took a shine to Ray. Actually, if she had looked past Ray toward him, Shane would have probably questioned why. Shane was well aware of his best friend's good looks and charm and how just about every girl in town had the hots for him. And it wasn't just the schoolgirls, but the ladies too. Shane saw the teachers bend over Ray's desk more closely than the other boys' desks and pay him extra special attention. He saw the waitress at the Catfish Grill stick her tongue through her gum, blowing and then wrapping her lips around the bubble real slow, popping it then drawing the gum into her mouth as she took Ray's order, eyeing him with lowered lashes. He watched Reverend Dole's wife pat him on the arm and fan herself as she invited Ray to make sure and let her know anytime if he needed anything. Then she'd pat his arm again, taking her time to move her hand across his shoulder and around to his back and then draw her hand down slowly and finally pull away. *Anything,* she would repeat slowly.

Shane knew Ray had his way with lots of girls—Sadie Toalson, who lived down in the row of little white clapboard houses across from the railroad tracks; Winona Fredricks, the girl who was several years older than him but who always needed help with a fallen tree limb or getting a box down from a high closet shelf. And he dated Morgan Kingsley for several months when they were juniors until Morgan's daddy—a high-paid lawyer of the local Westfall nobility—put a stop to his fair princess dating a boy that would no doubt amount to nothing.

So when Lydia moved to town and lots of folks saw her for the first time out at River Leap wearing that red-and-white-striped bathing suit, the town rattled with all the talk. Town folk had seen Phyllis Campbell around a time or two, hanging onto Russell's arm, but nobody ever knew she had a daughter. Well, boy howdy did she ever.

Shane was aware of everyone in town looking. You couldn't take your eyes off Lydia. Shane had been in the water out at River Leap that day, splashing and wrestling with Sam, Ronnie and Donnie Tyler, and Ray when, through the sparkle of water droplets that splashed around their heads in the summer heat, he saw three girls, two he knew and one he didn't, walking down the grassy bank carrying towels. He squinted as water got in his eyes because the other guys hadn't seen her yet and kept splashing. Suddenly, Shane's vision went watery and green as Sam jumped on him and pushed him underwater. Shane came back up spitting and cussing at his little brother, flinging the water out of his eyes and hair, looking back up toward the river shore. Now she was bending over taking off her shorts, and what a sight that was to see. She flipped her towel and laid it on the grass next to the other girls' towels. Then she stood and stretched.

The splashing stilled as the other boys followed Shane's line of sight. They all stood in the water and gawked. Shane was a lost cause. That girl had no idea what she'd done to him with the mere movement of raising her arms above her head and then lowering her fingertips to touch her shoulders as she arched her back.

She and the girls lay down on their towels, and Shane and the guys commenced to making fools of themselves to try to get her attention. Ray got a hold of a beach ball and tossed it in between the guys, and they batted it back and forth until Ray sent it flying her way. Sam had yelled for a little help, and the new girl kicked the ball back like some cotton-candied fantasy from a Frankie and Annette beach movie, her long leg and pink-painted toenails sending the ball skyward and back toward the river where Ray caught it. Shane and the guys stood there like idiots waiting for Ray to resume the game, but Ray side-armed the ball and waded out of the water with a cocky James Dean swagger, his buddies and the beach ball game long forgotten. The rest is history. Ray never looked at another girl for the rest of his school days, and Lydia never looked at another boy. Or so everybody thought.

It didn't stop Shane from lusting after her. And it didn't help when Ray and Lydia became a definite and devoted couple. But despite having a girl, Ray's friendship was true, and despite Shane's unrequited love for Lydia, it also felt right that they all hung out together. Shane accepted that Ray got the girl. And he also accepted that they were all friends. Lydia liked Shane and his brother Sam just as much as she loved Ray. They would ride around town in whatever car Ray had fixed up, racing on the back roads and outrunning Deputy Culpepper, laughing in the hot summer breeze. They would call on Mrs. Meeks. They would hang out at the river together, they would meet up at the Coney Shack and order chili cheese dogs and vanilla Cokes and sit together in the same booth. Shane wasn't with them all the time of course, but Ray still remained his friend, and Shane was grateful for it. At least he thought he was. The hardest thing he ever did was keep loving his best friend while trying not to let his pining for Lydia get in the way and ruin things.

It seemed to Shane that he and Ray had been best friends forever, but it really started when the boys were in fifth grade and he invited Ray over to play in his yard. Given Ray's dubious upbringing, no mother of boys the same age as Ray could be judged for not wanting her sons to run in his crowd. It was with some alarm then that Mrs. Cooper looked out her kitchen window that frosty morning one winter long ago to see her two young sons climbing on the wood pile out back of their house along with none other than that Bellamy boy. She was a good Christian woman though, so eventually she invited them all in for hot cocoa. He wasn't the cleanest, but he didn't smell, leastwise not any worse than her own two boys. And she soon saw that Ray was fairly polite, if a bit rough around the edges. Somewhere between drinking cocoa, learning that Shane and Ray were in Miss DeLaney's fifth grade class together, and watching them lie on the floor playing with Lincoln Logs, Mrs. Cooper decided there wasn't anything wrong with Ray and it was fine that her boys kept company with him.

And so Ray could often be found at the Cooper house with Mrs. Cooper plying him with pot roast or ham sandwiches, because back then, before puberty and muscle definition, Ray was one skinny boy. A shirt and a pair of jeans would surreptitiously be put in a nondescript brown paper sack along with an apple and some oatmeal cookies and handed to Ray as he left her house to head back to his home.

Shane was aware of the tar-papered shack Ray lived in down by the river with his father. He was also aware that Ray's talent at fishing had more to do with putting dinner on the table than it did with sport. Some of the people in town saw Ray as a victim, but Shane saw him as a survivor. When Ray stepped forward to claim due punishment for his hydrangea shenanigans, Shane had thought for a second or two about stepping forward too, but he froze. It went without saying that Ray was braver than he was.

Shane lamely settled up with Ray the next day by offering to buy his lunches for the next week, and he also helped him work in Mrs. Meeks's garden. Truth be told though, this was only because Sam had called his older brother out on what chickens they had been to not fess up, saying Shane needed to do something to fix this and it wasn't fair to Ray. The brothers had started wrestling and punching each other in their bedroom, knocking books off the desk along with the prized baseball that Sam had caught at a Cardinals baseball game last summer, and Mrs. Cooper had come marching in their bedroom, yelling at them to stop it. After Sam's verbal shaming, Shane did admit, if only to himself, that he was a sorry excuse for a friend, and so he pulled on his big-boy pants and made good with

Ray the next day. Ray had gamely accepted the offering, and there was no further reckoning regarding the situation.

Shane may have held a clear conscience about the hydrangeas, but Sam did not. Sam didn't have money for lunches, so he sulked mightily over his lack of backbone. When the time had come to confess, Sam had frozen too, watching his brother and then growing angry at not seeing him step forward. He hadn't needed to wait for Shane to step forward of course, but it was habit for the little brother to follow the older brother. By the time Sam's principled thoughts caught up with his gumption, his confession would have seemed suspiciously awkward, so Sam stood there, hating both his brother and himself for their gutlessness.

Sam was in third grade when Ray came into their lives. Sam had a love for his older brother, but when it came to Ray, it was unadulterated reverence. He'd never seen anyone more cool, compelling, thumb-your-nose-at-life, or all-out ballsy as Ray Bellamy. Sam's every waking hour was spent figuring out how he could look like, be like, sound like, and act like Ray. If Ray bought a *Two-Gun Kid* comic book down at Lee's Grocery Store, then Sam wanted one too. When Ray climbed the fire escape at the back of the movie theater and gripped the gutters as he traversed the roof line to drop into the side window so they could get into the movies for free, well by golly, Sam had to do it too. His fingers ached for days and his heart liked to never settle down for fear of falling the two-story distance to the asphalt below, but he would follow Ray anywhere.

Sam knew that he was the tag-along little brother and was pretty sure Ray and Shane just barely tolerated him most of the time, but Sam didn't care. He sensed with the unknowingness of an unworldly boy that sticking with Ray could somehow show him the world. When Ray jumped off the rocks at River Leap, Sam was scared to death but closed his eyes and jumped for all he was worth, his heart beating ninety miles a second all the way down. When Ray worked on his cars, Sam was right there handing him tools, head under the hood or whole body under the car, tinkering right along with Ray and listening to everything he had to say about the engine, chassis, and model. There was always something to be learned just by being in Ray's orbit, and Sam wasn't going to miss out on it.

Ray's attention toward Sam consisted of a patchwork of good-natured yet taunting older friend, teacher, and cheerleader for Sam's repeated youthful attempts to impress. Sam was awed by the fact that Ray would even notice him, much less find him worthy of commendation. When Ray found a mongrel pup down by the river and presented it to Sam, not Shane, Sam walked on air for days. Sam named the puppy Roy Rogers, and the dog followed Sam around as earnestly as Sam followed Ray.

When Lydia came to town, Sam was thirteen and had just begun the budding dance with puberty. He thought some girls were pretty all right, but he hadn't yet been bitten by the time-honored bug of infatuation that filled a young boy's head with nothing but thoughts of sex. However, Sam was quickly initiated into the lovelorn realms where the other teenage boys so helplessly found themselves when he first laid eyes on Lydia Campbell that day down at River Leap. It wasn't just that she was new and pretty and looked mighty fetching in that red swimsuit, although that was all certainly part of it. It was how Lydia had stood up and boldly held out her hand to Ray. She hadn't sweetly and shyly grinned and giggled, but had stood tall and presented herself as an equal force and fellow confederate. With one confident handshake, she had aligned herself with the town bad boy without the bat of an eye. Sam found this compellingly attractive.

Chapter 8

1956

No one could exactly say when Westley Culpepper decided Ray would be his number one adversary, but it seemed to be that he made it his duty to berate, bully, cuss out, ticket, and just short of torture Ray as much as he possibly could. Perhaps Westley saw in Ray everything he wasn't. Ray—fleet of foot, charming of wit, handsome of face and body—could easily be resented by one such as Wes. But probably the attribute most envied by Wes was that Ray didn't care one iota what the rest of the world thought of him. In contrast, Wes was a big man, awkward and lumbering, who had no sense of humor whatsoever and failed horribly in his misguided attempts to impress the world. He cared very much what everybody thought of him, and unfortunately, it was rarely good. He wasn't smart enough to know this, though, and simply kept trying harder. These attempts always fell short of their mark, which would have caused a more self-aware person to change his behavior. But instead of taking responsibility for his actions, Westley blamed others, pushed harder, and just got meaner.

Town folk, humbly unable to grasp the nuances of human behavior, tried their best to walk a wide circle around Wes to keep from experiencing his wrath. Some assumed Westley's bullying toward Ray started with the Mrs. Meeks hydrangea debacle, but others said it started before when Ray was younger. Still others pointed to the arrival of Lydia Campbell as the beginning of hell on earth for Ray.

Westley took his step-uncle duties seriously, and he did not like his new step-niece hanging out with the likes of that low-life Ray. He told Phyllis several times that Lydia being with Ray was nothing but trouble. Phyllis, having raised her child on her own the past eight years and not needing a man to tell her how to do it, told Wes in that straightforward fashion of hers that he could stick it up his redneck ass and keep his nose out of business where it didn't belong. As you can imagine, this did not sit well with Wes's lofty self-image.

Truth be told, Westley was perplexed by Phyllis. She didn't act like a proper woman, which in Westley's egotistical point of view meant kowtowing to your husband, taking care of him, and not talking back. Well, Phyllis was made of back-talk. She was so fast and facetious at her retorts that Wes couldn't keep up with her. By the time he'd thought of a response that he thought would put her in her place, Phyllis had moved on to three more comebacks, which usually had everybody else around them laughing. Westley didn't like a mouthy woman. And yet, there was something attractive about Phyllis. This confounded him to no end, because he would swear to anyone who cared to listen that he had no desire to be near Phyllis at all—he was in fact a bit scared of her. To a dim-witted birdbrain like Westley, Phyllis could be perplexing indeed.

The scene with Westley telling Phyllis what to do about Lydia dating Ray was stopped short of escalating when Russell raised a peace-keeping hand in between his brother and his wife. Russell thanked Wes for bringing this news to their attention and said he and Phyllis would talk about it. Everyone knew that had a snowball's chance in hell of happening, because Phyllis did not take advice from Russell on how to raise her daughter, and Russell very wisely did not give it.

Russell didn't really like his little brother. He and his sister had been doing just fine until the little red-headed terror had been born to parents getting on in their years. Joann Culpepper could have been knocked over with a feather when she found out she was pregnant at the ripe old age of forty-eight. At that point she'd already raised a son and daughter to the nicely independent ages of twenty-year-old Suzanne and eighteen-year-old Russell Jr. But pregnant she was, and Westley Jordan Culpepper was born big, red-haired, pink-faced, screaming and squawking—an indication of what was to come for the rest of his life, short-lived though it would be.

Perhaps Joann and Russell Sr. were too doting and spoiled the child, perhaps they were just too tired—most likely a little of both—but Westley grew into the town hellion. He seemed to have been born demanding attention, but with tired parents and siblings who had moved out of the house, Westley did not get the attention he needed, so he commenced to kicking up a bigger fuss. He was loud and rude, and he saw everything he did as a joke or a prank despite the fact that he was not funny at all.

Kids didn't laugh at his jokes, but they laughed at his inability to bounce a ball or catch a ball or throw a ball or anything else to do with typical boyhood games. Wes didn't like being laughed at and quickly learned that if you punched someone in the face before they could laugh at you, well, then you were not only spared their mockery, but you soon gained their allegiance out of fear.

As he grew, his development into a narcissist advanced well and his desire for attention never waned. He demanded that he get the front desk in Mrs. Barnes's second grade class despite the fact that he was tall for his age and towered over the shorter kids sitting behind him. He scratched his fingernails on the chalkboard despite the fact that it sent everyone in the classroom into shrieking shivers. He butted his way in the cafeteria line and insisted on being given not two, but three extra helpings of meatloaf and mashed potatoes despite the fact that he was already a pudgy little kid. Everyone gave in to his demands because it was just easier that way.

Joann tried, but Westley seemed determined to be a brat, and then as he grew older, an all-out terrorizer. Would she have treated him any different if she had known Westley's life would be cut short in his mid-thirties? There was no way of knowing, but what was known was that Westley was more than Joann could handle.

A stint in the military school in Boonville helped somewhat, which led to a stint in Korea. While Joann worried about her son being in the war, her more realistic point of view was that it was the North Koreans who needed to worry. Wes blustered his way up through the ranks and somehow made it to staff sergeant at the young age of twenty-two. His fellow soldiers felt his rank came less from a talent for leadership and more from a combination of pig-headedness and stupidity—no matter how much danger he was actually in, he just charged ahead and barreled into battles. After getting the heel of his boot shot off while jumping into a foxhole, Wes was sent home with a purple heart, a left foot somewhat smaller than his right foot, and a head a great deal bigger than when he'd left.

Joann had some respite when he was over on the other side of the world fighting the communists, but now Westley was back and harder to manage than ever. Joann thanked the heavens above when Wes got Melva Dean pregnant, because now Wes had to get married and move out and get his own house—now he was Melva Dean's problem. A baby boy was the result of Melva Dean's pregnancy, and another boy followed soon after. This required a job, and with his military background, Wes found himself the deputy of Westfall. He tried his best to get put on the ballot to run for the sheriff's position, but Sheriff Tyler—along with the mayor, the county commissioner, and other local leaders—put a cap on that right quick and told him to simmer down and learn the ropes. As deputy, Wes, all hellfire and self-importance, seemed to create as many problems as he fixed, but for the most part the job fit. For several years, life rocked along fairly smoothly. That is until Wes found Ray Bellamy in his crosshairs.

It was an unfair fight Westley waged against Ray, what with Wes's lust for power and having the weight of a deputy badge to give him self-deceptive one-upmanship. But that's not to say Ray was at a loss for applying his own vengeful antics, producing sometimes comical effects, much to the satisfaction of Shane and Sam and any others who happened to be around.

It will long be told in the annals of Westfall's history the time Ray got the deputy good, when Westley came to pick up his car from Earl's North End garage. Ray happened to have eaten boiled cabbage and smoked sausage for lunch that day, and the buildup of digestive gasses timed itself quite nicely when Earl sent Ray to drive Wes's car up from the edge of the filling station lot. Ray had already been letting a few stink bombs while he was talking to Shane and Sam, who had walked over that day and were waiting for him to get off work. When Ray sent a wide grin to his friends and then trotted off to get the car, the Cooper boys knew something was up.

Ray got in the car, started it up, and pulled it up to the waiting Deputy Culpepper, but not before letting loose one of the stinkiest farts the likes of which would burn any decent man's nose hairs this side of the state's southern border. Ray hopped out, shut the door against the tainted aroma, and handed the keys to Wes, who got in and drove off. Westley made it all of three seconds before the car came to a screeching halt and he jumped out, waving his arms about his head and face like he was fighting off a swarm of bees.

"Got-damn, somebody done shit in my car! Earl, what the hell!"

This bit of information tipped off Shane and Sam as to what Ray had done, which caused the boys to bend over their knees entangled in breathless laughter.

Earl came marching over to Wes and commenced to give him a good ass chewing. "What is wrong with you, Culpepper? Yelling like that! I got a business to run here, and I don't appreciate you insinuatin' we don't deliver high-standard service here at the North End."

"This might be the problem," Ray said, opening the car door from the passenger side and pulling out an old T-shirt, waving it back and forth above his head and pinching his nose, which brought more laughter from the boys as well as a chuckle from Earl, who was trying his best to subdue his appreciation for Ray's talents.

Wes frowned. "That weren't what's causing that smell. That's just my shirt."

Ray nodded. "Yeah, that's what we're taking into account here."

Wes walked over and grabbed the shirt from Ray and threw it back in the car.

"I think you're giving me the stink eye, Culpepper," Ray said, which was just about the undoing of Shane and Sam as they continued with no success to stifle their guffaws.

Wes glared at the laughing boys, then at Ray, and then over at Earl, causing Earl to hold up both hands in a truce. "Look, Wes. The car's running, and if I may say so, better 'n when you brought it in here. Just head on out and next time you need a fill up, come on in and I'll fill 'er up for free."

Wes gave a sanctified yank of his waistband, then got back in the car and screeched off, but not before rolling down his window and sticking his face out in the more agreeable air, still yelling, "Got-dammit!"

Earl turned to Ray with a grin. "I've a mind to fire your ass, 'cept that there was the best thing I think I ever seen. Go get you a Baby Ruth. That was damn funny."

Ray's shenanigans might have been amusing to some people, but Westley didn't have a sense of humor at all where Ray was concerned. It was only a matter of time before Wes exacted his own type of revenge. He would huff round, bound and determined to keep the town of Westfall, including his step-niece, free from low-count miscreants like Ray Bellamy. It was never long before Wes would find him, like that day he caught him speeding down Route K coming out from River Leap Park.

The wigwag lights were turned on, Ray slowed to a stop, and Culpepper got out of his deputy car with all the pomp and pageantry of a five-star general. It affirmed his sense of duty when he saw that Lydia was in the car. Chewing furiously on his gum, he got out his pad and clicked his pen.

"Got you this time, you little punk."

Ray raised both hands off the wheel. "Aw, why you gotta be like this, Westley. I thought you and I had something special."

Westley sniffed at him. "You in quite a hurry there, Bellamy. Do you know how fast you was going?"

Ray just shook his head. He was tired of this drill, as Westley chased him down at least once a week. Westley rarely caught him, but he wished the deputy would find some other project to keep him entertained, although this time, and to be truthful most of the other times, he had been speeding. He'd had in mind to hit the gas and let Westley chase them, but they were heading into town, and Ray knew with no other side roads on which to make a getaway, there was no way he was going to outrun him. "'Bout forty-five I s'pect," he finally answered.

"Way off. Waaaay off. You were going easily seventy."

"That's a crock."

"I'd ask you to use a tone of respect when you address me, son!"

Ray rolled his eyes. "I'm not your son."

Wes chuckled and moved his gum to the other side of his mouth. "Yeah, that's right. You're the son of the esteemed Ollis Bellamy, town drunk and all-around piece o' shit."

"That's no way to talk when a lady's present."

Wes turned red being called out in front of Lydia. He tipped his hat. "Pardon, miss. Step out o' the car, Bellamy!"

"What?"

"You heard me. Out!"

Lydia leaned across the car seat. "Uncle Wes, we're sorry. Ray was just driving fast in order to get me home. I told my mamma I'd be home an hour ago, and I know she's gonna be worried." Lydia hoped family references would cool Westley down a bit, but it didn't seem to help.

"This doesn't concern you, Lydia. Just stay in the car." When Ray stepped out, Wes pulled him to the back of the car to where he hoped he'd be out of Lydia's sight. He grabbed Ray at his throat and drew his face up close to Ray's. Ray had to turn aside to avoid the coffee-/double-mint-gum-/bologna-tainted breath.

"Now you listen to me close, boy. I'm going to write you a ticket, and you're going to take it from me like you've got some common sense although we both know you ain't got a lick o' sense in you. You're gonna take this ticket and you're gonna go down to the courthouse and you're gonna pay it and you're gonna do it all with a smile on your face." The whole time he talked, Wes squeezed Ray's neck. He enjoyed seeing Ray's face turn red, then bright red, then purple. It was with great satisfaction that he heard Ray gasp and choke. He continued his hold. "And you're gonna quit speeding and you're gonna leave Lydia alone!"

Ray reached up and pulled at Wes's arm. Finally, with a violent thrust, Wes pushed Ray away from him, sending Ray sideways against the trunk of the car, coughing and gagging and desperately trying to catch his breath. Westley wrote the ticket and smashed it into Ray's hand. Then he went around to the passenger side of the car, opened the door, and pulled Lydia out. "You're comin' with me. I'll get you home to your mamma right quick. Come on."

Lydia tried to pull away from Wes. "No! Leave me alone. You can't order me around."

But Wes continued to pull until he got a firm hold, and he led Lydia back to his cruiser, placed her in the car, and soundly closed the door. He sped off, leaving Ray leaning against the trunk of his car, and Lydia straining to look back at him. Ray opened his hand to see the crumpled ticket held there. He wadded it even smaller and threw it in the weeds alongside the road.

Lydia didn't tell her mom or step-dad what had happened. She knew that any chastisement given by Russell or Phyllis to Wes would in turn be handed down to Ray by Wes. But she did call Shane as soon as she got back to her house and told him what had happened. Shane jumped on his bike and found Ray in his car out on Route K, still there where Lydia had said. Shane got in the passenger side of the car and saw Ray sitting there, hot and sweaty and silent and seething.

"Lydia called me," Shane said.

Ray closed his eyes and silently nodded. "I hate that mother-fucker," he said, his voice hoarse, quiet and low.

Shane had enough sense to grab two bottles of Coke and put them in his bicycle basket before he left, and he now grabbed a bottle opener from the car ashtray, popped the top on both bottles, and handed one to Ray. Shane had been witness to Deputy Culpepper bullying his friend too many times. And he hated it.

"That man is seriously disturbed. Say the word," Shane said, "and we'll kill him." Then he tipped his bottle up and drank. Ray, whose throat was still on fire, managed to take a few sips. The caffeine and sugar from the soda along with the fervent support of his friend began to bolster him. They looked at each other in silent bond and nodded. Hate was a strong word, but that was indeed what the boys felt for Westley Culpepper. The boys put Shane's bike in the trunk and headed back into town.

Chapter 9

1956

Despite living with an alcoholic father who took his frustrations out by hitting him about the head and neck, and living in a town where the Deputy Sheriff made it his life's mission to bring holy hell down upon him, life during that winter and spring of '56 and '57 wasn't too bad for Ray. He could now see a purpose, a reason for living. And that reason was Lydia. He was blissfully in love and wanted nothing more than to graduate high school that spring, get a job and make money, marry Lydia, and move away from this awful little town to start a family and live happily ever after.

When he saw the $220 price tag on the little solitaire diamond engagement ring in the window of Lamb's Jewelers, he got serious about keeping consistent hours at Earl's filling station. He was still working with Mrs. Meeks and was learning about a lot more than pretty flowers. Mrs. Meeks sold her flowers to the local florist, and Ray's sharp mind began to develop plans about how to widen that market. He didn't know anything about running a business, but he watched Mrs. Meeks, and he watched Earl and also paid attention in school. He soon started putting together concepts such as supply and demand, profits and margins, forecasting, ordering, inventory, and production.

He also got serious about getting a good car, one that would last and not break down or have its brakes fail and roll into the Current River, and he found it in a 1948 Chevrolet Bel Air. It was two-toned teal—dark on the bottom, light on the top—with cream-colored vinyl seats. Sure it was rusted out all along the rear bumper, its muffler dragged, the passenger-side door didn't quite shut right, the windshield was cracked, and the seats and the headliner were ripped and sagging. But he got the motor to turn over with a lot of oil and some tinkering, and with a little TLC throughout that winter, Ray got it in pretty good shape.

It was in this car that he told Lydia about his dream of leaving Westfall and his desire to take her with him. Lydia was in love too, and although she was a junior in high school and wanted to wait and graduate, they declared their love for each other and began to plan a future and hold tight. It was in this car that Deputy Culpepper chased them down once again on the country roads of Riley County.

It was a moonlit summer night and Ray wasn't having it. Ray sped up, as much as the Bel Air could, and took a left onto a hilly, wooded road that headed down to New Madrid county. As soon as they turned on the road, Ray cut the headlights. Lydia gasped at first because driving in the dark was scary, but then an enchanted smile spread across her face. The full moon lit up the trees and the road in a magical silvery light. She snuggled closer to Ray, their Bel Air gliding across the earth like a dreamship filled with hope and promise. The car took a dip down a hill in the road and seemed to disappear into thin air, and once again Deputy Culpepper was thwarted.

Lydia liked to die of blessedness when Ray held her in his arms. She usually wasn't the one to get the guy, but she had. She was the lucky one. He was the best-looking boy she'd ever seen. His kisses made her heart flutter; his arms around her made her feel safe. His hands on her were like blazing fires, and she thought she would burst with the heat of it all. She loved him with all her seventeen-year-old heart could love, which was mighty much. She hated the way the world treated Ray. And she loved Ray that much more when he took the hateful parts of the world—his father, Uncle Wes, the impatient math teacher, some of the uppity mothers—and graciously rose above it all and acted as if the world was one great dance. It was the dance of a young man looking forward to a great future. And she couldn't wait to be a part of it.

But life being life, it wasn't smooth sailing, and although it could be argued there were many parts of the story that were turning points, it all probably started going south that one early spring day in April. It was a Saturday. Lydia had gone on a day trip to Cape Girardeau with her mother to shop for prom dresses. Ray, Shane, and Sam had plans to hang out for the day. Shane and Sam had chores to do in the morning, but as soon as they were done, they would come over to Ray's house.

The house where Ray lived was one of twelve built by the Missouri Veterans Success Corps, a small state organization that helped war veterans get re-established into citizen life. The MOVSC found this small piece of land on the edge of Westfall that, though it abutted the river, was not a popular area given the overabundance of mosquitoes and other vermin that collected in that overgrown, slow-moving bend of the river.

The houses each consisted of a main room that was a combined sitting room and kitchen, and two bedrooms. No closets—clothes were hung on a hook on the back of the bedroom door. One overhanging bare lightbulb hung above the sink, one above the sitting area, and one in each bedroom, and each cast a yellow gloom about the sorry little structure and turned the cheap paneling to a most unbecoming shade of old mustard. A fireplace in the wall between the sitting room and bedrooms contained an odd set of vents on the bedroom side that allowed heat into the bedrooms, although heat might not be the best description, as insulation apparently was an afterthought. No indoor bathroom, but instead a row of shared outhouses out back of the twelve houses, six doors and six holes. The kitchen sink did have a pump, and if one was so inclined, they could heat water on the wood-burning stove and pour it into a galvanized tub in the middle of the kitchen floor to take a literal half-assed bath as only half of your ass could fit in the tub at a time.

The MOVSC had good intentions, but it was hard living. On the bright side, it was the hard work of pumping that danged kitchen sink several times a day along with chopping and hauling wood for fuel that gave Ray his well-defined physique.

The day had started with Ollie cutting off a couple slices of Spam and frying up some eggs for breakfast. Payday had come for Ollie at his job down at the Riley County Charcoal and Briquette Factory, so there was food on the table. When Ollie had finished eating, he announced he was going into town to buy more groceries. He reached up into the cabinet and pulled down a Kellogg's cereal box from which he pulled a five-dollar bill. Ray promptly snatched it from his hand.

"Hey! That's my money. How'd you know it was up there?"

Ollie just laughed at him. "Your hiding places aren't very hidden. And yeah, that might be your money, but the food is for both of us!"

"I gave you ten dollars last week. Where's your money? You gonna drink it all?"

Ollie raised his hand toward him, but Ray deftly deflected. Now that he was eighteen, he was taller and stronger than his father and the beatings had become rarer. The two gave each other a stare down for a full five seconds until Ray swiped the cereal box from Ollie's hands and walked into his bedroom. He slammed the door—as best as you can slam a hollow panel of fiberboard hanging precariously on corroded hinges—and stood seething in his room. How long had his dad been stealing his money? This was money that would get him and Lydia out of town. He would have to find a better hiding place. When Ollie got a hankering for a drink, he would turn the entire state of Missouri inside out to find money.

Eventually Shane and Sam, along with Sam's dog Roy, showed up, and they all drove up to River Leap to spend the rest of the morning doing a whole lot of nothing. They waded around in the river, but it was too cold to swim, so they dug around in the park trash cans to see if there was anything of value. There wasn't, so they threw sticks in the river for Roy to chase, skipped rocks, and discussed whether Shane should ask Laura Roberts or Debbie Fontaine to prom. They soon made their way up to the River Leap rock outcroppings and commenced to climb around on them, doing all manner of stupid teenage boy stuff—chin-ups off the rocks that stuck farthest out over the river, and daredevil handstands on the edge of the highest cliff. None of them noticed when Deputy Culpepper made an appearance.

"You boys best get your butts off them rocks, ya hear! City ordinance says so." Just as usual when Wes made an appearance, all fun and pleasure were sucked right out of the air.

Ray gave a dismal sigh and looked up at the thick-bodied red-headed man standing a few feet above them. "City ordinance says no jumping off the rocks. We're not jumping."

"I said get off the rocks!"

"Or what?" Ray asked. It wasn't the smartest thing to ask, because Westley had a deputy's pistol, plus a whole lot of pent-up rage and desperation to prove what a big man he was.

"Don't try me!"

"Three against one, Culpepper. Do your best." Ray finished with a cocky tilt of his head.

Sam had to turn away and look out across the river to keep from laughing. The redder Wes's face turned and the more he blustered about in failed attempts to one-up Ray, the funnier it got.

Nobody moved, the boys kept staring at Wes, and Wes kept staring back. It was a lesson learned too late that when a bully is cornered, he'll do his best to hide how weak he truly is and strike back in an outburst of madness. Before anyone could blink, Wes drew his pistol from his holster, aimed, and shot. Everyone jumped, the sound of the gun reverberating up the river valley. The dog Roy let out a yelp and fell lifeless at Sam's feet.

Sam's mouth dropped open, the incredible thing happening so fast that he could barely grasp it. "You shot my dog!" he yelled and dropped to his knees to cradle his fluffy black-and-white friend.

"You shot my dog," Wes mocked in a baby voice, then twirled his pistol, blew at the end of it, and slammed it back in his holster with a show of nitwitted bravado. "Oh, get over it, ya little baby. I saved you some trouble. Ain't nothing but a mangy mutt that shits all over your mamma's backyard and tears up the trash cans. It's good he's gone."

"Goddammit, Culpepper! You son of a bitch!" Shane yelled, clambering over the rocks to where Sam kneeled next to the dog.

Wes turned his gaze on Ray. "There's your 'or what,' you little pissant. Trying to dare me. You miscalculated, big time! You said three against one, but with the dog it was four. So I evened the odds." He let out a perverse laugh. "That'll show ya!"

The hatred that filled Ray was palpable, but he was also filled with extreme remorse. He'd no idea Culpepper would take his insolent rage out on Sam's dog. Ray knew how much Sam loved that dog, and now what had just happened was his fault. His mind spun for what his next move should be. He wanted to punch Wes in the face, he wanted to grab his gun, wanted to spit on him and kick him. His chest heaved with disgust.

But before Ray could do anything, Sam picked up Roy and, cradling the dead dog in his arms, climbed up the rocks and stood in front of Westley. Sam stared at him with all the hatred his fifteen-year-old heart could muster. Wes looked down at him. He was going to say something trite, but then Sam took another step closer to him. Sam now stood only a few inches from Westley's chest, the dog's lifelessness on full display. There was a sudden heavy silence in the air as Sam turned cold and fierce. He had become a warrior whose blood could almost be seen pounding through his tense body. Wes gave a weak laugh and took a step back, and Sam shadowed him, his contentious stare never wavering from Wes's face.

Wes tried to look away, but it was as if Sam held some kind of spell on him. "Call . . . call your brother off, Shane," he said, unable to hide the tremor in his voice. "If you all know what's good for you, you'll call him off!" He put his hand on his pistol again, and this rattled Ray and Shane out of the spell that had surrounded them with Sam's intense display of hostility.

"Let's go," Ray said, and he and Shane stepped up onto the higher rocks where Sam and Wes stood, Ray gently pulling at Sam's arm.

"Come on, Sam," Shane said as he carefully maneuvered himself between Sam and Wes. Sam finally released his murderous stare upon Westley and took a step away, and then the three boys headed together down the pebbly path toward their car, allied in their hatred for Westley Culpepper.

"I'm gonna kill that son of a bitch one of these days," Shane said as they walked down the path.

"Not before I do," Ray said.

"I'm gonna beat ya both to it," Sam said, his jaw clenched. "I'm gonna bash his head in."

They got in the car, Sam sitting in the back seat, still holding Roy. As they drove off, Sam lowered his head to the black-and-white fur and cried.

Chapter 10

1957

The Westfall Warriors graduating class of 1957 had done a great job of decorating the high school gym for the prom. Streamers of green and white—the school colors—hung from the doorways and rafters. The art students had painted five different display boards, each six feet tall, with dioramas of the town, the school, and the river, and these were set up all around the gym. Mr. Walters's band, the Boogie Six—made up of the highly eclectic mix of a piano player, a guitar player, a fiddle player, a clarinet player, and a trumpet player—provided the music, which included the class song: Doris Day's "Que Sera, Sera." Mr. Walters's voice was a mite more baritone than Doris's, but it was an acceptable rendition nonetheless. The band thrilled the students by also offering up the latest hot tune by a boy with the strange name of Elvis Presley—"All Shook Up." The students squealed and jumped out on the dance floor and delightedly hopped and skipped and bebopped to the lively song.

Principal Buhlig was not happy about all that teenage gyrating out on his gym floor, but he was patting himself on the back for his brilliant idea of placing punch bowls on the refreshment tables filled only with green-tinted water before the students arrived. After the gym began to fill up, Principal Buhlig watched flasks come out of the boys' pockets to surreptitiously pour liquor into the bowls. Then Buhlig removed the punch bowls, poured the now sullied liquid down the sink, and replaced it with the more chaste choice of every teenager—good old lime Kool-Aid. Buhlig wasn't born yesterday, and he couldn't keep the smug expression off his bespectacled mug. There would be no gyrating, at least not with the help of alcohol, on his watch, by golly.

Lydia looked with love and pride at her handsome prom date. Russell had provided Ray with a white sports coat and a pair of black slacks from his clothing store. Lydia had given him a pink carnation, care of Viola Meeks. Lydia didn't think a boy could be any more dashing or handsome. She wore a pretty blue organza dress and a blue ribbon in her hair. Ray had given her a red rose wristlet corsage, again, care of Mrs. Meeks.

Lydia held the night close and appreciated it for what it was. Ray would graduate this spring, but she had a year to go. This night would bring an end to the high school days as she knew them. She and Ray were now hard at work saving money for when they would finally be together. Lydia had gotten a job as a wash girl down at Yvonne's Cut 'N' Curl. Three afternoons after school and every Saturday morning, Lydia would wash, condition, and comb out the ladies' hair and hand them off to Yvonne, who would work her magic with wired rollers, push pins, and a hair dryer. Lydia got twenty-five cents per wash and could make about a dollar a night, depending on the number of clients. On Saturdays she would sometimes make as much as two dollars. All this money was for her and Ray.

Shane's prom date was Debbie Fontaine. They had doubled with Ray and Lydia, driving together in Ray's car, all of them sneaking a sip from a bottle of Johnnie Walker out in the parking lot before heading into the gym. Debbie was a fine date, pretty in her green dress and dark hair, and she provided the perfect mix of fun chuckles and interesting conversation. But Shane couldn't help stealing a glance over Debbie's shoulder now and then to watch Lydia and Ray dance. Lydia looked like a movie star in her pretty dress, her blonde hair all shiny and curly. Shane had to focus to contain his desire to hold her in his arms just like Ray was doing now. He watched as Ray leaned down and nibbled at Lydia's neck and wished, oh how he wished, he could be kissing her like that. Ray was Shane's best friend of course, and there was nothing to do about it but lust from afar. Ray and Lydia belonged together, and that's the way it was. Some guys get the girl, others don't. He turned his attention to Debbie, who he had to admit was pretty cute with those freckles sprinkled across her nose. Maybe she'd let him go to second base tonight.

After the dance, the two couples drove over to the Catfish Grill—not very fancy, but no one had gas money to go up to Poplar Bluff like some of the other students had done. Besides, if you were hungry, which the guys were, there was nothing better than the fried catfish sandwich basket, complete with fries. The girls got Cokes and snuck some of the guys' fries and were enjoying talking about different happenings at the prom dance when the crystal perfection of the night was dashed by the sight of Ollie Bellamy walking into the grill.

He was drunk, of course, and loudly preaching his latest sermon about politics and how it was a fine thing that that asshole senator Joe McCarthy had died. Eisenhower had never liked him, although he pretended to, but that was just for his political gain. In Ollie's estimation, the whole world was going to hell in a handbasket, and he was doing his darndest to warn the good town folk about this impending doom.

There was a collective eye roll throughout the grill as nobody wanted to hear Ollie's pontifications, least of all the students who'd enjoyed a grand prom and now just wanted to continue the fun by sharing their fries with their dates. Ray ducked his head in hopes his father wouldn't see him, but Ollie soon spied him, raised his voice, heightened his posturing and gestures, and sauntered over to the table.

"Well, lookee here, aren't you youngins all gussied up. I was fixin' to head over to Mutt's and get me a drink, but I'm glad I came over here first to see the show. Where'd you get them fine clothes, boy?"

Ray dropped his fry into his basket, wiped his hands on his napkin, and eyed his dad. "Where'd you think I got 'em? From your closet, of course." Then Ray puffed out his chest and ran his hands down the jacket's lapels.

Ollie squinted at him for a moment or two, not liking the chuckles this got from the other patrons sitting nearby. There was no way to counter Ray's damnable clever talk without making himself look bad, so Ollie decided to deflect and shifted his gaze toward Lydia, taking in her hair, her dress, her pretty eyes, her pink lips; she for sure and certain was a sight.

"Well, that's good, that's good," Ollie said and nodded toward Lydia. "Because you need to look good next to this here fine-lookin' young lady. The unfortunate truth is you can't hold a candle to her, and I don't in God's name see what she sees in ya, but you gonna have to stay on your toes in order to keep her. Gonna take more 'n a fancy suit jacket." Then Ollie turned to the rest of the patrons, spreading his arms out wide and giving a sideways bow. "Ain't that right, folks? We all know where little Ray come from, and we all know I'm the smarter and better-lookin' one, for sure."

Somebody groaned. Somebody gave a sarcastic clap. Then somebody called from across the diner, "Get your dad outta here, Bellamy!"

Everyone at Ray's table let out empathetic sighs. Ray could certainly best almost anyone who conversationally confronted him, but it was different with Ollie, as Ollie never realized he'd been bested. Plus, despite his drunken habits, Ollie had a smart streak running through him, and everybody knew this. Ollie could carry on with one overture after another until you just didn't want to listen anymore. Once he got on one of his drunken tirades, there was nothing to do except either let him blow off steam or remove him from the scene. Ray knew this all too well, so with an annoyed shake of his head, he took a last sip of his Coke, kissed Lydia on the cheek, asked Shane if he'd see that Lydia got home, slid out of the booth, and took his father home. That was not how Ray had planned on prom night ending.

Richie Silbaine and his date Linda Atkins were also at the Catfish Grill, and Richie offered to take Lydia, Shane, and Debbie home. The three of them sat in the back of Richie's car, Shane in the middle of Lydia and Debbie. Everyone thanked Richie for driving them. They all laughed, complained about what a hellacious jerk Ray's father was, and then tried to sing "All Shook Up." It was a proper attempt at trying to save the night, but Lydia couldn't help looking out her window with a heavy heart. She had planned for this night to be the night for her and Ray. With the help of her friend Jenny, who had snuck into the men's bathroom up at Earl's North End gas station and bought condoms from the vending machine, Lydia had been planning a romantic climax, literally, to the evening.

She had been putting off Ray for some time when it came to sex. Lydia couldn't think of anything more scary than to become pregnant, especially since her mother told her often how much, yes, she loved Lydia, but getting pregnant when you're eighteen and not being sure if you loved the guy is not the best way to start out. This didn't stop the hormones from raging, though, and

Ray and Lydia certainly experienced some hot and heavy times in the back seat of his car. Lydia wanted it as much as Ray did, but they had to wait. She told him time and again, they had to wait. Ray was always a gentleman about it. A frustrated one, but a gentleman nonetheless. She had been secretly smiling to herself the whole night at how she was going to present the condom to Ray. Granted this whole condom thing seemed awkward and a bit orchestrated, but Jenny, who'd had more than one fling with a boy, told her that once the boy got the condom on, they didn't give a lick how orchestrated things were.

Now instead, she sat in the back seat of Richie's car next to Shane. Shane was a good friend, and she was glad he was there. She turned to him and they exchanged knowing glances of disappointment in the night's ending. With a sigh, she placed her head on Shane's shoulder.

Shane reached over and patted her knee. And he patted her knee again. And then he kept his hand there. The car lurched over a pothole and Lydia's head wobbled against his shoulder. The feeling of her against him was electric. His body actually buzzed. He willed himself to steady his breath and act like all he was doing was comforting his friend. But it was more than that, and he certainly knew it. Desire overwhelmed him, and he finally moved his hand from her knee to rest it on his opposite thigh, his hand strategically covering his bulging crotch, evidence of his shameless thoughts. And they were shameless. What kind of a lowlife asshole was he? Making a move on his best friend's girlfriend? This is what he kept telling himself during the rest of the car ride. *She is my best friend's girlfriend. She is my best friend's girlfriend.* It did nothing whatsoever to diminish his hunger for her.

Chapter 11

1957

Summer 1957 was a busy summer for Ray and Shane. They had graduated and were now considered fully into adulthood, complete with jobs and a positive trajectory toward the future. Shane had several part-time jobs and would be heading to Southeast Missouri State that fall on a scholarship in business, courtesy of his father who was an accountant down at the Riley County First National Bank.

Ray still worked up at Earl's North End filling station and still pursued the finer points of gardening. In a rare moment of support, Ollie had brought home a paper from the university extension service about a course in horticulture. He had slapped the flyer down on the kitchen table with great self-importance, stating that since Ray was "so gosh-danged diggity-dog set on working with them flowers and such," he could take the eight-week course offered over in Wayne County and be a master gardener by the end of the summer. Ray gladly signed up for the course, and he also got a job working at Beatta Noonan's farm on a referral from Viola. Viola had taught him a lot about gardening, but he was learning even more about potassium and potash and lime and growing cycles. Beatta was a third-generation German immigrant, and her family had bought land acre by acre over the years and set up orchards, gardens, and greenhouses. They were a large supplier of fruit, vegetables, and flowers to the community and the surrounding states. Ray was floating high with all the opportunities he had that summer. With Lydia having one more year of high school, Ray's year of working would provide a substantial nest egg with which the two of them could get married and head out to more inspiring horizons. He thought with an aroused smile of last night, when he'd held her in his arms, the heat of passion searing through them both. He couldn't get enough of her. She was the prettiest and smartest girl he'd ever known, and he thanked his lucky stars every night that she was his.

It wasn't all work that summer as the quartet of friends—Ray, Lydia, Shane, and Sam—often found themselves on the river, swimming, or on float trips in canoes. The boys swore that the river actually flowed in their veins, and Lydia never tired of how cool and pretty the river was. On one bright summer day Lydia sat in the front of the canoe with Ray in the back and the Cooper brothers paddling alongside. She held her paddle high above her head and let out a whoop. "I love this river!" she exclaimed, and the boys smiled. She stood up, a sight to behold in her shorts and swimsuit top, and with an arcing dive up and out, went splashing into the river. She surfaced, splashing the boys, and they joined in, the sounds of their laughter echoing up the valley. Life just couldn't get any better.

It was later in the summer, in August, the first day of the Riley County Fair, when Ray drove back into town from his job at Beatta's farm. A certain bullying small-town deputy caused him to be late, and this in turn would change the lives of Ray and his three treasured friends. Isn't it just like fate to send you a kick in the head when you think all is butterflies and rainbows?

That Friday night at the county fair, Lydia had no way of knowing that Ray had been arrested and now sat in the Riley County Jail thanks to Deputy Culpepper. But she had to sigh as she looked at her wristwatch and saw that Ray was almost an hour late. Going steady almost a year now, Lydia knew she loved Ray with all her heart, but she had to admit, there was a kink or two in his shining shield of armor. Of course, no one was perfect, and Lydia knew all too well the challenges Ray had to deal with—his good-for-nothing daddy, never having enough money, having cars break down at the worst times, and enduring the tortures of Deputy Culpepper.

And yet, sometimes it wasn't always bad luck for Ray, but rather a mixture of bad timing and bad decisions, some of which he had control over if he so chose. The delight he took in daredevil adventure was one of the things that made her swoon, but it also, truth be told, needed to be reined in. After all, he was a high school graduate now, and the future—their future—called. Fun was fun, but it was time to do a little growing up. Maybe a lot of growing up. Lydia's aim was to get through her last year of high school as quickly as she could make the world turn and get enrolled in a nursing diploma program. She and Ray could get married and buy a house and start a family. None of these goals had room for one-upping a small-town deputy by driving your car too fast, or dealing with a non-supportive drunkard father.

The sun, still out late this time of summer but slowly starting to set, cast magenta and amber colors over the fair field. She looked across the field toward the road where cars were driving in to the fair, hoping to see him soon. Behind her, people were laughing as they enjoyed their chili dogs and threw balls at milk bottles in an attempt to win a hula hoop. People squealed as the Ferris wheel went around and hollered in triumph as they bested the strongman high striker. Carnival organ music filled the air and made her head spin with delight. The smell of popcorn and corndogs filled the air. She loved the fair! It never entered her mind that she might have to enjoy the fair without Ray. They were part and parcel, joined at the hip; people even spoke their names as if they were one word—RayandLydia. She felt incomplete without Ray. They had made plans. Ray would meet her here by the concessions. She hoped for another night of passion like they had shared the night before. Ray could be vexing, but there was no denying the fire he lit within her belly.

It was then that she saw Shane walking toward her from across the midway, pink and purple flashing lights of the tilt-a-whirl casting him in a cotton-candy silhouette. She watched as he halfway extracted a pint of Jack Daniel's from his jeans pocket, slyly showing it to her before shoving it back down, an eager and playful grin shining on his face.

A few hours before, Ray had deposited his weekly check from Beatta's farm, keeping five dollars in cash for his night of fun with Lydia at the fair. As he walked out of the Riley County First National Bank, he didn't notice Deputy Culpepper leaning in the shadows, back against the outside bank wall. Suddenly, Westley was behind him and grabbed Ray's arm. In the blink of an eye, Ray felt a cold metal ring being slapped on his wrist. Too late, he tried to jerk away, but Wes held tight and grabbed Ray's other arm, pulled it behind his back, and clasped the handcuffs together.

"What the hell?" was all Ray managed to sputter.

"You are under arrest, Bellamy."

"What for?"

"For failure to pay a speeding ticket and not showing up in court to pay your fine. You are now under the jurisdiction of the Riley County Sheriff's Office, to be jailed until said fine can be paid. I finally got you." To say Wes cackled with glee would be an understatement.

Wes led Ray to his deputy cruiser, opened the back door, and tried to shove him into the back seat. Having a nature that did not sit well with being caged, Ray set up a fight, twisting and bending and shoving. Wes had a strong hold on him though, and suddenly he pulled a knife from his belt and held it against Ray's side.

"Don't push me, boy. I've a mind to use this blade right now and put an end to your sorry little ass. I'd be doing the world a favor." Ray twisted and pushed again, and in the tussle, the blade caught him, slicing across his forearm. The sight of blood startled them both, but it only managed to rile Wes further and he shoved harder, sending Ray tumbling backward into the back seat. That was when, thankfully, Ray saw Sam coming out of the Rexall drug store sipping a root beer float. Ray sat up and called his name.

"Sam! Go find my daddy. Tell him I need money to pay a fine."

Like a cartoon character, Sam's mouth about dropped to the sidewalk. In the two seconds it took to decipher the crazy scene in front of him, his love for his friend and his hatred for the deputy rose up like an erupting volcano. This called for drastic measures, and with the only weapon at hand being his root beer float, he sprinted across the street, pretended to stumble, jostled the drink, and sent it sailing in the air. His mark was true, and Wes gasped and sputtered as sticky root beer and ice cream splashed on his face and down the front of his shirt.

"Gosh dang!" Sam proclaimed as he held his hands out in a feigned apologetic gesture. "Ain't that the shits. I paid a whole thirty-five cents for that."

Despite his predicament, Ray laid his head back on the seat and hooted amid Wes's cursing and wiping at his face and shirt.

"What the hell, Cooper! God damn you!" Wes shook both hands, flicking off the root beer. "Don't be surprised I don't haul your ass into this car right alongside Bellamy! Gawd dang it!"

"Sam, I'm gonna need money. Go find my dad."

"How much?" Sam asked.

"More than you have, Sam-u-el," Wes said, still swiping at the root beer dripping down his shirt as he got in the car. "Get outta the way, I've got a fugitive to deliver to jail. Go on, now!"

Wes even had the audacity to turn the siren and lights on as he backed out of the parking space and drove dramatically toward the town square, where the jail—an old rock building attached to the lower level of the courthouse—awaited Ray.

Ray sat back in the seat with a huff. "You goddamned fuckin' loser, Culpepper. If you ain't the shittin'est piece of slime dog I ever met! God damn you! God damn you all to hell!"

Wes just chuckled all the way to the jail, which wasn't long because it was a whole block and a half from the bank. But in that short space he managed to achieve his goal—showing the townspeople how big and important Deputy Westley Culpepper was keeping all of them out of harm's way.

The deputy made quite a show of pulling Ray from the car and hauling him up the stairs to the courthouse. They continued through the main hallway all the way to the back where the sheriff's office was. Going down a back flight of stairs, Wes pulled the key ring off the hook, opened one of the two jail cells, and pushed Ray inside. He slammed the cell door behind him.

"You gonna take these cuffs off me?" Ray demanded, twisting his arms from around his back.

"Nah. Sit there and think a bit about what you're in there for. And maybe you'll come to the conclusion that you're not so high and mighty after all. Them cuffs are good for ya. Now, then," and he looked at his watch, "it's right at about four thirty-seven. Courthouse closes at five sharp. Looks like you got less than twenty-five minutes to pay that fine or . . ." He gave a mocking shrug. "Or guess it looks like you'll be in here for the whole weekend."

Wes studied him from behind the bars. They were old and rusty.

In fact, the cells weren't used much, which might explain why Culpepper was so fired up to catch himself a prisoner. He had so few chances to show everybody how strong and essential he was to this town. The fact that Ray Bellamy was his prisoner pretty much made this the best day of Wes's life.

Ray stepped up and pressed his face to the bars. He sniffed. "Hey, Culpepper." He sniffed again. "You smell like . . . root beer." He watched as Wes's jaw tightened, then he stepped away and sat down laughing, snorting and guffawing with all his might. "Don't get all mad about it, Culpepper. This is a sight better. I can't begin to tell you the times we all thought you stunk so bad. Like a pig, you stunk!" Ray continued to laugh. "Like a pig, I say. This here's way better!"

Wes marched off, Ray's cackling echoing in his now red ears.

The town of Westfall had begun like most small rural towns in mid-America, with a courthouse on the town square, and the square being the center of the town. But after an earthquake that caused a mild shift in the lay of the land, the Current River had taken to flooding every third spring or so, enough that it ran up into the south part of the town, and the houses in that area took the worst of it. So the southern side of town was eventually abandoned as the residents moved and built their homes to the north and east of town where they were safe from flooding. As a result, the town square and the courthouse sat a bit cattywampus to the town layout.

The jail was built on the south end of the courthouse some sixty years ago. It had seen a bit of action back in the 1920s as bootlegging was sorely frowned upon, at least by law enforcement. Prohibition ended of course, and the business of locking up folks dwindled to the occasional burglar, car thief, or rabble rouser. The jail was made from river stone, and the handiwork applied to it was the best in the state. The courthouse might blow away in a tornado—built of pine with bricks here and there for aesthetic purposes—but the jail would stand staunch through any storm and most likely be there until hell froze over. Except that the bars were made of poor-quality rebar. Each jail cell had a window that looked south of the square, out past the grocery store and down to the river. There was no glass in these windows as prisoners usually didn't stay very long, and those that did just had to take any foul weather as part of their punishment. Time and weather had done its worst to the bars. If a man had a hammer, he could probably bang away at the bars long enough to eventually create an opening in the deteriorating metal.

Ray suddenly noticed a commotion outside his jail cell window. It was Sam, jumping up high enough to be able to see into the cell. "Ray! Where you at?"

Ray scuttled over to the window and stood on his tiptoes. "I'm in here. Sam, you little life saver! Hallelujah!"

"What do you want me to do?" Sam asked amid his jumps to gain a better view.

"Go back up to the office and ask Miss Grant how much my fine is. And then go find daddy and ask him to get money to pay it. And hurry, the office is about to close. If I don't get it paid, I'll have to stay in here all weekend."

Sam took off at a run but then slid to a stop when he heard Ray calling him back.

"And tell 'em I'm bleeding and I still got the handcuffs on. Turd-ass Culpepper cut me when he put me in the car, and he still has me handcuffed. If I gotta pee, I'll have to piss my pants."

"Fuck him!" Sam said with a shake of his head. "What a prick! What a goddamned deranged lunatic. Got a brain no bigger'n the size of a flea's ass! I'd like to cut him, son of a—"

"Go! We ain't got much time!"

Sam cut off his verbal murder of Wes, then turned and ran around to the front of the courthouse and up the steps. He pulled open both of the double wooden and glass doors, ran down the wood-planked floor, heard his panting breaths echo up to the high ceiling, and pretty much catapulted himself into the courthouse office. Both Judy Grant and Sheriff Tyler, who were discussing a report, looked over aghast at the Cooper boy looking as if he'd just outrun a jackal.

"Ray's bleeding and hestillgothandcuffson and he won'tbeabletopee and howmuchishisfine," was what they thought they heard the boy say.

Sheriff Tyler, in that slow, gentlemanly way he had about himself, held up a hand and said, "Calm down, son."

At this point, Sam was now bent over, trying to catch his breath with one hand on his knee, the other pinching at his waist. He had run from the bank and now here, and he had a howling set of stitches in his side. He raked his fingers up through his sweaty blonde hair, creating a bit of a crazy scientist look, and gasped out, "Can't. Gotta get the money for the fine or else Ray's gonna have to spend the weekend in the jail. What's his fine?"

Sheriff Tyler frowned and looked over at Judy for confirmation. "What's this?"

Judy pushed her glasses up the bridge of her nose. "Wes brought him in on account of him not paying a speeding ticket. You just missed him." She picked up the folder on her desk and handed it to the sheriff.

Sheriff Tyler opened the folder, held up a piece of paper, read it, turned it over, and read some more, all the while Sam wanting to yell at him because he was moving much too slowly for his liking. Tyler looked over at Sam. "You say he's still handcuffed?"

Sam nodded. "Yes!"

Tyler heaved a huge irritated sigh and rubbed his forehead as if trying to erase a headache, something he'd been doing a lot since Westley Jordan Culpepper had joined the team. He stepped over to his desk and pulled out a ring of keys. "His fine is sixty-eight dollars for an unpaid speeding ticket last summer. He needs to pay the fine before I'll let him out. Ray's done enough of this kind of thing that he knows better. I'll go take the cuffs off him and let him know."

"Office closes in fifteen minutes," Judy said, eyeing Sam with a slightly peeved expression. She had a date with her boyfriend to meet him at the fair, and she wasn't going to miss it. "Fifteen minutes, ya hear?"

Sam nodded, then turned and commenced to do more running.

Ollie was not at his house, and Sam finally found him up at the fair, working the ball and milk bottle booth. "What are you sayin'?" Ollie asked Sam when he gave another fast-talking rendition of the course of events. "How much is his fine?"

"Sixty-eight dollars."

Ollie frowned. "I ain't got that kind of money. Leastwise, not on me. Damn kid needs to learn his lesson. You done missed your time, anyways. It's ten past five; Judy's for sure closed up the courthouse office. Quit yer hootin' and hollerin'. Go enjoy the fair. We'll get the money on Monday."

Sam lunged across the counter at Ollie, grabbing his shirt, surprising them both along with the couple standing at the booth throwing baseballs at the milk bottles. "He's my friend and I want him out of there!"

Ollie frowned and pulled Sam's hands off his shirt. "Well, he's my son, and I say it ain't gonna hurt him one bit to spend the weekend in there. Now get outta here!"

Sam stood and glared. Ollie stared back. Sam did not back down. Finally, Ollie gave a dramatic sigh, reached under the counter, and pulled out five dollars from a cigar box. "That's pretty much my pay for the night. He's gonna owe me. That's all I got. Now go on. Git!"

It was a start. Sam turned, trying to think of what he should do next. He was all too aware of the passing time. In truth, Judy Grant had stayed an extra fifteen minutes at the office, allowing for the hope that Sam might have actually gotten the money in time. But after waiting until quarter after five, she'd done all she could for the Cooper boy and his friend, and Ray would be okay anyway because he was a tough kid. She turned off the lights, closed and locked the office door, walked down the wide hallway, locked the courthouse door, and headed over to the fair.

Sam had decided he'd go back to his house because he had some money saved and he'd add it to Ollie's money. Maybe he could find someone else to help make the collection grow, and then somehow he'd make the clock go back in time and get Ray out before the courthouse office closed. He had been saving his money to buy a car, and even though it was only twenty-six dollars, he was proud of himself for having achieved this notable cache. It was more money than he'd ever had in his life at one time. But now, there wasn't any question of whether or not to offer the money up for Ray. Sam had never quite lived down the fact that he'd let Ray take all the blame for tearing up Mrs. Meeks's flowers. This was a small way Sam could repay him. And not just by offering up his savings, but by not letting him sit in jail the whole weekend. He turned toward town and ran home as fast as he could.

He flung open the front screen door and ran past his parents, who were sitting in the living room watching *The Adventures of Rin Tin Tin* on their black-and-white TV.

Mr. Cooper removed his pipe and sat up with a frown, and Mrs. Cooper stood up with a gasp. "What happened?"

"Ray's in jail and I gotta get him out!" Sam did the best he could
to explain the course of events for the third time that night. He
told them about Ollie's five dollars, and that he had twenty-six
dollars he wanted to add to it and still needed thirty-five more
dollars. At this point, Mr. Cooper corrected his son's math and
stated that he needed thirty-seven dollars, which he could get for
him. But all that didn't matter because, according to Sam's story,
Judy would be long gone from the office. Sam's nerves were pretty
much frazzled by now, and Mrs. Cooper could see that her son was
near bursting. She could also see that he'd been crying. She placed
a hand on his shoulder and gently squeezed with a calming touch.

"We can get the extra money. And I'll call Birdie Tyler. No
telling where Sheriff Tyler is, but Birdie's worked in the office with
her husband before and most likely has keys to the office and will
know how to process the paperwork. I'm hoping she'll be willing
to help. We at least have to ask."

Birdie Tyler, lovely and esteemed wife of Sheriff Tyler, was in
the same bridge club as Emily Cooper, and Emily thought nothing
of calling Birdie for help. And after hearing the preposterous tale
in which she felt sympathy for Ray and exasperation with Westley,
she thought nothing of getting the keys and meeting them all
down at the courthouse. Birdie found Ray's arrest folder in the
office, took the fine money from Sam, stamped the record as paid,
and put the money in the lock box in Judy's desk drawer. Then
they all went down to the jail to liberate Ray. There were hugs
and nervous laughter, and they offered to take him to the Catfish
Grill to get a sandwich, but Ray said no, he had to go find Lydia,
and he'd get something to eat at the fair. In all the commotion of
getting arrested, Ray had forgotten that he had five dollars in his

pocket that could have helped pay his fine, but the ladies insisted that wasn't needed and he should go enjoy himself.

Sam wanted to go with him, but he didn't want to be a third wheel. He was happy his friend was out of jail, but the night had spent him and he went home with his mother, took a bath, and crawled into bed, lying there considering the crazy things of life for about two minutes before he fell asleep.

As Ray drove over to the fair, he passed Deputy Culpepper, who was standing at the edge of the entry gate to the fair talking with Mutt Templeton. Ray saw Wes just a second before he started to turn into the fair entry, so instead of turning into the fairgrounds, he kept driving down Current View Road. He looked in his rearview mirror and cussed a blue streak as he was sure Wes had seen him. For once he just wanted to spend a nice evening with Lydia without Culpepper shoving his knuckleheaded nose into everything. He decided he'd drive around to the east side of the fairgrounds, park the car, jump the creek, and enter the fair that way, and he hoped that would throw Culpepper off his trail. But there in the rearview mirror, he saw Culpepper's car coming after him. Ray steeled himself for the chase. As he increased his speed, he looked left and saw Shane and Lydia sitting on the hill just on the edge of the fairgrounds. It looked like he had just kissed her. Ray almost drove off into the ditch as he craned his neck to look back at them, so he turned his gaze back to the road. What the hell? For now, he had to keep on driving. He'd ask for an explanation later, for surely there was one.

Chapter 12

1957

Lydia realized she was in trouble near the end of September. Having last seen her period back in July, she hoped its absence in late August was a nonsensical blip of mother nature. But its failure to appear in late September was indisputable and earth-shattering evidence that she was pregnant. God help her, but the thing that was splitting cells inside her was not wanted at all. Lydia had heard enough tales from her mother about how—though Phyllis loved Lydia with all her heart—there was nothing worse in this entire universe than being a teenage mother, and a single one at that. Combined with the town gossip spreading like wildfire across the whole of Riley County and probably all the way down to Paducah, Phyllis's alarm at this turn of affairs would very well be her undoing, and Lydia's as well.

While lying in bed, pondering her predicament with a heart that wouldn't stop beating at ninety miles a minute and a headache that threatened to split her skull wide open, Lydia went over one solution after another. Checking off option number one, then option number two, then three and four, she would lay her hands on her belly and feel absolutely nothing, physical or emotional. That, along with the fact that she hadn't felt one whit of morning sickness, breast tenderness, or any other signs that normally came along with pregnancy, affirmed for her that this whole debacle just simply wasn't meant to be. And so, with her course of action decided, she skipped school the next day and headed over to Ray's house.

She started out resolutely, determined to take charge of her body and her future, but was only four blocks from her house when she started crying. Wiping furiously at her tears, she realized in that moment that she hated men. All of them. Even Ray. They had this offhand attitude about sex and their bodies. They could take possession of another body—all superior and privileged in their need to take pleasure—implant a seed, and walk cavalierly away from the whole thing. And the repugnance of it all was that she had to turn to a man to help her out of this. She set her jaw, wiped her tears, and began walking again. Then she started crying again. Then she marched on.

The trembling that had overtaken her body by the time she reached the weedy gravel driveway that led up to Ray's house was now sorely visible. She was not looking forward to the conversation she had practiced in her head on the walk over—it had changed at least nine times, one angle sounding fine, then a different spin sounding better, then nothing of it sounding acceptable at all. Somehow she had to extract help without starting World War III in the tiny town of Westfall. Her eyes red-rimmed, she looked at the little dilapidated tar-paper shack and sighed ruefully. This vision made her question exactly what she was pinning her future on. Of course Ray was more than this sad little house. Of course he was. He was her present and her future, despite occasional misgivings she had from time to time. This was not going to be easy, but she knew Ray had saved up some money for their future, and if their future ever needed help, it was now.

She knocked tentatively on the faded frame of the screen door and stood with the late summer breeze ruffling her hair, which was a good thing because by now she'd worked up a sweat and suddenly felt claustrophobic from a rising heat within her. There was no answer so she knocked again, this time with force and attitude. Open the door and help me! Then the door opened and it was Ollie who stood there, gray T-shirt and jeans, eyes red-rimmed like hers, but his no doubt because of drinking too much booze. Yet another man she didn't like. She shook her head as if to dismiss him.

"I'm looking for Ray. Is he home?" Her voice sounded like her throat was lined with sandpaper.

Ollie reached down and pulled his suspenders up over his shoulders. "Ain't home. He's probably up at Earl's, if I was to guess."

Lydia looked away with a perturbed sigh. She supposed she was going to have to go traipsing all over town looking for him. That would take time, and she didn't have time.

Ollie rubbed the stubble on his chin and studied her. He knew her as Ray's girlfriend. Pretty. Seemed smart. And despite him never admitting it out loud, he thought she was a fair good match for his son. They both seemed to have a good head on their shoulders, hard workers. He often saw her with a bright smile and a lift to her walk, and he secretly cheered her on in her young naive innocence. Nice that the world hadn't soiled her soul.

Ollie was familiar with soiled souls, his own being the first at the hands of a cold and abusive father. A shame Ollie hadn't learned enough to stop that pattern with his own son. But Ollie's keen eye noted the smiling, high-stepping girl he was used to seeing about town now had a dark mood hanging over her. Something had happened to her, there was no mistaking it, and there was no longer an innocence that showed in her expression. This here girl standing in front of him was in trouble deep. No disputing that fact.

"I think . . ." Ollie worked his mouth a bit, trying to sum up what he wanted to say. He took a half step out past the screen door and looked around. Nothing about but the river, dark green and slowly moving around the bend among a heap of tangled brush and small cedars. A bird called somewhere, and a few leaves slowly drifted down from an elm tree, a sign of an early autumn. Satisfied the coast was clear, he stepped back into the doorway and looked up at Lydia.

"I'm supposin' you might be in a bit a trouble."

His words had a rather galvanizing effect on her. Lydia had not said one word to anybody about this, and yet hearing someone say the very thing that was haunting her was strangely comforting. She blinked at him, feeling the trembling in her body start to subside.

"Listen . . . um, I think, if it's what I think you is needing . . . I might be able . . . to . . . you know."

Lydia's mind, baffled at Ollie's correct conjecture and half-baked suggestion, was unable to string together any sensible thought. Her head and heart blazed. The whole thing was getting on her nerves, and she sent him a frown that meant business. Then she realized she'd been holding her breath and she now felt faint. She teetered and began to sway.

"Here now," Ollie said and reached out to take hold of each of her arms. He guided her to a wooden crate sitting beside the doorstep, which he turned over, dislodging an empty glass bourbon bottle that rolled away, clanking down the gravel driveway a few feet. He gently pushed her down to a sitting position.

"Take a deep breath, lean your head down."

She did as she was told, and the trembling took over in massive resurgence.

"Wait here," he said and disappeared into the house.

Lydia heard some rummaging around, a drawer opening, something that sounded like a box being opened. She couldn't quite tell, but Ollie seemed to be looking for something. She raised her head and looked out on the river. She was struck by the incongruent peacefulness of the scene. She slowly blinked as she studied the river curving around the bend. She could just go there, she thought, looking at the river's dark-green depths with longing. Well now, this had not been an option on her checklist. Just a quiet slipping into the cold current. She could just drift away and then she would be gone, and she would sleep and no more would the powers of men have a hold on her.

Somehow she found her breath and was remarkably soothed by this thought. It mattered a great deal that she had control over this whole thing. It was lack of control that had gotten her into this mess. She took a few clearing breaths while the sounds of Ollie rummaging around in the house continued behind her. She thought she heard him cuss, and she had to smile at the ludicrousness of it all. Perhaps it was hysteria taking over, but she couldn't help thinking how comical this little scene was, and she heard herself chuckle, which dismayed her. How in God's name had she ended up here?

She continued to look at the river, the current beckoning.

Then as suddenly as he had disappeared, Ollie reappeared, and she looked up at him. She had thought he was getting her a drink of water, but instead, he had money in his hand.

"This here's fifty dollars. I think it should be enough. Go on up to Viola Meeks's house. She can help."

Lydia's mouth dropped open, and she slowly stood up. She stared down wide-eyed at the money. "Mrs. Meeks?" she finally was able to squeak out.

Ollie nodded. Again, he took a step past the front door and looked out, making sure no one was around to see or hear about this transaction. After all, what he was talking about was against the law.

Lydia reached out and took the money. It was a slow moment as if in a dream, where your arms simply wouldn't move fast enough, and your awake self is yelling at you to hurry up before the moment passes. She held the money in her hands and studied it. Then she looked up at Ollie.

"Thank you. I'll . . . pay you back. I mean, how can you . . . is this okay?"

Ollie waved his hand. "It's okay."

Lydia stood there, unable to move her legs, caught again in that dream where nothing works the way you want it to. Her emotions continued their roller-coaster ride that had started several weeks ago and had been brought to their heights on this day. Part of her wanted to crumble to the ground and cry and scream. She didn't want to do this! She didn't want to have to do this! She wanted to curse mother nature, and men and sex! She hated herself and her life and this dirty little man standing in front of her.

"It isn't fair!" she said, unable to determine where the words had come from or, for that matter, why in the world she was standing there proclaiming them to Ollie Bellamy.

"Well now," he started, and looked out past her to the river. "Ain't no need in hanging on to what was never fair." He reached out his hand and ever so slightly touched hers. "It'll be okay. Just go now."

Lydia blinked at him, and realization came to her. Though older, she saw the same bright blue eyes that she saw when she looked into his son's face. She'd never noticed, but his cheekbones were nice, and there was a softness about his mouth. Yes, age and bitterness and drink had lined his face in leathery creases, but she had never seen what lay just below that rugged skin—a man who had lived through hard times and had not done a very good job of it, but in some mysterious way had managed to carve out a living and had never, not even one time, been mean, salacious, or demeaning toward women.

She thought back now to how he had helped Mrs. Meeks deliver her flowers and vegetables, how he had helped push Mrs. Cooper's car out of the snow, how he had carried campaign signs to people's yards that declared Jenna Rainright the best person for county collector, how he'd returned her step-grandmother's wallet that she had dropped on the bank floor, how he always left a whole dollar tip for Maggie down at the Catfish Grill. Until now, Lydia had only seen him through the lens of how he treated Ray, which was not at all good. But now, seeing him through a different lens, a different light began to develop around him. This man, as obnoxious and vexing as anyone could be, had never been anything but polite and supportive to women. This new realization made Lydia slightly cock her head like the Victrola dog.

"Huh," Lydia breathed out.

She continued to stare at him, and he shifted his feet a bit, getting uncomfortable at her stare, which was a switch because Ollie was usually the one who made people uncomfortable. She finally pulled herself out of her epiphany and was brought back to the thing at hand.

"Anyway." She held up the money in her hand, noticing a strange, clean smell coming from it. "Thank you. I . . . thank you." She looked back out across the river, trying to work up the courage to say the next words. "Oh, and . . . um, do me a favor, and don't . . . can you, I mean, might as well . . . can you not tell Ray about this?" She hadn't planned on this, but since the course of events had taken the turn they had due to Ollie's help, she felt it was for the best.

Ollie raised his chin and hooked his thumbs behind each of his suspenders, then nodded. "Sure enough." Then having reached the limit of his ability to provide comfort, he stepped back into the house and closed the door.

Lydia blinked at the door, then down at the money she held in her hand. She felt like she had been standing there for the length of a lifetime. Her heart picking up its quick desperate beat again, she turned and walked up the path to the road with a strange lightness to her step. Still filled with trepidation at what she had to do, she now felt a little more in control. This strange turn of events made her realize the world wasn't exactly what she thought it was. She understood now that there were so many more layers to people than she could ever imagine, both good and bad. Herself included.

Chapter 13

1957

Mrs. Meeks's house was about two miles out on the edge of town in a small cluster of houses where other black families lived. While it wouldn't be totally correct to say that black people were welcomed in Westfall, they were at least tolerated. But in 1957, there was an actual law on the books that said black people had to be out of the town of Westfall by sundown.

Hence the small cluster of houses was a bit of its own village, with the Second Baptist Church along with a cemetery perched on a small hill just above the houses. Eula Glover taught school to the several children up at the church, as well as running a quilting bee on her back porch. Shadrick Bradley and his two sons fixed cars in the shed out back of their house. Jeb Featherston raised chickens and sold them and their eggs. And folks came to Mrs. Meeks to get medicinal care from her herbs and nurturing ministrations.

A flat green space on the west side of the houses served as a baseball field for the children to play in, along with a dirt track that circled the field. There were bleachers, a gazebo, and a few picnic tables back under the trees where children and families gathered to play music, play ball, sell vegetables, and swap stories. A creek bordering the field ran usually as a lazy trickle, but could transform into a bubbling cascade after a rainstorm. This creek made its way to a confluence with the Current River, where the black folks would cool off on the river banks on hot days a few miles down from the white folks' River Leap Park.

This area of land had been allowed to the black families by the white people as it had the tendency to flood. But mother nature, having no apparent favor to one race or the other, produced a small earthquake back in the early 1900s, causing a slight upheaval of the land that created a natural berm on the edge of the river. This kept the river inside its banks as it flowed past the houses, now flooding farther south, pestering the white people. The black people in their little village had to tip their hat to mother nature's hijinks.

Lydia made her way up the road, the morning getting warmer and warmer, causing the light jacket she wore to be no longer needed, but nonetheless, she kept it on, pulling the collar high in an attempt to hide her identity. She walked up to Mrs. Meeks's porch and softly knocked.

"She ain't at home."

Lydia heard the voice but at first didn't see anyone. Tracking the voice to the porch of the house next door, she turned and saw a woman stand up and walk to the porch railing. The woman took a last puff on her cigarette, then with a flick of her fingers, sent it flying into the side yard.

"If you're looking for Mrs. Meeks, she's up in St. Louis visiting her son for a few days. Anything I can help you with?"

Lydia stared at her for a moment. She recognized her from a time when she had come out to help Ray and Shane and Sam in Mrs. Meeks's garden.

"I . . ." Lydia started. "Do you know when she might be back?"

The lady shook her head. "Not sure. My name's Mary. And if you're needin' what I think you're needin', I can help."

Lydia now began to wonder if she didn't have a large P for pregnant stamped right smack dab in the middle of her forehead. It sure hadn't taken Ollie long to catch on, and now Mary seemed to have nailed the predicament in a matter of seconds. Lydia mulled this over for a few moments, a mixture of embarrassment, wariness, and nervousness causing her indecision. But the main emotion that once again bubbled up and took over was anger. Anger that she had no control over her own body, and that everybody else seemed to have license with her body except her. Anger that society and its laws kept her from having control over her body or her future. She would never say this out loud, of course. Indeed, she wouldn't have even been able to put words to her thoughts. Society had done a good job of making all this be the woman's fault. And it took, buried itself deep into her consciousness, and she believed it. The anger fell limp to the porch floor, and she felt nothing but shame.

"If you need help with what I'm thinkin' you need help with, then time is of importance. The sooner the better. I know what I'm doin'. I've helped Mrs. Meeks." Mary was not telling the absolute truth. She had in fact helped Viola before, but Mary did not know what she was doing. Mary shrugged. "Of course . . ." She turned and sat back down in her rocking chair. "If you want to wait . . . well, no tellin', of course."

"No," Lydia said finally. "I don't want to wait. I want this to be over."

Mary stood back up. "You got money, right?"

Lydia nodded. "Forty-five dollars," she said, in case she had to haggle. The quick shake of Mary's head told her she would have to haggle.

Tears rose up, and Lydia drew in a deep breath. What if she didn't have enough? "Fifty is all I got," she said through an angry sob, then she turned and headed back down the porch steps.

"Now hold on," Mary said. "Fifty'll do. Come on up here." She beckoned for Lydia to hurry. "You'll be all right. You ain't the first girl to be in this situation, and you won't be the last."

Lydia brought her hands up to her face, and as she walked up Mary's porch steps, the tears poured out. Mary placed an arm across Lydia's shoulders and held open her screen door.

"You'll be all right," she said again and led her through the door.

Things moved in a haze after that. Lydia remembered a kitchen table being pushed up against the wall and a quilt and a sheet and brown paper being laid down on it. At some point Lydia laid on top of all those layers, the crinkling of the brown paper starting out as a buzzing in her ears, and then rising into a dizzying crescendo. She drank something, whiskey maybe. It burned her throat. She remembered the murmurings of Mary down at the other end of the table, she remembered the prodding and poking, pressure and stinging. Maybe she cried out, maybe she bit her lip, but there was something in her mouth, maybe a rag, that she was biting down on. At first, it felt like it was taking forever, and then it seemed like in no time Mary was helping her sit up and move over to sit upright on a chair. She remembered a cool cloth on her face, and it feeling good on her sweaty forehead. She remembered cramping. She remembered Mary telling her she could take a shower but not a bath until the bleeding stopped, which would be for a week to ten days. A pad was put in her panties, and on top of that a rolled and folded towel, and then Lydia was standing. And then she had her jacket on and she was walking. Out to the porch. Down the steps. Out past Mrs. Meeks's house and the other houses, and out to Route K. She walked back toward town. The yellow of the early autumn sun seemed particularly bright, not helping her headache. A feeling of horrible relief mixed with a cramping backache all swirled together in an overwhelming haze. She kept walking.

Chapter 14

1957

S he hadn't thought this part through, and she began to feel tired and weak. The walk back to her house seemed infinitely long. Despite the heat, she pulled her jacket collar up to her cheek, again trying to hide her face as much as she possibly could, but danged if she didn't hear a car slowing down behind her, then pulling up beside her.

"Hey, pretty lady," the driver called.

Lydia turned to see, of all people, Sam driving a brand-new silver-blue Chevrolet Impala. When Lydia looked back on this serendipitous meeting out on Route K, with Sam looking quite cocky in the driver's seat, she would remember that he had not only saved her life, but had put into motion steps that would eventually change it. For the better.

"What are you doin' out here?" he asked, stopping the car and peering out the passenger window at her.

In reflex, Lydia pulled the collar closer but bent down and looked into the open window. "The better question is what are *you* doing out here? Where'd you get this car?" Lydia amazed herself with her acting. Despite feeling the pad in her panties filling up with blood as she stood there, and the cobwebs of the previous hour's events still fuzzing up her brain, she managed to pull off the persona of a young lady who just happened to be out for a stroll and hadn't a worry in the world.

Sam grinned and spread out his hands, palms upward, as he showed off the car. "It's Mr. Miller's. I've done this for him once before. New car comes into Poplar Bluff, and he needs someone to bring it down here for him to sell off his lot. He pays me two dollars to drive it down. Ain't that something? Two dollars to drive this beauty. Wish I could buy it." He rubbed the shiny dashboard, then stroked the slim steering wheel.

"How'd you get up to Poplar Bluff?"

"Drove up in Charlie's milk truck early this morning."

Lydia nodded and pretended to admire the car. "You're skipping school."

Sam tapped his forehead then pointed at her. "And so are you. You got a better reason than making two dollars?"

Lydia forced a chuckle, although the longer she stood there, the more dizzy she began to feel. "Maybe I was making money too."

"Doing what?"

Lydia shook her head. "It's a secret. Me and Mrs. Meeks are working on something." Which wasn't altogether untrue, she supposed. It was a secret, but it wasn't Mrs. Meeks, it was Mary, and instead of making money, she had spent quite a lot of money, but these discrepant details didn't need to be disclosed now, or ever. However, she would surprise herself many years later by doing just that, telling Sam the whole story.

She felt herself sway, and she placed a hand on the car. "How 'bout you giving me a lift home. Would Mr. Miller be okay with that?"

Sam reached over and opened the door. "What Mr. Miller don't know won't hurt him. 'Sides, I don't care what he thinks. I'll take you anywhere you want to go no matter what anybody thinks." Sam puffed up and felt several years older and several inches taller at being able to escort Lydia. He chose to disregard that he was two years younger and several inches shorter than her. Made no difference—this was his fantasy, and he could be as old and as tall as he wanted.

Not a moment too soon, Lydia stepped into the car and gratefully rested her legs, which had been threatening to fold up underneath her any second. She gave him a thankful smile and they drove off, Sam feeling like the king of the world driving the prettiest girl in town in a beauty of a car.

They hadn't gone barely a mile when Sam's bright fantasy started to fade and he picked up on a darkness that seemed to hover around Lydia. She had now slipped into silence, closing her eyes and leaning her head back against the car seat. Stealing a sideways glance her way, he saw tiny beads of sweat on her upper lip and noticed tendrils of hair stuck to her sweaty forehead. He wanted to reach out to her, to touch her hand and offer reassurance for something that he didn't understand. He knew this was not the normal Lydia he had come to know. His heart swelled with love and protection for her that he knew had always been there, but had been suppressed. Not because she was Ray's girl, but because Lydia was one of the strongest girls he'd ever known and had rarely been in need of protection. She'd always been the protector, the one offering strength to Ray and him and his brother by way of a wise phrase, a supportive cheer, a better plan.

Now she looked broken. This sent an apprehensive tremor through Sam. Something was definitely wrong with her, and he didn't like it. She remained silent for the rest of the ride, and he dropped her off in front of her house, frowning at the way she pulled her coat tight around her as she walked haltingly up to her door.

The next morning at school, Sam sat in Mrs. Teegarten's social studies class, a class he shared, much to his delight, with Lydia. However, she hadn't shown up that morning, not at her locker nor now in first-hour class. The longer the class dragged on, the larger a sense of dread began to grow in the pit of his stomach. He had thought about her all last night, unable to sleep soundly, and he'd thought about her this morning as he got ready for school. Something wasn't right. No longer able to concentrate on the merits of the three parts of the federal government that Mrs. Teegarten was passionately explaining with the help of a chart she had been using for the past twenty years, Sam closed his book, went to Mrs. Teegarten's desk, and whispered that he thought he might be getting sick and needed to go to the bathroom. With a slight look of alarm—Mrs. Teegarten had cleaned up enough student vomit in her day—she took a step back from him and quickly whisked him away with a flick of her pointer stick.

Westfall High School was a handsome two-story brown brick building with white trim and tall windows. The front entryway opened up to a wide hall with smaller halls branching off, one to the right and one to the left. Two wide staircases rose up on either side of the great entry hall, and at some point in the school's history, someone had decreed that the right staircase was to be used only for going up to the second floor, and the left staircase was to be used only for coming down from the second floor. This rule made for a more orderly trafficway when two hundred students changed classes six times a day. However, when it was not class change time and those two hundred students were not on the stairs, the rule made no sense. Principal Buhlig didn't care, a rule was a rule.

Sam walked out of Mrs. Teegarten's classroom, which happened to be next to the up staircase, but he had no time to adhere to a rule when it made no sense, so he ran down the staircase two steps at a time. As he turned the corner on the landing to head down the last flight, he ran right smack dab into Principal Buhlig.

"Mr. Cooper, I'd thank you to turn around and go back upstairs and come back down the correct staircase."

Sam thought surely Principal Buhlig had lost his ever-loving mind, because it didn't make sense to go back up and then down the other staircase, especially when there was no one else on the stairs. Sam shot him an incredulous look and kept going down the up staircase.

"Mr. Cooper!" Principal Buhlig's raised voice and stern expression stopped Sam. "Would you like to apologize to me for disobeying?"

Sam let out an impatient breath, studied this ridiculous scene for a moment, then said, "Not any more than you'd like to kiss my ass!" and he pushed past the shocked principal, knowing he'd take his knocks when he got back to school, but he didn't care. All he cared about, all he could think about, was Lydia. He had to get to her, and he had to get to her now.

Lydia hadn't had to fake the cramps when she told her mother that morning that she didn't feel good and wanted to stay home. Lydia was rarely sick, and she didn't like to miss school, so Phyllis had easily believed her. Phyllis and Russell eventually left for work, and Lydia gingerly made her way from her hot attic bedroom down to the couch in the living room. The storm door was open, and a slight breeze came in through the front screen, which helped some. She had a wet cloth on her head and she felt as limp as that dishrag. She was still bleeding, and despite the fact that Mary had said the flow would lessen each day, it was showing no signs of slowing down. She placed a towel and then a folded sheet on the couch and laid down, praying for strength to return to her body.

At some point, the room began to turn yellow and started to tip and swirl. She felt weightless and disoriented. She thought she heard knocking on the screen door and a voice, but everything was garbled and gray and shadowed. The face of her grandmother, dead now some seven years, loomed in front of her. Was that who was talking to her? Then her grandmother's face dissolved and it was Sam's face looking down at her, his hand on her shoulder shaking her. How did Sam get here? And why was he here?

"Go get Ray," she managed to whisper. "He'll know what to do."

Perhaps she slept for a year, perhaps it was only two seconds, but then Ray was there, picking her up off the couch, cradling her in the sheet and towel she'd been lying on. Then they were driving. There were so many black moments in among everything, time and space no longer made sense. Was that Sam again? Were they in a car? Someone was crying. Was it her? No, it was Mrs. Meeks. How did Mrs. Meeks get here? No, it wasn't Mrs. Meeks crying, it was Ray. Then things went black again. There was more pain down there. Someone, something was poking her. She smelled strange smells. Herbs perhaps? Some kind of tea? Alcohol? Sounds, muffled voices, someone touching her shoulder, touching her stomach, her legs, someone kissing her cheek. Black again. Black again. Black again.

Chapter 15

1957

Ray had been scared a lot of times in his life, but thus far he'd been terrified only twice. Once was when Mr. Willis, notable town crank and curmudgeon, fired a shotgun at him when he found him stealing vegetables from his garden late one night. By the noise of it, Ray had thought he'd gotten his fool head blown off, but somehow all the buckshot missed him and he ran for his life, ears ringing and several carrots stuffed down the front of his shirt. The other time was when he ran and jumped off the top part of River Leap. He knew the instant his feet left the rock that he'd made a mistake. He hadn't gotten the full lift from his jump that he had anticipated, and in the two point three seconds it took for him to fall to the river, he clinched in alarm as he flew way too close past the craggy cliffs. His leg hit one of the rocky edges as he went down, causing him to career waywardly down toward the river, where large rocks hid just underneath the water. He had gotten turned upside down, and he saw the underwater boulders rush up at him, knowing his head would be split wide open as soon as he hit the water. Again, just as the buckshot from Mr. Willis's gun missed him, so too did this underwater pitfall. Ray managed an unlikely threading of the needle and fell through the water into a space of about two feet between the boulders. A few inches to either side, he would have surely cracked his head open, broken his neck, or both. Underwater, he had to swim down deeper to work his way out from the dark maze of boulders hiding in the murky green water. He finally came to the surface, spitting and splashing amid the cheers of his buddies. He never jumped from that high at River Leap ever again.

Now, after delivering Lydia pale and weak to Mrs. Meeks, he sat on her front porch, knee twitching, knuckles against his teeth, and he could surely say that this was the most terrified he'd ever been. He wasn't sure which was worse, the moans that came from Lydia inside the house, or the times when it became deathly quiet. He had asked Mrs. Meeks if he could do anything, and she had given him a few directions to gather towels, start some water heating, and to grab her jars of herbs and medicine from the shelf in her kitchen. Then she had told him to go outside and wait.

Sometime later, Mrs. Meeks came out to the porch and sat down next to him. "Ray, listen to me carefully. You're going to take her home. Tell her mamma that she had an abortion. She should be okay, but she'll need to rest. She lost some blood, but I got it stopped."

Ray frowned and shook his head. "What happened?"

Mrs. Meeks took a deep breath. "Well, that child in there wasn't able to go to the doctor to get a proper procedure. She went to someone else who didn't know what they were doing." At this, Viola turned her head toward her neighbor Mary's house. Mary had been out on her porch when Ray got there with Lydia. As he had walked up Viola's front porch steps carrying the pale figure, Mary had slipped into her house silent as a shadow. Viola would be talking to her later.

"Lydia had an abortion that wasn't done right. There was tissue left inside her that caused her to bleed. I've fixed it, and like I said, she should be all right."

Ray's knee continued to maniacally bounce up and down, and he nodded, but he didn't understand. He was having a hard time putting all the pieces together. "I . . . I . . ." He turned and looked through her screen door. He couldn't see anything but knew Lydia was in there. Then he put both his hands up to his face and tried to stifle a sob. "Is she gonna be all right?"

Mrs. Meeks nodded. "I think so. But you need to tell her mamma everything. She needs to know what she's dealing with. Mrs. Culpepper's a hardy woman; she's been around the block a time or two. So tell her what I said. And tell her to watch Lydia. If the bleeding doesn't stop, she has to take her to the doctor. No use worrying about the law—if Lydia doesn't get better, she's got to go to the doctor. You hear me?"

Ray nodded. His throat was tight in an effort to keep it all together, but the tears were now streaming unbidden down his face. "Thank you."

He stood up then and entered the house, the screen door squeaking behind him. He carefully picked Lydia up and took her to the back seat of his car. He drove her back into town and back to her house. He carried her up to her attic bedroom and kissed her on her forehead. He sat there while she slept. She was definitely resting more peacefully than when Sam had led him to her writhing on her couch earlier that morning. After a while, he went downstairs and sat out front and waited for Phyllis to come home.

Thankfully, Phyllis appeared about a half hour later, walking up the sidewalk, coming home for lunch. Phyllis worked down at the Culpepper Clothing Store with Russell, and it made for a nice arrangement. Phyllis enjoyed the work as well as the company of her husband. Russell sometimes accompanied her home during lunch, but not always, and today was one of those days when Phyllis came home by herself. She paused when she saw Ray sitting on her doorstep, then her heart started beating double-time when he slowly stood with the most injured look on his face.

"What's the matter?" she asked.

"Can we go inside?" Ray asked.

She ushered him inside and gestured for him to sit on the couch, and she sat in the chair. Then Ray started his story. He was halfway through the third sentence when Phyllis drew in a deep breath, jumped to her feet, and ran upstairs. Ray sat on the couch and hung his head. After fifteen minutes or so, Phyllis came back downstairs, her face a mixture of worry and anger. He looked up at her with as much apology as he could muster.

"I'm so sorry, Mrs. Culpepper. I—"

Phyllis held up her hand. "She was able to tell me some things, but she's very tired. She needs to rest. I'll keep an eye on her. My baby girl will be all right. I—" She studied Ray for a few seconds. "I . . . I know how to help her. I know what she needs." She caught a sob and shook her head, then smoothed her hands down the lap of her dress and sat down. "You men don't know anything except to . . ." She looked out the window, trying to suppress an anger from long ago. "Anyway, tell me what you know. What happened?"

Ray splayed his hands upward and rested them on his knees. He told her about how Sam had come and got him, how he'd found Lydia here, and that he'd taken her to Mrs. Meeks. He ended with what Mrs. Meeks had told him to tell her. When he finished, she went to the kitchen and got him a drink of water and brought it back to him. He drank it, not realizing how weak he felt.

"You should probably go now. You've been through a lot as well. We'll get through this. It's gonna be okay. And listen, you keep your mouth shut about this, ya hear? Ain't nobody in town gonna be talking about my girl."

Ray nodded, took a last sip from the glass, set it on the coffee table, then stood up. "Mrs. Culpepper, I need to tell you something." He ran a hand across the back of his neck. "It wasn't mine."

Phyllis stared at him, her eyes growing wider by the second. She seemed to tip, then she sat down and looked around the room. "Oh," she managed to say, and she looked up at him. She wasn't sure she could believe him. After all, the two of them clung to each other like teenage lovers do, and Phyllis surely knew what that was like. Ray looked like a rag doll, a puppet whose strings had been let go. The handsome boy she knew, the one who loved her daughter, stood there bereft of any energy or strength. It didn't make sense. "Okay," she finally said.

Ray turned then and walked out of the house and got in his car.

He had not planned to leave, leastways not in the way that forethought and ideas intentionally formed themselves in his mind. It was as if his body moved on its own, automatically going through movements that he did not resist because he did not realize they were happening until after they had happened. He found himself at his house and in his room and opening his suitcase before he had time to think about it. He found himself stashing his clothes in the suitcase and looking down and realizing that his suitcase was now packed. He found himself going to the wrapped bar of soap underneath the bathroom sink—his hiding place for his money behind two other bars of soap—and unwrapping first one and then all three bars of soap to realize that Ollie had found this hiding place and stolen his money. He had thought it was a smart place to hide the money as Ollie rarely used soap. He yelled and cussed. But his exasperation at this soon subsided into indifference, and he was moving past it, again before he realized it. Now he was out in his car, now he was driving.

And then, there he was sitting at the top of River Leap looking down into the dark green swirls of the current that rolled in a hushed ripple over the hidden boulders deep in the water. The day had turned cloudy, an autumn breeze starting to pick up and turn the air cold. Then he stood and reached beneath a rock shelf, pushing smaller rocks and dry leaves out of the way. In a deep, small pocket in the rocks, he wormed his hand through the hollow area then pulled out a small black box. He opened it to reveal a small diamond solitaire. He held it up, but there was no sun to make it glint and catch fire like it had when he had come out to look at it before. He'd had sense enough to hide it out here where Ollie couldn't get a hold of it. He wished he'd done the same with his money. And then the ring was being flung out, out past the rocks and boulders and down to the river. As before, he'd done it without thought, and it was done before he realized it had happened. He watched the ring hit the water with no qualm, no reluctance, no feeling whatsoever. It was as if his whole being, in an attempt to protect him, shut everything off.

He climbed down off the boulders and walked down the rocky path—past River Leap Park where he had first seen Lydia in her red striped swimsuit, past where he'd had the best times with Shane and Sam playing in the river—and he got in his car and drove away. He was gone before he realized it, and except for one very short and secretive visit in 1964, he would not come back until eighteen years later.

Chapter 16

1975

Shane walked into Riley County Hospital Room 4 to see Ray sitting up, cradling his arm in a sling and looking over at Maybelline as she removed the blood-pressure cuff from his arm.

"Mornin', Deputy Cooper," said Maybelline. You can ask him a few questions, but not too much. He needs to rest." She walked over and turned off the bright overhead fluorescent light, a faint pink sunrise beginning to glow into the window and the little lamp on the bedside table the only light in the room. "He just woke up, so he's a mite groggy." Then she left the room and the two men stared at each other for a long, silent moment.

It was Ray who finally broke the silence. "So you're deputy now?"

The voice was the same, but Shane could see now that, even though Ray seemed to be in great shape, his eyes had aged. Their brilliant blue had faded somewhat.

Shane took off his hat and worked the brim around in his hands. "Thought maybe I could show everybody how to do deputying right. It's harder than you think. Don't get me wrong, I'm not excusing Culpepper of anything, and we know what a turd ass he was, but this . . . it's hard."

"Well, good for you." Although it didn't sound like Ray was pleased or really even cared.

"Culpepper of course isn't around anymore," Shane said.

The two exchanged a long look. "Yes, I know," Ray said.

The silence became awkward. Not knowing what else to say or do, Shane placed his hat on the bedside table, reached over and pulled a chair closer, and sat down. He reached into his front shirt pocket and took out his little spiral notepad and pen. He flipped open the cover, clicked the pen, and drew a breath. "I just need to take a report. About the shooting."

Ray stared at him then snorted a chuckle. "That's what you want to ask me? After all these years, that's it?" He waved it off with his good hand. "No matter. I didn't come back for this. I had to think real hard to decide to come back at all, but I wasn't going to miss Mrs. Meeks's funeral. I somehow stupidly thought I might get out of town without having to see any of you, or my dad. But of the half a dozen or so people I've run into, danged if you all weren't right smack in the middle of everything."

Ray thought back to the night before, walking into the hospital and seeing Lydia sitting there at the nurses' station. The shock of it, her bright face, and her name tag proclaiming *Lydia Cooper* amidst the pain of his bloody nose and wound in his shoulder sending his emotions into overdrive.

He looked at Shane now and saw the passage of time. His gut wrenched and he suddenly, desperately, wished he wasn't here. He raised up his shoulder and pointed his chin at his bandage. "And obviously things haven't changed. Still the same one-horse, god-forsaken, idiot-filled, low-life town it's always been."

Shane tried not to acknowledge any of the emotions rising up within him. Defensiveness and anger mixed with sadness and joy all tumbled together to create a swirl of confusion that made it hard to think. He was so glad to see his friend, and yet . . . Shane laid the notepad in his lap and looked down, as if searching the green tiles on the floor for answers.

"Look, Ray, I'm awful damn glad to see you, but . . . I just gotta ask, where the hell have you been?"

"I've been around," Ray said. The words were clipped and cold.

The two men studied each other, eighteen years of hurt feelings and ponderings of deception sitting like an impenetrable wall between them.

Finally, Ray shrugged. "Ask me anything you want. I'll give you answers. Funny how that works, isn't it, how you get all the answers. I didn't get any answers some eighteen years ago. I had to come to my own conclusions, seeing as how you and Lydia did such a fine job of keeping your secrets."

Shane's brain paused and sputtered, anxiety rising up within him. "What are you talking about?"

Ray sighed impatiently. "The baby." His jaw set in a hard line as he squinted at the person he thought had been his best friend. "It wasn't mine." Ray raised his chin with self-assured smugness.

Shane stared mutely, his breath held, frozen in a time warp from that summer so long ago when he'd heard Lydia'd had an abortion. He remembered being sick with worry for her, for Ray, for all of them. And now, with nauseating clarity, it all came together for him. All those years that Ray was gone, he now knew why. Like some piercing whistle screaming through his ears, Ray's accusation split through Shane's skull, and his eyes widened as he looked at his friend. He slowly closed his spiral notebook.

"Ray, me and Lydia . . ." Shane put a hand up to his face and thought he might cry. He started shaking his head and continued to shake it until he was bobbing his head like a crazed puppet. He tried and tried to think of something to say, anything that would make this better. He held his friend in a sorrowful gaze. "Goddamn, Ray, no."

Ray frowned at him.

Finally, Shane stopped his shaking. "Me and Lydia never did anything like that back then."

"I saw you. You were both together out at the fair. And then, after that night . . ." Ray took a deep breath and looked out the window. The sun was now touching the eastern horizon, and daylight was beginning to brighten the room. He turned back to look at Shane, but his vision settled somewhere in the middle distance, just past Shane's shoulder.

"It changed. Something changed after that night. She barely wanted me to touch her. And then she turns up pregnant and has an abortion. And you, I remember how you wouldn't look at me. Something was up and I knew it. So many lies. I couldn't take it. I couldn't stay. I just couldn't."

Shane sat up in his chair. "Ray, you need to talk to Lydia. Why didn't you talk to her then! Goddamn you, all this time. I thought Culpepper was the reason you left. Ray . . . ?"

"Quit trying to defend yourself! Just quit!" Ray suddenly couldn't breathe, and his head began to throb. He wanted out of this room, out of this town. He wanted to be back in Kentucky, back in his house by the lake. "No," he said fiercely. "Tell me anything you want. Lie all you want, but I know. I know it's true! And you waited just long enough to get married to make it look respectable."

"Married?"

Ray nodded. "Viola told me. She wrote me a letter, said Lydia had married the Cooper boy. So I guess it's all true, right?" He tried to be smug, but, despite his years of certainty regarding these events, he was aware that his self-righteousness was beginning to slip. Something wasn't at all right.

Shane, totally spent, leaned back in his chair and fixed Ray with a weary gaze. The silence surrounding them hummed with anguish. "Wrong Cooper boy," Shane said. "Lydia married Sam."

Chapter 17

1957

That day Ray brought Lydia back from Mrs. Meeks and told Phyllis his story, Phyllis stayed by her daughter's side like the mamma bear she was. She washed Lydia's face with a cool, wet cloth, held her hand, talked to her and soothed her, made her drink small sips of water. Phyllis's heart beat double-time as she went over what Ray had told her. Her mind did flip-flops as worst-case scenarios filled her head, causing her to tremble with breathless anxiety. And yet, she was confused. Could she believe Ray? What had really happened? She needed Lydia to wake up and talk to her. And most of all, she needed her daughter to be okay. Her daughter was her world.

At some point in the afternoon, Phyllis, who had been losing a fight with denial, feared that something might still be wrong with Lydia. Viola, as trustworthy as she might be, was still nothing more than a small-town woman with no more than a high school education. When it came to her daughter's health and life, Phyllis needed more assurance than the well-intentioned ministrations of a kindly old lady.

Despite Lydia's protests of wanting to stay in bed, Phyllis was able to help her stand up, and they walked to the car—a cream-and red-colored 1955 Oldsmobile that they rarely used unless they were driving up to Poplar Bluff. She drove downtown to Dr. Scott's office, thankful that it was on a side street in a rather nondescript building.

Phyllis entered the office with Lydia leaning on her. Cecilia Wiggins, Dr. Scott's receptionist, was sitting at her desk typing up a report. Cecilia turned to them, her lavender-gray curls—wound tight and sprayed to the high heavens courtesy of Yvonne's Cut 'N' Curl—looking even more purple thanks to the fluorescent light. Cecilia's eyes widened at the sight of Lydia's pale form.

"Can we see Dr. Scott?" Phyllis asked.

Cecilia stood up, pushed her black-framed eyeglasses up the bridge of her nose, and gestured for them to step past the receptionist desk. "Follow me, dears. I'll get you set up in an examining room. Dr. Scott's with a patient, but I'll let him know you're here."

Elias Scott was not a native of Westfall. Born on a farm in West Plains, Missouri, he surprised his agricultural-minded family by showing a natural proclivity toward biology, chemistry, and all things medical. He was top of his class at the University of Missouri Medical School and could have picked almost anywhere to do his residency. He chose Boston, but was whisked away by the war soon after arriving there, which was just as well because he knew he would have never become a Red Sox fan—everyone knew that the St. Louis Cardinals were the best team in the world. After being a medic in the war and experiencing its life-sucking atrocities, the call of a simpler, more peaceful place beckoned. Westfall and the Current River were just what the doctor ordered, literally.

Westfall did not have a hospital at that time, so Dr. Scott practiced in his office downtown on Maynard Avenue. He did everything from stitching up boys' knees to checking for pneumonia in the elderly and, if need be, sending them up to the Poplar Bluff hospital for more in-depth care. He even delivered babies in the little office, an undertaking made less stressful by way of a cloth soaked in diluted chloroform held near the nose of the laboring women.

Throughout his time in Boston, World War II, and small-town Westfall, Dr. Scott had seen it all. When Phyllis brought Lydia into his office, he knew exactly what was up, what had happened, and what to do. Mrs. Cecilia Wiggins was pretty sure too, and although she tried to remain professional, there was no denying the judgment in her pickle-pursed lips and the righteous lift of her powdered chin. Mrs. Wiggins was a good church-going woman with high standards, but she conveniently seemed to forget that her own son Orville had been born seven months after she'd married Mr. Wiggins. In Mrs. Wiggins's eyes, her sin had been atoned for and was nobody's business. New sins, however, could be great entertainment, and one could only guess if Lydia would become gossip tomorrow.

Phyllis knew this, and she would be setting up the defenses should she hear any woman talking about her daughter. Lydia's health was top priority of course, gossip be damned. For the third time in two days, Lydia's cervix and uterus were set upon. After Dr. Scott's examination, he found that Viola had done fine and proper work, an antibiotic was prescribed, and Lydia was taken home to finally take a well-deserved rest.

The body being the masterful machine it is, Lydia was up in a few days—back to school, back to life, and spending her time waiting for Ray to come back to her.

Chapter 18

When Ray did not return after a month, then two, then three, the town folk assumed it was because of Deputy Culpepper. It was no secret to anyone how Wes had it out for Ray. Everyone knew that if he didn't get in a daily dose of harassment toward Ray, he became even more of a spoiled bellyacher. Many other citizens of Westfall had experienced Wes's bullying, so it was understood why Ray had left, although it was a head scratcher why he hadn't taken that pretty Campbell girl with him.

Wes was quite aware that people attributed Ray's departure to him, and he took full advantage to strut around like a peacock, making sure everyone knew what kind of power he wielded. But when the exhilaration of this dubious victory began to dwindle, Wes realized he needed another triumph to keep himself in the spotlight, and he began to look for other conquests. He found one while visiting Yvonne's Cut 'N' Curl.

Stepping into the salon, bell tinkling to announce his entrance, he nodded to the ladies. He was there to pick up his wife, Melva

Dean, as it was his habit to walk her home, being the good and protective husband that he saw himself as. Melva Dean glanced at him, her lips pressed around several bobby pins, and indicated with a nod of her head that she was almost done. Wes took a seat in one of the chairs, picked up a *Life* magazine, and settled in. The murmurings of the ladies chit-chatting mixed with the buzz of the hairdryer blended into a nondescript hum until he heard Cecilia Wiggins mention Dr. Scott and Lydia, and his ears pricked up.

"I'm not one to judge," Cecilia said, "but I would bet my best Easter hat that's why Lydia was in the office that day. Dr. Scott needs to stay as far away from that kind of thing as possible. I don't mean to gossip, you know, but it's been a while and I guess she's doing okay. Shame on her for finding herself in that predicament though. I thought she was a good girl, but when you hang around with the likes of that Bellamy boy, then I guess sooner or later you're gonna find yourself in trouble."

"I don't know why you're bringing Dr. Scott into this, Cecilia. He's treated you just fine all these years, and he's a good man. I'd say the blame needs to be on that colored woman, Viola. It's no secret what she does out there in her house. Such a sinner."

Both Cecilia and her gossiping friend would have clutched their self-righteous pearls if they'd been wearing them. Melva Dean gave a harrumph as she walked past the ladies, letting them know she had heard their tittle-tattle and didn't like it, but she knew it wouldn't do much good. She grabbed her purse and headed out the door with Westley walking closely alongside her.

Melva Dean didn't like these walks home with her husband, but Westley insisted upon it. He liked to keep a close watch on Melva Dean, something Melva Dean learned too late after she was already pregnant and married to the man. She was in a pickle then, because she had nowhere else to go. So she stayed in the marriage and endured what so many other women endured—marriage to a man who made himself feel big and important by putting his wife in her place. According to Westley, Melva Dean wouldn't be anything without him, and she didn't have any friends because she was too stupid. He would even stoop to physical abuse that included well-placed slaps whenever the fried chicken wasn't made to his liking.

As Melva Dean walked home with Westley that day from the Cut 'N' Curl, she didn't know that several years later he'd be gone. She didn't know how light she would feel with Westley no longer weighing her down.

Now, having walked a few blocks from the Cut 'N' Curl, and heading up Grand Avenue, Wes asked Melva Dean if she knew what the ladies in the salon had been talking about. Melva Dean knew very well what they had been talking about, but she knew her husband and she wasn't going to provide him any ammo to serve his bullying purposes. Fact was, Melva Dean had used Viola Meeks's services and had appreciated her care and support. Melva Dean played dumb, which was how Wes usually liked it anyway. He pressed, both for more information as well as on the forearm he was now gripping tightly. Being as they were out in the open, Melva Dean felt bold enough and jerked her arm away, telling him again that she didn't know anything about it, and that was the end of the conversation.

Leastways that was the end of the conversation Melva Dean had with Wes. As soon as she could, though, Melva Dean went straight to Phyllis and told her what she'd heard and what Westley was doing. At which, Phyllis commenced to hunting down Westley, finding him in the parking lot of Smith's department store. Seeing there was no one around to hear their conversation, she set upon giving him a dressing down that no self-respecting deputy, at least in Wes's mind, should have to endure.

"What do you think you're doing, Westley, asking questions about Mrs. Meeks? This is going to put Lydia right smack into a spotlight that she doesn't deserve. You stop this right now!"

"Simmer down, Phyllis. I'm not doing this to get at Lydia. It's Mrs. Meeks and that god-awful group out west of town I'm after. They're the ones that need to stop doing what they're doing. They're breaking the law."

"You want to stop people breaking the law? Well, you'd best stop, so I won't kill you. I'll *kill* you, Westley Culpepper, if there is even one bad word about my daughter!"

Even though Phyllis was several inches shorter than Westley, she drew herself up and stuck out her chin.

"God almighty, Phyllis. Steady yourself. If anything, this is to protect Lydia. If what I'm hearing is right, Mrs. Meeks didn't do right by Lydia, and that's why you had to bring her into Doc Scott's, right?"

Phyllis squinted her eyes at him. "You don't know anything about that."

"If Ray'd kept his hands off her, then she wouldn't have found herself in such a pickle, now would she have?"

"A pickle? That's what you call this? You're a son of a bitch."

"Damn, Phyllis, back away a second. Jesus, your red hair sure gets to flamin' a tad too hot sometimes. Just let me do my job. Lydia'll be fine."

Phyllis stared at him. "Keep her out of this, you hear! I mean it."

Wes held up his hands and shook his head. "Just go on and leave me to do my work, and you do what you do best. Which I assume," and his face spread in a smarmy grin, "is give my brother a decent blow job when he comes home tired from work."

Phyllis swung her arm up and slapped him across the face so hard it caused his ears to ring. Westley stumbled back, cradling the sting on his cheek with his hand. They both stood seething at one another, silent in their impasse.

Finally, Westley spoke with a gritted jaw. "Because you're kin, I'm gonna pretend that didn't happen."

"No," Phyllis said, her own jaw just as tight. "Don't you *ever* forget that happened. You keep it in mind every second you put my daughter in the middle of a mess that she had no call in. Every. Second." With that, Phyllis turned and walked away, every muscle in her body trembling with anger and spite.

Neither his wife's lack of help nor Phyllis's threats slowed him down though, and Wes went ahead with gathering information. It was a day later when he went out back of Viola's house, nearly scaring the living daylights out of her, walking up behind her as she weeded her vegetable garden.

In an instinctive move, she jerked her hoe up into his face.

"What in tarnation you coming 'round here for, stepping all over my bean plants? Lookee there, you've smashed three of the blue lakes. Get outta here!"

Wes was startled enough by the willful woman and her handy hoe that he did indeed take a step back, but then he remembered his position, which according to him was several steps above a small town colored woman. He hitched up his pants and began to speak his piece.

"I know what you do out here, and I know that you're breaking the law, and I'm saying right here and right now, it's gonna stop. You're sinnin' too, so be ready for the Lord to strike you down."

Viola lowered her hoe and blinked, trying to make sense of his crazy tirade. She silently gazed at her garden and decided the only thing to do—usually the best course of action for black people when faced with accusations from a white man—was to agree with him. "Well, Deputy Culpepper, you got me, I guess." She waved her hand across the expanse of her garden. "Might as well lock me up, 'cause this here vegetable garden and the flowers out front are surely the work of the devil."

Wes huffed and waved a brown paper bag in front of her. "Got this from your house as evidence, and you know what it is and you know what I'm talking about. I think you and I need to take a ride downtown."

Viola stood tall. "What for?"

"I'm arresting you, that's what for. Now come on." Wes slapped the hoe out of Viola's hand and grabbed her arm and pulled her toward him. Viola set up a squallering loud enough that the neighbors came out of their houses to see what all the commotion was about.

Wes pulled her around to the front of the house toward his car. He waved his hand at the alarmed neighbors. "Nothing to see here folks, nothing to see. Go on back and let the law do its job."

"Viola!" Shadrick, one of her neighbors, called. "What's the matter?"

Viola turned wide eyes toward Shadrick. "Call Jackson. Let him know Westfall's deputy is arresting me. Tell him to get a lawyer."

Wes pulled her harder. "Ain't no need for a lawyer. This here's a case that's gonna be settled right quick. I'm gonna put a stop to all your criminal actions. What a fine thing this will be to rid the town of the likes of you and all your desecratin' of young girls."

And just like that, Viola was shoved into the back seat of the cruiser. Wes drove her into town, of course with the siren blaring and the lights on. He marched into the courthouse, leading her down the back steps and into the very cell where Ray had sat.

"Now then, little honey, you sit right there and ponder on all the sinning you been doing, and understand there's a women's prison up in Jefferson City that's got a cell with your name on it."

Viola sat on the rough wooden bench visually shaking. Wes stood there, taking perverse gratification from what he saw as another victory.

"Mr. Deputy, you're a big man."

Wes frowned at her.

"No, I mean what I say. You're about six foot tall?" She stood now, staying a good distance from the cell bars, but nevertheless, in front of Wes.

"Six foot two," he bragged.

"Yes, well, see how big you are. So why you always having to put down on people smaller than you? You do it to try to make yourself bigger, but you don't have to."

Wes started to reply but turned to the sound of Sheriff Tyler's voice calling him as he walked down the stairs toward the cell. "Westley, what you got here?" Tyler took a look into the cell, drew a very long sigh, put his hands on his hips, then turned to Wes in question.

"Got us here a certified abortionist." Wes beamed.

Sheriff Tyler's bushy eyebrows rose nearly a full inch up his forehead. He stuck his little finger inside his ear and wiggled it as if to determine if he was indeed hearing what he thought he was hearing.

Wes held up the paper bag. "Got evidence too." Wes reached into the sack and pulled out a thin, steel rod with a hook on the end of it. "An abortionist's tool, and that's a fact."

Viola spoke up. "What you got my crochet hook for?"

Wes gave a questioning frown to the rod, then put it back in the bag with pursed lips. "Don't matter. I got witnesses who'll tell me all about Mrs. Meeks here. And one in particular is Lydia Campbell. Got her medical records at Doc Scott's office that confirms it."

Sheriff Tyler looked at Mrs. Meeks and cleared his throat. "Viola, I have heard a rumor or two about the goings-on out there in your neck o' the woods. Potions and powders and such. Deputy Culpepper's got some weighty accusations here. You got call to speak to it?"

"Well now, I have no call at all to speak to such nonsense. But I will tell you this: I don't make potions. I do make my own aspirin powders from the bark of the willow trees out by the river. I give them to people. And if I do remember correctly, your lovely wife, Miss Birdie, uses my aspirin powders for her sick headaches, and she tells me they help quite a lot. I don't think you can call making those powders anywhere near to doing abortions. And that there that he just showed you is a crochet hook. I make me several afghans and sell them at the church bazaar. And as for a Lydia Campbell, I don't know any such person."

Sheriff Tyler took a deep sigh. He did indeed know that when his wife had her sick headaches, she stirred some powder into a glass of warm water. Birdie ofttimes spoke highly of Viola's medicine and how grateful she was to have it. Still, Sheriff Tyler was pretty sure there was more to it. He looked down and studied the floor for a few moments. "Well now, since there wasn't any arrest warrant," with this Sheriff Tyler cast a glare in Wes's direction, "I'm going to let you go. However, I think there might be cause to check into this further. Abortion is a serious offense. Let's go on up to the office and make a report."

Tyler unlocked the jail cell and led Viola up the dank stairs, Wes following in a foul mood. Tyler instructed Judy to write up the report, titled *Riley Co. v. Viola Meeks; suspicion of the unlawful act of abortion; March, 1958. Investigation notes to follow.*

Sheriff Tyler instructed Viola not to leave town and offered to have Wes take her home. But, being as Viola didn't want to be anywhere near the insolent deputy any more than she had to, she respectfully declined and walked out of the courthouse, headed for home.

On the walk, she reflected on her conversation with Sheriff Tyler in the jail cell. She was a god-fearing woman as well as a sheriff-fearing one, and she did not take lightly lying to Tyler. But she held her head high—she knew she had not offered up one lie to the man and was proud to say it. It was exactly true that making aspirin powders was not at all like doing abortions. It was also exactly true that the tool Wes had was indeed a crochet hook. She kept her medical tools wrapped in a leather pouch and stored below a floor board in her kitchen. Wes had probably stepped on that very floor board when he came into her house earlier that day.

And finally, when she told Sheriff Tyler she did not know a Lydia Campbell, she again spoke in truth. Viola knew that Lydia's mother was married to Russell Culpepper and that her name was Phyllis Culpepper. Not being up on all the comings and goings of the white folks in town, she didn't realize that Russell was Lydia's stepfather, and so she had assumed Lydia's last name was also Culpepper.

She was just about to reach Route K when she sensed a car coming up slowly behind her. It was Deputy Culpepper's cruiser. He pulled up beside her and rolled down his window.

"Sun's about to go down here pretty quick, Viola. You best hurry up and get on outta town. You know what happens to your kind if you're still in town after dark."

Viola kept walking, not looking at him, not saying a word. She was aware of the car continuing to follow her, setting her heart to drum a hundred miles a minute. Then Westley whoop-whooped the siren a few times, laughing when he saw Viola jump. He pulled the car ahead of her and raced on, his sick laughter trailing behind along with the exhaust fumes in her face.

Viola walked on. When she got home she would have to call her son Jackson in St. Louis, tell him she wouldn't be visiting him this month, and see where he was at on getting her a lawyer. She pulled her sweater tighter, wondering what kind of hellfire and mayhem she was in for, all because of one egotistical deputy's lust for power.

Chapter 19

1958

The town of Westfall was the county seat, but there was no presiding judge at that time. Sheriff Tyler made a call up to a friend of his, Robert Swindle, who was a judge in Poplar Bluff, one county over. Yes, his name was indeed Swindle, and though Robert tried to get people to pronounce his name with the emphasis on the last syllable—swin-*dell*—nobody ever got it right. The judge went through life knowing his name provided comic entertainment to lawyers and defendants alike, not to mention the implication of suspicion. At some point in his professional career, he finally decided to let it be, because when the honorable judge, a paragon of fairness and decency, was out fishing on the river enjoying a rare moment of peace and quiet, he didn't care if his name was pronounced like swindle or kiss-my-ass.

After hearing the details of the situation, Judge Swindle scheduled a time to come down to Westfall the next week. In the meantime, Sheriff Tyler would call on a list of witnesses that Westley had provided to get statements. At this point, it would be an inquiry to determine if there needed to be a trial. Trial or not, news got out, and an electric buzz filtered through the little river town faster than a hot knife through butter. This was more excitement than they'd had since Mrs. Dole accused her husband, the preacher at the First Baptist Church, of having an affair with one of his parishioners. Westley loved it, especially since he would be a top witness.

The large, wooden-floored room with high arched windows in the courthouse doubled as a courtroom and a multipurpose room. School graduations had taken place here, community meetings were held here, the Boy Scouts met here, and, much to the annoyance of the courthouse staff, Mrs. Francis taught tambourine lessons to sixth-grade girls here on Wednesday afternoons.

On the first day of the inquiry, Judge Swindle gathered with Sheriff Tyler, Deputy Culpepper, Westfall City Attorney Jacob Lightfoot, Mrs. Meeks, her son Jackson, and the lawyer he'd brought down with him from St. Louis, Mr. Allen Brown. Witnesses had been told beforehand that they were requested to sit in on the inquiry to answer questions, but each had a specific time to appear inside the courtroom. Judge Swindle made it clear this was not a trial, and it was not open to the public. Nevertheless, folks gathered out on the courthouse lawn underneath the large oak trees in hopes they'd catch a snippet of the goings-on. It was to their delight when one of the windows was raised a bit later in the day due to the courtroom getting stuffy. The one black metal oscillating fan was doing little to keep the courtroom comfortable on a day when Missouri decided to enact its occasional spring tom-foolery of producing a temperature of eighty-six degrees in March.

The first person to be questioned was Westley Culpepper. He beamed at the knowledge that he was in the middle of all the hullabaloo, but was disappointed to learn that the proceedings would not be a proper court showdown. The judge wasn't even sitting up at the bench, but instead sat at a table in front of the courtroom. Sheriff Tyler and Mr. Lightfoot sat at one table to the left in front of the judge, and Viola, Jackson, and Mr. Brown sat at a table to the right. Westley sat in a chair next to the table where the judge was sitting.

Judge Swindle explained that the proceedings were to determine if there needed to be a trial. He hoped to have all information collected that day. He then turned over the questioning to Mr. Lightfoot, who began by noting that Deputy Culpepper had brought Mrs. Meeks in under arrest and placed her in the city jail. "Under what premise did you arrest her?" asked Jacob Lightfoot.

"Well, because it's a known fact that Mrs. Meeks there does abortions, which we all know is against the law." Wes took great delight at seeing the lawyers writing notes on their legal pads after he spoke.

"And how is that a known fact?"

Wes nodded. "Well, because it's just known. Oh, and I've questioned several people around town who will tell you the same. You've got their names and all."

"Yes," Judge Swindle said. "We'll be questioning them."

"Now," Jacob continued, "you stated that you know of one particular citizen who obtained Mrs. Meeks's services. Would you tell us who that is?"

"That would be Lydia Campbell." Wes's face turned red, not being too happy about trashing the name of his step-niece, but it had to be done in the name of the law. And besides, though Westley would never say so, it was more about getting back at Ray.

"And how did you come to know that Miss Campbell had obtained Mrs. Meeks's services?"

Wes patted his knees with both hands, quite proud of his investigatory work. "Got the records from Doc Scott's office."

Both lawyers scratched away at their legal pads.

"All right. I also understand that you obtained a surgical tool from Mrs. Meeks's house."

"Yes," Wes told Jacob. "An abortionist's tool." He nodded with affirmed aplomb and sat up even straighter.

"Okay. Mr. Brown, do you have any questions for Deputy Culpepper?" Jacob asked.

Allen Brown shook his head and gave a slight wave of his hand. There might have been a person or two in the courtroom who were questioning Mr. Brown's expertise, but he knew exactly what he was doing.

Judge Swindle nodded. "That'll do, Deputy. You can sit there next to Sheriff Tyler. But before you do, would you call in the next witness out in the hall."

Wes sat there for a second, dissatisfied at the short length of time of his questioning. He finally stood up, walked over to the door, opened it, and asked Ethel Broadus to come into the courtroom.

Ethel, a tall, very thin, young black woman, walked into the room, her expression and posture telling everybody she absolutely did not want to be there. Wes gestured forthrightly to the chair beside the judge's table, where she timidly sat.

"Miss Ethel Broadus, do you know why you're here?" Jacob asked.

Ethel shrugged. "Deputy Culpepper said I had to come. Said it was my sworn duty to society."

Jacob nodded. "Yes, okay, but Deputy Culpepper has told us that you told him you have used Mrs. Meeks's services in the past. Did Mrs. Meeks perform an abortion on you?"

Ethel looked over at Viola sitting at the table. Ethel's large brown eyes welled up. "I'm sorry, Mrs. Meeks, the deputy said I had to say so. He even paid my mamma a dollar for me to say so."

Judge Swindle looked over at Westley, who was holding up both hands.

"No money exchanged hands, your honor. It didn't have to. Ethel's neighbor verified it for me. Mary Grimes told me that Ethel had been up to Viola's house and she knew what had happened there."

"Mary Grimes told you this?" Judge Swindle looked over his notes. "I don't have her on the list of people to be questioned."

Westley shook his head. "Don't need to have her. Ethel here can tell you." Westley neglected to state that Mary Grimes had not been as easy to bully as Ethel was, which was why Ethel was here and Mary wasn't.

"Ethel, can you tell me what type of services you obtained from Mrs. Meeks?" Jacob asked.

Ethel looked over at Viola, who was sitting at the table looking harried and nervous, and yet there remained the sweetness of a friend Ethel had known all her life. With a quick glance at Deputy Culpepper, Ethel turned to Jacob. "Mrs. Meeks is like our doctor. If we got a cold, she'll give us some good tea and broth. If we got a headache or a stomachache, she'll give us some good powders. This one, if you put it in some lemon tea, it'll settle a sour stomach right quick. She helped deliver my mamma's two babies who were borned just two years ago."

"But what type of services did *you* get from Mrs. Meeks?" Wes nearly shouted, which caused Ethel to jump and the judge to slap his hand on the table.

"Mr. Culpepper!" Judge Swindle said. "You need to sit over there and keep quiet and leave the questioning to the lawyers. Now, Ethel, you can continue."

Ethel looked over at Viola again. Aside from her mother, Viola had been one of the people who had taught Ethel the fear of God, and to do right, which included to not lie. So she said, "I went to Mrs. Meeks when my monthly time was awful heavy. It gave me terrible pains in the back. She gave me some tea and powders, and it fixed me up pretty good." This was most certainly not a lie, and Ethel sent a tentative smile toward Viola.

The people in the courtroom sat silent as if waiting for Ethel to go on, but she appeared to be done. Judge Swindle looked at Ethel. "Is that all you have to tell us? Is that all you went to Mrs. Meeks for?"

Westley let out a coughing harrumph, which caused Ethel's eyes to grow wide again. She didn't look at him and smoothed the material of her dress in her lap. "Well, she also . . ."

Everyone in the courtroom moved an infinitesimal inch closer toward Ethel. "She also taught me to crochet afghans for the church bazaar. I sold one for seventy-five cents once."

Judge Swindle sat back straight in his chair, clasping his hands together over his middle-aged paunch. "All right then, Ethel. Mr. Brown, any questions?"

Allen Brown again waved his hand and shook his head to pass.

"Deputy," Judge Swindle said, "would you let Ethel out of the room and call in the next person."

Wes stood up, doing a lousy job of trying to hide his disdain for the young lady, what with his heavy stomps toward her and a low growl growing inside of him. Ethel blanched as he came toward her, and she jumped up from her chair, doing her best to beat him out of the room before he could get near her.

Next into the room came Dr. Scott. He nodded to the group and sat down.

"Thank you for being here, Dr. Scott. Are you aware that we've called you because one of your patients may have obtained abortion services from Mrs. Meeks here?"

"Yes, I am."

Jacob looked at his notes then looked up. "All right then, Deputy Culpepper states that Lydia Campbell, who is a patient of yours, went to you after she got an infection from an abortion from

Mrs. Meeks. Can you tell us about that?"

"I cannot."

"Doctor, did you provide medical treatment to Lydia Campbell on . . ." Jacob checked his notes. "September 27, 1957? It says so here in her medical records."

"I did treat Miss Campbell."

"Was it for a botched abortion?

"It was for a dilation and curettage, or a D and C. The patient was suffering from heavy blood flow. It says so right there in the records. Records which, by the way, were taken from my office without my permission."

Allen Brown stopped writing at this point, placed his pen down on his legal pad, and looked up at the judge. "Your honor, may I ask that this questioning cease? There is no case to be had here."

Judge Swindle looked around the room at the people sitting at the tables. The black metal oscillating fan whirred to the left, paused, then whirred back to the right. Judge Swindle scratched at his temple. He was certain he knew what was going on. And he was also certain that compassion had a place in his courtroom. He also knew that sometimes people are not altogether evil, and sometimes some people are. He looked over at Deputy Culpepper, then over at Mrs. Meeks and her son and their lawyer. He thought about Lydia Campbell, who had, interestingly, not been called in for questioning.

Westley, sensing that his time to shine was quickly stumbling to a halt, blustered as he tried to say something relevant. "But what about the tool I got from Viola's house?"

"Inadmissible evidence," Jacob Lightfoot said. "It was obtained without a search warrant."

Judge Swindle closed his folder and gave a nod to the folks sitting at the tables. "I'd say we're done here. You all right with that, Jacob?"

Jacob nodded.

"Mr. Brown, I'll assume you and your client are okay with being done with this?"

Allen nodded.

Judge Swindle turned to Viola. "Mrs. Meeks, you tread very closely to practicing medicine without a license. I'd highly recommend you cease and desist providing medical services to the public."

"Then I suppose that means Dr. Scott here will be seeing the people in my neighborhood?" Mrs. Meeks asked. "Because as far as I know, he doesn't take colored patients, and that's why I tend to them."

Before Judge Swindle could react, Mr. Brown quickly cleared his throat, nervously patted the front of his three-piece suit, then held up a hand. Mr. Brown admired her gumption, but knew this was not the stage for Mrs. Meeks to display it. "I will advise my client on the ceasing of her medical services immediately, Judge."

Judge Swindle slowly stood, a steely gaze shadowing his face. Mr. Brown stood as well, gesturing to Viola and her son to stand also. Gathering his folders, notepad, and pen, he gave a quick nod back to Judge Swindle. "Thank you for your time." Then he placed a hand on the small of Viola's back and could not usher her out of the courtroom fast enough.

It didn't register even a tiny blip on the Westfall radar when the next day Ethel was found beaten and thrown into the creek, and Viola's house caught fire, because no one in Viola's neighborhood was going to report it to law enforcement—it was sure as certain that law enforcement was the cause of it.

Neighbors rushed to Viola's house with a bucket brigade and did the best they could, but not before the north corner of the house was destroyed. The burned roof, broken-down ceiling, and soggy floors stood as a reminder of what happens when a town bully is denied his glory.

The lilac bushes and irises up next to the house got singed, but nature, being the rock star she was, got the plants looking ship-shape in no time. Shadrick placed a temporary tarp over the corner of the roof, and he and Jackson—along with friends and neighbors—managed to cut, saw, and hammer their way to a mostly repaired house. Despite Viola's washing the walls and floors with vinegar, the smell of smoke would linger for years, adding to the list of reminders that she was a black person living in a white-ordained world.

Viola did her best to fix up Ethel, and it was a miracle that she was still alive. Despite Judge Swindle's instructions, Viola stitched up Ethel's cuts and placed balm on her bruises, but the worst of it was her eye socket. The swelling would go down, but Ethel would live out the rest of her days with her eye slightly askew due to the damaged muscle.

As for Viola's abortion services, it was never known for certain if she continued or quit. It is known that about a year or two later, Sheriff Tyler's niece visited Viola. The niece had brought her cookies, so who's to say it wasn't a white girl making a friendly visit to a sweet black lady?

Chapter 20

Lydia couldn't quite say when she figured that Ray was gone for good. Was it a month later? A year? It could have been the very next day, as time passed in a blurred jumble and it was hard to know. She did know that she no longer trusted the bucket of bologna fed to her by movies and novels about happily ever after and romance and flowers and being dependent on a man and giving all your love to him and letting him support you. No ma'am.

It wasn't that she didn't like men anymore. What she didn't like anymore was the girl she had been. She now dove deep within herself, not letting anybody truly know how she felt. She went to her job at Yvonne's Cut 'N' Curl and washed hair. She shunned her friends and held her books close to her chest as she walked through school and went to her classes. She endured meals at Grandma and Grandpa Culpepper's, where the whole family, including Westley, gathered for the weekly Sunday dinner.

Westley was part of the reason why Ray up and left. It wasn't just on her. As Lydia sat across the dining table from Westley—him licking his greasy fingers after chomping down on a fried chicken leg—she wished she could stare laser daggers at his head like one of Sam's comic-book superheroes. She couldn't stand the man. He had done her wrong, mighty wrong, and she wished him dead.

She kept her head down and her mouth shut; it was her full intention every day to not call attention to herself. It didn't help one day when Sam got in a fight because of her. Ricky Owens and Sam were in the cafeteria when Sam heard Ricky talking about Lydia.

"I heard Ray left 'cause she was messing around on him. Guess the darling Lydia is nothing but a slut."

Sam hauled off and punched Ricky square in the mouth, Sam quickly learning just how much it hurt to punch someone. He drew his fist back and shook it. But he didn't care, and the next thing anybody knew, Sam barreled his entire body into Ricky, bucking at him like a crazy bull. They both slammed to the ground and all kinds of mayhem commenced. They rolled around on the floor, kicking and punching as people gathered about and started yelling.

No one saw Lydia enter the cafeteria, walk up to the middle of all the commotion, and slam her books down on the tiled floor. This caused a loud booming sound very much akin to a gunshot reverberating around the high-ceilinged cafeteria. Everybody stopped their yelling, and Sam and Ricky, in mid-punch, stopped and looked at a red-faced Lydia. Both boys stood up. Ricky's nose was bleeding, and Sam was clenching and unclenching his fist in an attempt to stop the pain that was pulsing through it.

Lydia stepped up to Ricky, real close, nose to nose. They were both seniors and they had geology class with Mr. Elfrink together in third hour. Ricky thought she was a pretty nice girl, but what he saw in front of him was something more akin to the Cobra Goddess in the movie *Cult of the Cobra*. Ricky had snuck out with his older brothers to watch that movie last year, and he'd been having nightmares about it ever since. He took a step back and tried to think of something to say in his defense but it didn't matter, because it was clear Lydia was not having it.

"What'd you say about me?" Lydia asked. Her voice held a formidably low and controlled tone.

"I . . . I . . ." Ricky tried.

"Say it!" Lydia demanded. "If you've got cause to talk bad about me, don't be a chicken and say it behind my back. Step up, *Dick*! And say out loud what you just called me!"

The entire Westfall Warrior cafeteria waited. Ricky said nothing. He just wiped at his bleeding nose.

Lydia turned to take in the crowd, those near her flinching back. "Anybody else wanna take a crack? What do you wanna say about me?"

She looked over the crowd but, in truth, really didn't see anyone, because she couldn't focus. She could have easily dropped to the floor right then and there in a puddle of sorrow and gloom. Just a few months ago she'd had the world by the tail and her future sealed with the boy she loved. Now in the blink of an eye it was all gone and she didn't know who she was.

"No?" she asked the crowd. "You all just going to be chicken like Ricky here and wait until I walk away and then talk about me? Is that how it is? Fine, then. I've got two more months in this school. When you see me, you step aside. When you hear someone, anyone talk about me, you shut your mouth! Don't ever, and I mean ever, pretend to know what you think you might know about me. Is that clear?"

Several people awkwardly nodded. So much for trying not to call attention to herself. She bent and picked up her books, turned and looked at Sam, mouthed "thank you" to him, then walked back out of the cafeteria, the flock of students parting as if she was Moses walking through the Red Sea.

After that, things seemed to settle down, and there was little to talk about. Shane, who had left for Southeast Missouri State to study accounting per his father's wishes, lasted one semester. Missing Ray deeply and filled with rage toward Westley Culpepper, he came back to tell his mom and dad that he didn't like accounting and didn't like college. This did not sit well with Mr. and Mrs. Cooper, and when they watched their son slipping into a downward spiral of apathetic anguish, Mr. Cooper called up his brother Jerry, who had been in the military for over twenty years, and asked him for advice. Uncle Jerry Cooper got Shane on the phone and talked to him, and within a few weeks, Shane was enlisted in the United States Navy. Shane flew to Norfolk, Virginia, and after boot camp, he found himself assigned to the newly commissioned aircraft carrier, the USS *Forrestal*. For the next two years, he served as a fire controlman, helping coordinate the take-off and landing of navy jets and taking in sights around the world, mostly in the Mediterranean Sea and Pacific Ocean. It was the best thing that could have happened to him. If he'd stayed in Westfall, he might have killed himself, or Deputy Culpepper, or both.

Lydia finished out her senior year and went on to get her nursing degree, then moved to Columbia where she worked at the University Med Center.

Sam was left to live out his last two years of high school in the now forlorn little town without his brother, his best friend, or his fantasy girl.

Chapter 21

1965

Lydia found the town of Columbia, Missouri, to be a welcome distraction from the numbness she continued to walk in. After getting her nursing degree, she moved there with two friends she'd made in nursing school and rented a little house just east of the University of Missouri campus. They worked at the University Med Center, decorated the little house, cooked and shopped, and with sheer grit and a metaphorical toss of her head, life settled into a semblance of living. Looking at her, no one would ever know that she carried around inside her a very dark and heavy secret.

The university's atmosphere offered a sense of novel possibilities that were in total contrast to her life in Westfall. Lots of progressive energy livened up the college parties, as well as the many college boys away from their families for the first time. Lydia at first had no time for such things, focusing on her job and wallowing in lost love, but one day it didn't seem like such a bad idea when her roommate Audrey drug her to a fraternity party.

There they got drunk on too much spoly-oly, a drink revered by the frat boys, made with grain alcohol, sloe gin, and whatever soda or Kool-Aid was handy. It did a bang-up job of getting Lydia more drunk than she'd ever been in her life, but as she upchucked the sloppy red mess into the fraternity's bushes, Audrey carefully holding back her hair, something clicked. She would never get that drunk again, that was for sure, but she perceived there was a potion here for lost and forlorn girls, and she soon found herself caught up in the college party life, never acknowledging that she was now a good year past the typical college partying age. It made no matter.

College boys were ready and willing to provide her with activities much more entertaining than the god-awful loneliness she was now growing tired of. In a fabulously impetuous step into rebounding, she shook off her small-town compunction and boldly dated as many boys as she could. With each downtown college bar she went to, each college football game she attended, each time she danced in a hot and sweaty fraternity basement, each time she walked home in the early dawn, carrying her shoes and rubbing at her smeared mascara, instead of feeling remorse, she felt a freedom of sorts and began to feel a heaviness lifting from her shoulders. It felt better than anything had in a long time.

In her third year in Columbia, she felt a slow shift away from dating so many boys. Before she knew it, she had settled on a freshman named Brad who was as fresh as they came, but he was lots of fun in bed, and Lydia took full advantage of that. Brad, at his hormonal peak with a sex drive that didn't let up, provided all the fun a girl needed to forget her first love and the dumb little south Missouri town she so desperately wanted to put behind her. With the help of this new thing called the birth control pill, every roll in the hay with Brad chipped away at the angst she had carried with her from Westfall.

She did not love Brad, nor did she ever want to, and that was perfectly fine. He was actually a little on the stupid side, having to take Math 10 twice, never having paddled a canoe before, and not getting her sense of humor, which caused her to miss Ray and Shane and Sam all the more because they had shared a roaring and sarcastic wit. But sex seemed to be just the ticket, and she felt herself growing freer and freer and blossoming with a sense of confidence and control.

She began to gather that Brad had a hometown honey, something he had failed to tell her, but it made no matter to her. When he went home for the semester break, she was sure he took back up with Brenda or Belinda or whatever her name was. And she didn't mind it at all when he came back to campus after break and was right back at her door, shaking his tail and raring to go at it. He had brought her a box of chocolates, some flowers, and two tickets for the college basketball game. Then he picked her up in his arms, and she squealed with delight as he carried her back to her bedroom, her roommates eyeing each other from across the living room, smiling with pressed lips as they heard the playful carryings on in the bedroom at the end of the hallway. It was restorative to experience something totally physical that had nothing to do with her heart. It was a life where she was calling the shots, and she was thriving in it.

It had all been fun, but it was near the end of Brad's sophomore year when Lydia had pretty much made up her mind that she was tired of him. As she tried to decide if she was done with him for good, he made it easy on her by revealing one evening, as they sat in her bed eating sandwiches and chips, that he had not been in school all that semester. Being as she had seen him walk across campus carrying his textbooks, and had heard him mention a professor or two that he didn't like, she found this bit of information confusing.

"What?" she asked with a befuddled frown. "I don't understand. You're still living in the fraternity. They wouldn't let you live there if you weren't in school, right?"

Brad shrugged with a boyish smirk. "They still think I am in school. You have to show your grades to the fraternity director, and I just took old grade slips of mine from past semesters and changed the dates, a few of the classes, and the grades with my nifty ballpoint pen. They don't really pay that much attention anyway. I've just been pretending to go to classes." Brad was obviously very proud of his deception and puffed up his chest.

Lydia stared at him. "I'm still confused. What happened? Did you drop out?"

Again he gave his lame shrug. "I got put on academic parole a year ago because I flunked so many classes. I had this past fall to bring up my grades, and well, I didn't, so they kicked me out. I can't take classes here until next fall."

"How ... how ..." She shook her head, still trying to process. "How are you ... don't you have to pay the fraternity room and board?"

Brad nodded. "My parents are sending me money."

"They still think you're in school?"

Brad nodded again with a bright smile. "They don't know a thing. And who's smart, now?"

Lydia slowly slid off the bed and stood up. "Let me get this straight. You've been pretending to go to school, lying to your parents and the fraternity, and you've been over at my place most of the time and eating my food."

"I bring my own food sometimes. I bring cereal."

Lydia rolled her eyes. "Yes, I know you bring cereal. We've got boxes and boxes of Sugar Smacks and Rice Krispies all over the counter. We don't need that much cereal. And what have you been doing all this semester? You don't have a job. At least I don't think you do. Or have you been keeping that from me too?"

"Why are you getting your panties all up in a wad? What difference does it make to you whether I'm in school or not?" Now he got off the bed and they were standing toe to toe.

Lydia felt a Phyllis-type squabble rising up within her, but then her newfound independence stepped in and paused the moment. A slow satisfied smile spread across her face as she realized Brad had just proffered a most convenient exit from her life. "You're right, sweetie. It doesn't matter one bit to me. And that is why," and she took the sandwich from his hand, reached over for his coat, and handed it to him, "you are leaving now. It's been fun, and I wish you well."

Brad's eyes went wide. "Just like that? I—"

"Just like that," Lydia said with an unflappability that would not be challenged.

She did not miss Brad nor the partying lifestyle she had taken up these last few years. Perhaps she was a bit more mature, or maybe she preferred to think of it as having a more worldly perspective. First love had been fun, although heartbreaking; casual sex had been fun, although empty. Following rules and being a good girl had been one way; going against rules and being a bad girl had been another. Both had brought their fair share of shame and guilt, and fun and delight.

She knew she was seen as a slut, and Brad was seen as sowing his wild oats. So be it—she'd gotten what she needed out of that phase. But was there another way, or a combination of both?

And so once again, she decided to take a few steps forward but in a different direction, experimenting with a different style, a different focus. Feeling rather fatigued with the whole boys and sex and love and broken hearts business, she set her sights on something far less emotional, and looked to her job and her future. She took more classes in nursing and eventually became a registered nurse, and toyed with the idea of becoming a doctor.

She felt a settling in of sorts in Columbia. It was a nice town, and Westfall was far enough away that she could pretend it didn't exist, but close enough that she could visit in a day if she wanted.

Since leaving over seven years ago, she had been back to Westfall only a few times a year—usually for Christmas, Phyllis's birthday, and a few days around the Fourth of July.

During these visits, she would always stop by to visit Ollie and check up on him, leaving a ten-dollar bill and a bag full of groceries. Some visits he was grumpy and sullen, offering only a grunt or two toward her attempts at making conversation. Other visits he was perky and lucid, orating on and on about whatever local scandal or national political turpitude was taking place at the time that would surely be everybody's downfall. He would sometimes sit and talk about the past, without recollecting any specifics, and draw her back in a way that could actually be sweet. She often marveled that somewhere deep within the dishevelment of his brain, there were glimpses of brilliant reflection and insight. What a waste for this man to end up in a sorry little shack with barely a high school education. During one visit, she learned he had moved from the little house down by the river into a sublet on the second floor of the Victorian house owned by Miss Lipperton.

She asked the first time she visited Ollie if he'd heard from Ray, but this had been met with a zealous string of cussing so fierce that Lydia resolved to never ask him about it again. She didn't want to send Ollie into a conniption, and she told herself she didn't want to know because she didn't want to care.

She also was careful to avoid Shane and Sam during her visits. Their presence would bring up memories of Ray, and it was like an incomplete dozen of eggs, or a pea pod missing one of its peas. It was just never going to be quite right.

It was with great surprise and a small amount of distress then when she walked out of the Med Center one day after work and saw a young man leaning against a red 1959 Chevy pickup truck waving at her. She thought she knew him, but then . . . the short, goofy boy with an awkward but infectious grin that she remembered didn't quite match up with the tall, poised man, hair the color of summer wheat, looking quite handsome in a finely cut pair of light blue slacks and a crisp white shirt. She slowed her walk and stared. The smile was the same, and as she got closer, she saw that the dark-brown eyes held the same twinkle.

"Sam Cooper?" she asked as she walked up to him.

He smiled and held out his arms. "It's me. Can I hug an old friend?"

She figured this day would probably come at some point; no amount of dodging about in Westfall could completely assure they'd never run in to each other. But as long as she had been able to keep her distance from the Cooper boys, the easier it was to put it all behind her.

With a certain amount of anxiety she stepped into his embrace and let his arms fold around her. She was not at all prepared for how his warm touch caused the anxiety to slip away, and how the feeling of love and friends, the river and its clear current, canoe rides, fried catfish, cherished fun and laughter all washed over her and began to fill something inside her that had been so terribly empty until now.

Chapter 22

1965

Lydia took Sam to a small hole-in-the-wall diner on campus called The Shack. They got a beer and a burger and began a tenuous conversation, sidestepping old memories and highlighting what had happened in their lives during the past five years. Eventually they both began to relax when Sam said something that made her laugh. She had been a bit baffled with the awkwardness—this was after all the same person she had swum and canoed with on the river; the same person she had ridden with in Ray's car, whooping and hollering as they sped over country hills in an attempt to outrace Deputy Culpepper; the same person with whom she had chomped down on a watermelon they had stolen from McGavery's field. She was now grateful for Sam lightening the mood, as well as a bit astounded with his maturity and grace.

She told Sam about her nursing studies and promotions, her trips back to Westfall, and how much she enjoyed living in Columbia.

Sam told her that while he was still in high school, he had taken Ray's old job at Earl's filling station and had gotten to love cars as he tinkered, hammered, readjusted, and fixed. He had joined the navy just like Shane and had been assigned to the mechanical division, where he had learned all manner of welding, fabricating, pipefitting, painting, and metal design. Coming out of the navy, he had directed his skills to his own business of refurbishing old cars and trucks into show pieces that were beginning to attract quite a few clients. The money came in spurts, if at all, but he was enjoying working creatively with his hands.

Lydia watched him as he talked, and she couldn't help marveling at the incredible person he'd become. He'd been raised by attentive parents, but probably the navy was more responsible for fashioning this well-heeled, straight-postured, bright and innovative young man. It mixed well with the old Sam, the one she'd always known to be affable, caring, and perceptive. She just hadn't realized how much until now.

She also hadn't realized he'd had the makings for growing into such a handsome, well-built, well-spoken gentleman. Back in Westfall, he had always been that tag-along little brother, tripping over his own feet, goofily eager to please and impress, and quick to make a stupid joke; cute, but in a toothy, too-big-of-a-grin-for-his-face kind of way. Now, in the short time they had been together, he'd tipped his hat to every lady he met, opened the door for her, ushered her into The Shack with a respectful hand on the small of her back, and presented a wonderful display of polite and considerate company sprinkled with a tantalizing balance of wit, whimsy, and joy. She couldn't take her eyes off of him.

Later, she took him round to her house and introduced him to her roommates, who shook his hand just a tad too long and asked him too many questions, but Sam endured it all with a playfully smooth grin and captivated them with his funny stories. He eventually excused himself, thanking Lydia for the visit, explaining that he had come to Columbia to look at purchasing a 1938 Lincoln-Zephyr with a convertible top. Lydia offered for him to sleep on the couch, but he said no, he was meeting the car owner—a friend of his father's—at his place, and that was where he'd be staying. Lydia made him promise that if he came back to Columbia he'd let her know.

She walked him out on the porch, moths flickering at the overhead light. Although the night had been light and fun, they each now floundered a bit in the awkwardness of a goodbye between friends who hadn't seen each other in a long time. Did she hug him? She wanted to. Shake hands? The moment finally culminated when Sam held her steady in an electric gaze and said, "I've missed you, Lydia." He reached out with a gentle touch of his fingertips to the back of her hand, then he turned and walked down the sidewalk.

Lydia stood there, watching him in the shadows as he got into his truck and drove away. She thought he might have waved at her through his window, but she wasn't sure. She also wasn't sure about the way she was feeling. She stood there, watching the truck get farther and farther away. She waited, just as much to process as to hold off the chatter she knew would erupt from her roommates when she went back into the house—who was this Sam person, and why hadn't she told them about him before, and boy oh boy, was he ever handsome.

But how could she explain that Sam was a good friend who had been there during a very meaningful, very eventful part of her girlhood, a time when her heart had experienced more than she ever thought it could handle. How could she explain that she had never realized until now how Sam felt about her? How could she explain that she'd never thought she would have feelings for him, especially not after a three-hour visit. You can't explain anything like that. And so, caressing the place where he had touched her hand, she lowered herself to the porch step and sat there long into the night, her roommates finally giving up waiting for her and going off to bed.

It was three weeks later when Lydia got a letter in the mail from Sam. He would be up the last week of the month. Would she be around? Could they meet again for dinner? He had a meeting with a car owner on Friday. What were her plans for the weekend?

Lydia held the letter in her hands, contemplating this interesting turn of events in her life. What were her plans? That was a very good question, and depending on how it was answered, it could certainly have ramifications far beyond the weekend. She had never imagined that her plans would ever again involve a boy from Westfall, and she was very much intrigued. Should she follow that intrigue? Or was she overthinking the whole thing? Had Sam's touch to the back of her hand been only a simple goodbye from an old friend? Is that what she wanted it to be, or did she want it to be more?

She stewed on this for a couple of days, finally revealing to Audrey that Sam had written her. It just so happened that some friends of theirs were going on a float trip the weekend he would be in town. Lydia was trying to decide whether or not to invite Sam up for it.

Audrey had plopped down on the couch beside her, cradling a bowl of Jiffy Pop popcorn. Throwing a few pieces into her mouth, she chewed then grinned. "Well, if you don't invite him, I will."

Lydia shot her a deriding yet good-natured look, knowing that this of course cinched it for her. She was still unsure about Sam, but she did know she didn't want anyone else to have him. Long-distance charges be damned, she called him and invited him up for the float trip. She thought it a safe invite—they would be surrounded by other people and it was just a friend thing. At least that's what she tried to make it sound like on the phone call.

He met her at her house in his red Chevy pickup, and they drove in awkward silence. Finally, Sam broke through when he said, "You sure have worked hard at your nursing degree. I couldn't be more proud of you. Told everyone in town about how well you're doing."

"Thanks. I think my mom's told just as many people. She's proud too, and that makes me glad."

"Ever thought about becoming a doctor?"

Lydia turned to Sam's question with surprised eyes. "Doctor? No! I don't think, well, that's a lot of—"

"You're smart enough. You could do it. Being a nurse is good too. I don't want to downplay that. I just remember you being smart enough to be in Mr. Rudanovich's senior biology class when you were a junior."

Lydia secretly beamed at Sam's compliment, and smiled at the memory. "Wow, Mr. Rudanovich. There's a memory."

"I had geometry right across the hall from you, that's how I remember."

"You were smart too, Sam. I remember you and I being in Mrs. Teegarten's social studies class together and you always asking good questions."

Sam straightened up in the seat, placed his hands staunchly on the steering wheel, and began a proper recitation of the mnemonic Mrs. Teegarten taught them to remember the branches of the government. "Lazy elephants jump slowly and sit regularly."

Lydia laughed. "Legislature, executive, judicial, states . . ."

Then Sam joined in and they finished together. "Amendment process, supremacy of the constitution, and ratification."

They were caught up in it now, giggling as they remembered. "How 'bout the 'only up the up stairs and down the down stairs'?" Sam asked.

Lydia's eyes grew wide. "Oh my gosh, Principal Buhlig was the worst about that!"

They chuckled some more and drove on.

"Ahh, high school," Lydia sighed sarcastically. "Fun times."

They both laughed, eyeing each other in knowing camaraderie.

They gathered with her friends up at the river. Canoes were loaded with buckets of beer, summer sausage, Hershey bars, and other snacks; they would put in some nine miles upriver from their camping site. They headed out, and within one short minute, all sorts of buffoonery commenced. One canoe hadn't gotten three yards from the shore before it capsized amid the good-natured screams of its passengers, sending beer cans, towels, and packages of cookies down the river way. Sam and Lydia circled back, capturing as much of the loot as they could, handing it back to the drenched canoers who were now splashing everybody by whacking the river with their paddles. Another canoe ran into Lydia and Sam's canoe, knocking them sideways, and Sam laughingly got them back on course. Another canoe got stuck a few yards downriver in a log jam. Lydia and Sam rescued them, and they were proclaimed by the rest of the gang to be the eminent king and queen of the float trip.

"You need to let Sam paddle for you, Lydia," one of the wayward canoers called. "Big strapping young man like that can surely take his lady down the river."

Lydia and Sam looked at each other, caught up in a bit of embarrassment, but then Lydia smiled and shook her head with self-assurance, exclaiming, "My mamma told me 'love many, trust few, and always paddle your own canoe.'"

Everyone laughed, and Sam pointed his paddle at Lydia. "And her mamma knows, because she's one smart lady."

All seemed okay for a minute or two, but then a yell came up from behind, where a couple were jumping up and down because a snake had gotten in their boat. Sam and Lydia quickly paddled up against the current, and Sam looked in the canoe to see not a snake but a lizard. He refrained from explaining that snakes did not have legs, and instead dipped his paddle in the canoe, scooped up the lizard, and flung it back on shore.

He flashed a grin over at Lydia as they started floating back down the river. "Are these *good* friends of yours?" he asked.

Lydia grinned back. "Yes. Well, maybe no. I should say no self-respecting friend of mine acts like this on the river, nor do they confuse a snake with a lizard. Oh, they're all okay, I just think they're drunk already."

"Yeah," Sam said. "Wanna guess how many make it to the campsite alive?"

Lydia laughed and shook her head.

"Look," Sam said. "We're never gonna make it to the campsite before dark if we stay with this pack of yahoos. If cavorting out here like this was your intention, then I'm okay with that. But if it's not, let's get the hell out of here and enjoy this river."

Lydia's face brightened as she was reminded of a childhood bond with a kindred river rat. "Absolutely!" she said, and she raised her paddle at him and he raised his and they clacked.

Sam yelled, "Yahoo!" Their paddles went into the water in spirited synchronization, and in three strokes they were gliding swiftly with the current.

The trees on the river shore passed by in dense swirls of a hundred shades of green, the birds flew ahead of them, a fish jumped, a turtle slipped from his perch on a fallen log into the river, and the smell of honeysuckle blew in on the breeze. The screwball party was soon left behind as they rounded a bend, and it was just the two of them, two bodies moving as one in complete harmony with river, canoe, nature.

Sam started singing a song about finding his baby in the sugar shack across the tracks, a salute to the diner Lydia had taken him to when he'd first come to Columbia to visit her. His lyrics weren't quite right, but the words bounced off the tall cliffs they passed and rolled back down to them, the melody lifting them up. And for a brief and wondrous moment, when Lydia looked over her shoulder and smiled at him, and the clear, sparkling river current carried them along, all was right in the world.

That night around the campfire, Sam was the center of attention. Every girl there developed an immediate crush on him as he made them laugh with his stories about crazy things that happened in the navy, people in Greece and Malta where his ship docked, buying and selling cars to some questionable characters, and finally all the shenanigans he and Lydia and Ray and Shane got into in Westfall.

"Remember that time we found that old johnboat?" Sam asked Lydia. "It had a motor but no cover on it. We all took it out for a run on the river, Ray driving like a maniac, and then he hits a log. It bounces the motor up and the motor gears grind into Ray's elbow."

"Oh my," Lydia said, shaking her head. "All that blood. His arm was a mess. We got him into Doc Scott and he stitched him right up. We were all so scared, but that damn Ray was laughing the whole time."

"This one time, Ray and Lydia were in the front seat of some pickup he'd gotten for like five dollars—was it that old 1939 Ford, Lydia? The blue one?"

"Goodness, it was so rusty, how could you even tell what color it was?"

Sam grinned at Lydia. "Yeah, that's true. Anyway, they were in the front seat, and Shane and I were riding in the back. Ray was going too fast of course, and here comes Culpepper, chasing us down. Ray took off down some dirt road and I knew he was heading straight for the river."

Lydia squealed. "I knew it too! I was yelling at him to slow down, slow down!"

"But no, ol' daredevil Ray kept gunnin' it. He turns off the road just lickety-split, right into the middle of some field. Man, we couldn't see anything, so many bushes. Deputy Culpepper goes whizzing by back up on the road, didn't even see us. Now bushes and tall weeds thrashing past us as Ray keeps on going through this field and all of a sudden—" Sam slapped his hands and both arms flew outward. "Bam! He hits a rock, or a big log or something, and we go airborne."

Lydia slapped a hand over her mouth as she tried to stifle her laughter. "I was never so scared ..."

"Gosh dang," Sam said, taking a deep breath. "Man, Shane and I got knocked straight out over the truck, and we both landed in the river. Saved us from breaking our necks, I guess."

"And that truck went nose-first into the river. Good grief, how are we still alive today?" Lydia and Sam looked over at each other, laughing, faces flushed as they shook their heads.

"Yeah, after we pushed that old truck out of the river, Ray took us back into town and made it up to us by buying us each a soda."

"I think that was the first time I'd ever had peanuts in my soda," Lydia said.

"What? Peanuts in your soda?" asked a camper, not too sure of the palatability of this type of refreshment.

"Yeah," Lydia said. "It was you, Sam. You showed me about putting peanuts in my bottle of Orange Crush. Sounds weird, but I loved it. I haven't done that in a long time."

"This Ray guy sounds like a hoot," said one of the campers.

"Yeah," Sam said, looking over at Lydia. "A tad dangerous. But we all ... sure loved him."

"What do you mean loved? Did he die or something?"

"No," Lydia said, her voice dropping down to a more controlled level now. "He just left. He had . . . I don't know, I guess he'd had enough of that little town and that gawd-awful deputy and . . . and other things." Lydia looked down and started drawing in the dirt with a stick. "I'd had enough of it and left too. Didn't like the town. Didn't like the deputy."

"That deputy's not there anymore," Sam said, causing Lydia to stop her dirt drawing and look up. Sam studied her face. The fire crackled and snapped, sending sparks swirling up into the night sky, where they flared bright red-orange then fizzled out. "He kind of disappeared. There was an investigation, but I don't know that they found anything. No one knows for sure what happened. Someone said they saw his car out on Route K. I think they hauled it over to Melva Dean, Culpepper's wife. They searched around Mrs. Meeks's neighborhood, because you know there'd been bad blood out there." The glances Sam and Lydia exchanged may have appeared nondescript to the other campers, but they were heavy with unspoken recollections.

"They looked around the river," Sam continued. "In the woods there by River Leap Park, asked around. It was like he'd up and vanished. Did your mom ever say anything to you about it? I mean, being as he was your uncle and all."

"Step-uncle. And good riddance," Lydia said, throwing her stick into the fire. The campers turned their focus to her because her voice had come out hard and flinty. She was staring dark-eyed into the fire now, rubbing her thighs, bare in her blue jean shorts, and was beginning to slowly rock back and forth. "Good riddance, I say."

Sam slowly placed a hand on her shoulder, then let it slide down her arm to take a hold of her hand. She stopped rocking and turned her face to Sam, liking the feel of her hand in his. "No. My mom never told me. But then, we don't talk much about him."

He didn't kiss her that night, and she had wanted him to. She had to mentally shake herself, though, saying that this after all was Sam, little Sammy Cooper, for cryin' out loud! But when she looked at him, there was nothing little about him. He had grown so much, come so far from that southern Missouri small-town boy. And yet, her heart flew wide open when she saw that, as much as he had grown, he was still the same. Here was the boy who had saved her after the abortion, who had saved Ray by running all over town the night he was in jail, who had saved Shane by making him stand up and help Ray with Mrs. Meeks's garden. He had been the bravest of them all, and she was stunned that she had never seen it until now. How lucky, how blessed she was that she was finally seeing it, that he'd come back into her life. What she didn't know was that he'd never left.

On the drive back to her house the next morning, he told her he'd be in North Carolina the next week with Shane for some business stuff, something about a cousin who lived there selling them land he owned in Riley County. He said he might be gone for a while depending on how the sale went. Something in the way he said it got Lydia thinking that once again she'd misread the whole thing—they were just friends, and that was why he hadn't kissed her last night, and now that she thought about it, she hadn't wanted him to kiss her anyway.

She put on what she thought was her friend face—which to be honest was more of a shield around her heart—told him she hoped the sale was successful, and said to tell Shane hi for her. He walked her to her door, and things got awkward again. He told her he'd be back again soon, thanked her for a great time, gave her a quick peck on the cheek, got back in his truck, and drove away. Once again she sat on her porch steps and contemplated the whole darn thing. Her life had been just fine, thank you very much, before Sam had stepped back into it. She didn't need old memories being dredged up. Then why, she asked herself, was she feeling this strange mixture of confusion and elation?

She couldn't deny the little jump in her heart when a letter from Sam came a few weeks later. The words on the paper seemed to stay on an old-friends level, but she felt her heart grow warmer each time she read it. She chastised herself for acting like a teenager. One minute she was deriding the whole thing as silly, and the next she was checking the mailbox again. She wrote him a letter, he wrote her back, and she missed him.

Then another week then two went by, and there was no letter. He was busy, she told herself. She thought about calling him but then what would she say? Wouldn't it just be a call between two friends? Indeed, what would it be? She chewed on her nails and wondered, carried on with her life, questioned her heart, and searched the mail each day.

It was another week later when she came home from work and walked up the porch steps to see a bottle of Orange Crush and a pack of peanuts sitting on her doorstep. She drew in her breath and looked up. He was sitting there at the edge of the porch, arms crossed, leaning on the railing, grinning at her. Her heart began to beat double-time. Unable to suppress the delighted smile spreading across her face, she bent down and picked up the soda bottle and peanuts and looked over at him. "What a fine gift."

She walked over to him, and he didn't take his eyes off of her as he reached out and took the bottle from her. He deftly popped the top off the bottle by catching it on the edge of the porch railing, the bottle cap landing on the porch with a metallic whirring as it spun to a final stop. He took the first gulp of the soda, something you had to do in order for the peanuts to fit.

"Sorry you haven't heard from me for a while," he said. "The thing in North Carolina took longer than I expected. And . . . well, I thought I'd just come up instead of write." He held her in his gaze for another moment, then opened the pack of peanuts, poured some in the bottle just like he'd shown her those many years ago, and handed it to her.

She took a drink, and he watched as she lowered the bottle and chewed on the peanuts, her mouth struggling to keep the peanuts in and swallow because her delighted smile was growing wider and wider. His eyes followed a trail of orange soda that trickled out of her grinning mouth. Then he leaned toward her and softly kissed at the orange liquid. She turned and reached her arms around him, the bottle of soda sloshing against his shirt, but he didn't care, and he held her tight and their kiss was sweet and magical and heated. They were filled to the brim and yet at the same time, so light they could have sworn they were floating.

Any questions or second thoughts she'd had evaporated like a dewdrop in the sun. She leaned back and looked up at him, shaking her head in wonderment. "I . . . I never knew."

Sam pulled his gaze away from her full lips up to her blue eyes. "I always knew." Then he pulled her closer and kissed her again. And it was then that his fantasy—the fantasy that had begun so long ago when he'd first laid eyes on Lydia Campbell as she kicked a beach ball back into the Current River—came true.

Chapter 23

1964

O ne March before Sam had come back into her life, Lydia made a visit to Westfall for her mother's birthday. Now that Lydia was living on her own in Columbia, had her own job and was paying her own bills, she felt she had enough agency to make decisions about where she went and who she saw, and when she came back to Westfall, she flatly refused to be anywhere near Westley Culpepper. Her mother accepted it, having endured enough Sunday dinners watching Lydia stare daggers at the deputy. Interestingly, Westley seemed to dislike her presence as much as Lydia disliked his, and though he tried to puff himself up when he was around her, he just didn't seem to have the gumption to "put her in her place."

Phyllis was just glad to have her daughter in town. She was proud of who Lydia was becoming, and despite heartache from young love, she knew her daughter would be all right. Lydia and Phyllis were cut from the same cloth—a colorful span with a strong weave that grew ever more brilliant as life went on.

As her daughter was growing in her years, Phyllis would drop hints to find out if there was anybody Lydia had met that was worth marrying. Of course Phyllis knew marriage was not the end-all, be-all, having experienced her own first marriage that left quite a lot to be desired. Her mantra to Lydia was never to get yourself in a spot where you have to depend on a man, financially or emotionally. A woman's strength came from within, and with that, a man could be a slice of her life, but never the whole loaf. Still, Phyllis thought life was better if you had a good partner to go through it with, and so she wished this for Lydia. Not to mention her hope of grandchildren.

It was a delicate subject of course, what with the abortion, and Phyllis stepped into it quite messily during that visit in March. She mentioned how Birdie Tyler had three grandchildren—three mind you—and it just seemed like a wonderful thing. Noticing Lydia's pained expression, Phyllis quickly apologized.

"I don't mean . . . honey, I'm sorry. I know . . . I mean I don't know. I don't know what I'm trying to say. It's just that . . . well you and Ray . . ."

"Mom, Ray was not the one who got me pregnant."

Phyllis stopped and blinked. Then she nodded. "I know, he told me that. I'm not sure I believe him though. How can you be so sure? I mean—"

"Ray and I never had sex. At least, we did stuff. Just not . . . intercourse. It wasn't Ray. He was telling you the truth."

Phyllis sat on the couch beside her daughter. "Then . . . who was it? If you don't want to talk about it, you don't have to. But, it might help. I heard . . . that you and Shane—"

Lydia took a deep breath. "It wasn't Shane, Mamma." She felt her throat tighten, and she cast her gaze on a vase of flowers that sat on the coffee table. Tulips, soft pink, a sign that spring was upon them. She wanted to take the flowers from the vase and press them to her cheek, to smell them, to pretend that the story that swirled inside her was not there. She had done a very good job of it over the years. So well, in fact, that just a simple view of flowers could take her away from the pain, the angst. The horror. Perhaps it was time to let the horror out. Perhaps her mother was the perfect person to let it out to.

Phyllis sat silent, trying her darndest to tamp down the curiosity that threatened to spill out of her. She shook her head. "I'm sorry. I didn't mean to pry. Whatever . . . whoever."

"I was raped, Mamma." Lydia turned her eyes from the flowers and looked at Phyllis full on. "Westley raped me." Then she smoothed her skirt down across her lap and began to tell her mother the story.

Lydia would forever regret drinking the whiskey from the flask Shane had pulled out of his pocket at the county fair that August night so long ago. She would blame at least part of the night on that. She had drank too much and gotten drunk. She had lost track of time, track of her senses, track of all that mattered. The alcohol that ran through her veins fed that small kernel of irritation that had started with Ray being late and not meeting her when he said he would. The kernel would grow into full-out anger. How dare he treat her like this! She was constantly waiting on him, and yet he was so impatient with her. Hurry up and graduate, as if she had anything to do with the timing. Just run away with me now, he'd say. Have sex with me now, he'd say. I love you so much and I want you now. Now, now, now!

She would take another drink from Shane's flask, go on the Ferris wheel with him, let him shoot a BB gun at some balloons until he won her a stuffed rabbit. Take another drink. She thought she saw Sam at one point running through the fairgrounds, but she wasn't sure. She asked Shane if he'd seen him, but he wasn't sure either. They were both getting pretty drunk. They walked out of the fair and sat down at the edge of the park where a small hill led down to a back road. Out there the breeze was cooler and they could catch their breath.

Lydia was beyond annoyed now at Ray's no-show. Feeling tipsy and muddled, she leaned her head on Shane's shoulder. "Where is he?" she asked.

Shane touched her cheek and she turned and looked up at him. In a move that surprised them both and was undoubtedly fed by the whiskey they had drank, they kissed. As soon as their lips met, they knew it was a mistake.

Shane's mind seemed to close in on itself, and something inside of him slammed shut. This was not the fantasy, this was not all warmth and sensuousness but rather something cold and flat and not at all right. He sensed Lydia felt the same way, and they both drew apart, shame and regret immediately filling the space between them.

Shane shook his head and whispered, "I'm sorry." Then he stood, brushing grass away from his pants. He held out his hand and helped her up. They stood awkwardly, trying to not look at each other.

Finally, Lydia said, "I need to go home."

They walked down the small hill and along the very road Ray had driven past just a few moments before, and on into town and over to her house. When they got to her door, Shane stood, not knowing what to do.

"Lydia, I'm sorry. So sorry. That kiss—it should have never happened. I mean Ray and I . . . and Ray and you, well . . . And there was nothing—"

Lydia nodded. "I agree. It's okay. We're okay."

Shane still fretted. "I mean, should we tell Ray? I don't know, it's just that I don't want to hide anything from him, but you know, well, I guess there was nothing to it, right? Right?"

Lydia shook her head. "I don't think we should tell him. It would just . . . I don't know. It was a mistake. And it won't happen again."

"No! Absolutely." Shane placed a hand on the back of his neck, rubbing at the short bristles of his new haircut. "Well, then, you gonna be okay? Is there anything—"

"I'll be fine," Lydia reassured. "I'll just . . . I need to sleep this off, you know. The whiskey and all." She tried a smile, an attempt to make them both feel better. Not knowing what else to do, she turned and went inside.

Shane turned and walked down the driveway and toward his home. What a loser he was! Kissing his best friend's girl! He felt horrible. And the thing of it was, he had wanted it so badly. He could still feel the touch where her lips had met his, a dreadful shadow that would not let go.

He knew he was a chicken. And he knew now just how big of one he was. He hadn't had the balls to step forward when Sheriff Tyler asked who had torn up Mrs. Meeks's flowers. He'd offered to help Ray with the gardening but only after his little brother had guilted him into it. And he knew how mean Ray's dad was to him and how hungry Ray could get and it was his mother who stepped in to help, not Shane. He'd actually been a little embarrassed when he saw his mother slip Ray an extra sandwich and some cookies. If Culpepper had been after Shane the way he was always after Ray, Shane would never have been able to withstand all the badgering and would have folded like a baby. He shook his head now. He would never be the man Ray was. He was weak, and he hated himself.

After Shane left her, Lydia walked into the house to find that her parents weren't there. They might have gone down to the fair, or over to some friends' house to play pinochle, which was a Friday-night ritual of theirs. She didn't want to go to bed; the night's travails were still stirring in her head, and she would no doubt end up tossing and turning and trying to figure out how the night had gone wrong.

She came back out on the porch and sat in the wicker swing. A few of the neighborhood houses' lights were on, a car drove down the street, somewhere there was a cricket going crazy trying to find a mate. She could barely hear the sounds of the fair wafting up the hill into town—the music from the Ferris wheel, a ding and then distant applause as someone hit the high striker hard enough to reach the top. She could hear the hum of voices, of faint laughter, and wished she was there with Ray. She wished she hadn't drank so much, she wished she hadn't ended up with Shane, and she wished she hadn't kissed him.

Meanwhile, Deputy Culpepper was driving through the back roads of Riley County, cursing up a storm when Ray managed once again to lose him. How in the world had he gotten out of jail? He couldn't imagine that Ray had been able to pay his fine before the courthouse closed. Westley had been working the fair and riding high knowing that son of a bitch Ray Bellamy was sitting in that god-awful cell. It had been the highlight of his crusade!

Sweaty, spent, mired in bitter indignation, he drove back into town, slowly searching the roads for any sign of Ray. He came upon his brother and sister-in-law's house and saw Lydia sitting on the porch swing. Something within him came absolutely undone.

She knew as soon as he got out of the car that something was horribly wrong. Westley slammed his car door behind him, stood with legs spread and arms akimbo as if he was setting up for a gun-slinging shoot-out. "Where's Ray!" came a voice that did not belong to any earthly being Lydia knew. This here was a madman. Alarm coursing through her, she sat up in the swing, Westley starting toward her, and something told her to run.

The space between the swing and the door grew astonishingly long as Wes ran up the walk in double-time. Seeing that she could not open the door and make it into the house in time, she ran across the porch—calling upon a strength she didn't know she had—and leapt over the porch railing, clearing the bushes and heading into the dark backyard. She hadn't made it four feet when Westley grabbed her hair and jerked her head back. She let out a scream, but he pulled her around to him, smashing her into his chest. He clamped down on her with arms of steel, wrapping her in a suffocating clutch.

In Wes's warped brain, it made sense that if he couldn't have Ray, the next best thing would be to have Lydia.

He fell to the ground with her in his arms, smashing her and knocking the breath out of her. She tried to scream, but her lungs failed her. She tried to kick, but his weight was too unyielding. With maddening revulsion she felt him grab at her skirt and grapple with her panties, felt rough fingers ply apart her thighs. She felt his hot breath on her face and tried to turn away.

"You're so pretty and snooty. You and your mamma come to this town and start stirring things up. My brother was just fine before you all showed up. He didn't need you. All he needed was me. He was a good brother. And Ray, he's got no place going after the likes of you. Ray's nothing but a tick on my ass, and I had him just where I wanted until you showed up. And you, all pink-faced and innocent and all. Well, I know better. You're a whore. A slut, you hear me! Laying with that trash Ray Bellamy makes you a whore, don't you know that! I tried to tell ya, 'Stay away from Ray,' I said."

His mouth was pressed to her face, his words tumbling over one another like a drunken sermon, convincing himself that he was only taking his due. By God, he was an upstanding man of the law and he was trying his best to make this town a reputable place, but people like Ray and Viola and so many others were making it hard work for him, so he deserved this!

Lydia turned her face away, but he only pressed his rough mouth to her other cheek now. He pulled at his pants zipper then heaved himself upon her, pushing in, piggish grunts accompanying his movements.

Lydia tried with a strength that just couldn't best his weight to push him away. She choked on a sob and turned away again, and in the dark of the night, saw the little flower garden her mother had planted. Tall, colorful zinnias, monochrome in the dark night, stood against the white picket fence. The vines of the rose bushes curled in thorny curves, their pink-red petals somewhat scruffy against Missouri's unforgiving summer heat, but yet they held on. Daisies and black-eyed Susans bent slightly toward the ground, hopeful of finding a bit of dew on the nighttime grass. While Lydia was being raped, she looked at the flowers.

Finished, Westley rolled himself off of her, taking great gulps of air. Then he began to stand, but Lydia, now released of his suffocating weight, beat him to it, pulling at her panties as she stood up. She swayed for a moment, taking in deep breaths, a shaking hand reaching up to her mouth. Then, gathering as much saliva in her mouth as she could, she let spew the muckiest glob of spit she could muster into his face. He held up his hand but not before it made its mark. Then she kicked him square in the crotch, scowling with disgust at the sight of him standing there, wincing and weaving with his pants down around his knees, hands protecting his now throbbing balls.

One would think a girl might run then, but Lydia did not. She took two steps toward his doubled-over form and sneered at him. "You're a weak, little, sissy mommy's boy hiding behind a stupid deputy badge. And you stink." She drew in a half breath, half sob and put her arms around herself as she began to shiver uncontrollably. "You're a loser and you'll always be nothing." Then she turned and walked away, her legs trembling, the rage within her causing her to shake so violently that she could barely put one foot in front of the other.

Wes was finally able to stand straight after Lydia's well-aimed kick. He placed a hand on his lower belly and moaned and watched her walk away. He breathed heavily as he took in her straight back and squared-up shoulders and grew even angrier as he saw she had not been put in her place. He yelled arrogantly, "You tell anyone about this, little missy, and it'll be Ray who pays. You hear!"

His words called across the dark yard echoed inside her head. They echoed the whole time as she went inside the house, locked the doors, went upstairs, took a bath, and crawled into bed, pulling the covers up to her chin. They were the last words she heard as she fell into a fitful sleep. They were the first words she would remember when she woke up. They were words that would follow her around for a long, long time.

Lydia had never told the story to anyone, never breathed a word of it before this. The sound of her words, the release of the scalding, raw episode now ran like a river, its current cascading over boulders and hills, a release akin to the breaching of a huge and mighty dam. While she had talked, tears had dampened her eyes, but now as the story ended, torrents of tears flooded outward. It was huge. This cathartic sharing, finally, finally absolution from her pent-up heart. A lightness came to her with the unburdening. Her muscles felt lithe and limber where once they had been stiff and weak. Her bones now felt strong and resilient where once they had felt brittle and rigid. Because not only was the story now out and told, it was told to a ferocious mother who would take the weight and shoulder it. Looking at her mother's stricken but determined face, Lydia knew this. For the first time in a long time, Lydia felt safe and unafraid. She sat amazed in her newfound buoyancy.

Phyllis had sat stunned during the story, her heart breaking with each word, interjecting "Oh, my God" and "I'll kill him" and "My poor Lydia" as the story unfolded, but as it ended, she now had her hands up to her face and was full-on sobbing along with Lydia.

It was Lydia who calmed first, and she gently pulled at her mother's hands, taking them down to her lap. "Mom, I need to tell you something. Listen to me. I need you to hear me. I'm okay." She dipped her head to look into her mother's bent face. "Do you hear me? I'm okay."

Through her tears, Phyllis searched her daughter's face and shook her head. "But how? My God, my God! I can't believe this! I'll kill him!"

Lydia rubbed her mother's hands in hers. "I am all right, and you want to know how that can be?" Lydia drew in a long, replenishing breath. "Because of you, Mom."

Phyllis looked through red and puffy eyes at her beautiful and magnificent daughter and tried to make sense of what she was telling her.

"Mom, I heard you say once to some lady, 'I'll pay for my own sins, but I won't pay for my husband's.' I've always remembered that. And I've lived by it. And that's what it is. It is not my sin. It is not of my making and I don't carry it with me. Do you understand?"

Phyllis took a deep breath, but tears started anew. "My darling Lydia. This horrible, horrible thing. My words? They comforted you?"

Lydia tilted her head and projected an expression of grateful acknowledgment. "They strengthened me. It is you and your take on life. I watched you, Mom. You're dauntless. And you raised me to be that way too. And I love you for it."

Phyllis leaned in and hugged her daughter. She never would be able to express how proud she was of her. She had tried to be a good mother, but, like all mothers, was often frustrated with her own failings and flaws. Lydia sitting in front of her, scarred but strong, gave her hope.

"There was something else that helped me too. Strangely enough, it was the river. I used to go out to River Leap and just sit there. It gave me a sort of peace, I guess, watching the current flow on by. It was at the river where I started to become stronger. I looked out on all that beauty, all that power of all that water going downstream, and it was comforting in a way. And it sort of . . . felt like that power began to run through me. I don't know if I can make you understand, but the river kind of saved me in a way. The river and you."

Phyllis smiled. "It is a wondrous river, isn't it?" She took a deep, clearing breath, thankful for the river, for its prevailing beauty. She was thankful for her daughter's strength. She was thankful for her own seemingly brilliant motherly way, but in truth it had been a simple following of her heart.

"I wish you'd have told me."

Lydia nodded. "I should have. I'm glad I'm telling you now. Now is a good time because you get to see that I'm all right. I left town, I got away, and I'm doing okay."

"But Lydia, sex . . . and relationships . . . He ruined that for you."

Lydia looked directly into her mother's eyes. "No. No, he didn't. What he did to me wasn't sex. And I've never thought of it in the same realm. I've never let it . . ." She pressed a finger to her lips and gave a mischievous grin. "Well, you must know, I've enjoyed quite a lot of fun sex since going away. That has not been ruined one bit." Lydia searched her mother's face to see if she understood, and Phyllis released a dubious smile.

"You've never fallen in love though. Never . . ."

Lydia gave a smirk. "We could just as well blame that on Ray, couldn't we?"

Phyllis twisted at a tissue she had taken from the box on the coffee table. "Lydia . . . what about the abortion? How are you doing with that? I totally agree, of course, but are you okay?"

Again, Lydia forthrightly held her mother in her gaze. "Westley forced a lot of things on a lot of people. Bullying, harassment, his sense of righteousness. My God, he nearly choked Ray to death, and he killed Sam's dog. The abortion? It was my decision and I made it clearly. I was not going to allow him to force a pregnancy on me."

"He still has power over you though. You didn't tell anyone, and so he walks around free like nothing ever happened."

Lydia nodded. "He still scares me. I don't like being around him. So in a way, yes, he does have a sort of power over me. That's why I stay away. I can't stand to be anywhere near him. It's best that I stay away." Lydia held her mother in a steely gaze. "I've thought of killing him several times."

Chapter 24

Ray sat in the hospital bed, mouth hanging open and eyes wide at what Shane had just told him. He wasn't sure he'd heard Shane right at all. Lydia and Sam married? Sam? But Mrs. Meeks's letter had said—ah, now it was coming clear. Lydia hadn't married Shane, and suddenly the great mountain of self-ennoblement that Ray had been sitting on all these years began to crumble. As his realization came into focus, all the bitterness he'd lived on these past years began to dissolve. The chip on his shoulder began to crumble with it, first tiny bits, then larger bits, then huge parts tumbling down one over the other.

And he sat there in stony silence. If he didn't have that mountain to sit on, that chip to carry around, that absolute certainty that everyone had done him wrong, then who was he?

He looked up at Shane and frowned. "How? What?"

"I was as surprised as you. Little brother Sam just slipped right in there and stole her heart. I had no idea he'd been visiting her up in Columbia, but he was. Next thing I know, we're in town visiting Mom and Dad, sitting there at the dinner table, and he tells us he has a girl that he's serious about. Then he tells us it's Lydia and I 'bout fell out of my chair."

Ray shifted in his bed, his shoulder now beginning to throb. "How does . . . I mean, what does Lydia think of all this?"

Shane's eyebrow raised and he pulled back his chin. "What does she think? She's in love. He's in love. They make a great couple, good partners. And that boy of theirs, he's a rascal and cute to boot."

Ray was still trying to grasp all that he was being told when there was a commotion out in the hallway and both men turned their attention to the doorway. Maybelline entered and wiggled her fingers at Shane. "Uh, Deputy Cooper, um . . ." She cast a glance over toward Ray and then back at Shane. "Brenda be calling from down at the jail. Says Mr. Bellamy, Ollie, he's in a bad way. She thinks maybe . . ." Another glance over at Ray. "She thinks maybe he might be having a heart attack. Says his chest hurts and he can't breathe."

"You got him locked up?" Ray asked. "Man, you all don't waste any time in this town. Even Culpepper never managed to cage my daddy."

"Well, he never shot no one 'til now," Shane offered. "Leastways, not that I know of."

"He in that old god-forsaken jail?" Ray asked.

"No, a new jail got built, about seven years ago. That old jail, well it's long gone and I bet you're glad of it."

"Yeah . . ." Ray said, and drew the word out to an exasperated sigh, the heaviness coming back in the room. "The night of the fair . . . ?"

Shane's face froze as bad memories rose up within him.

Maybelline cleared her throat. "Deputy, Brenda's needing to know what to do. She don't want Mr. Bellamy down there dyin' on her."

"No," Shane said, mentally shaking off a dark cloud and turning to Maybelline. "None of us want him dying on us down there at the jail. Can Zeb go down and get him?" Shane reached over and picked up his hat. "Hell, I guess I'll need to go down with him. No doubt he's fakin' it and he'll probably run off and I don't want Zeb feeling bad about letting him get away."

Shane headed toward the door, hearing Ray mumble "He can't run very fast" with a slight chuckle.

Maybelline nodded and said, "And I'll call Lydia. She'll want to know if anything's wrong with Ollie."

Ray was taken aback by this. "What's that?"

Shane turned to Ray with a slight shrug. "Well, Lydia's been, um . . . well, she's always had a soft spot for Ollie. Danged if I know why, but she has. Not sure—maybe since . . . well, since you left there wasn't no one to take care of him." Shane shook his head. "She brings him food, stops by to check on him now and then. It's not like they're buddies or anything, but she, well, she checks on him." He turned to Maybelline. "Yeah, go ahead and tell Lydia. She'll want to know."

Ray followed this disclosure with perplexity, and he shook his head in bewilderment, realizing that this little town wasn't exactly as he had left it.

Despite his tendency to partake in overzealous dramatics, there was indeed something wrong with Ollie. Shane and Zeb drove him quickly to the hospital where, paradoxically, he was placed in the room right next to the son he'd put in there by shooting him the night before. After examining him, Dr. Scott noted the fifty-seven-year-old man was experiencing ventricular tachycardia. He gave him a shot of lidocaine, and it calmed things down for the time being. The little man lying in the bed looked more like seventy-seven, thin and pale, but Dr. Scott was aware of enough inner orneriness that would most likely keep Ollie alive longer than a lot of others.

Back up at the front desk, Lydia picked up the ringing phone to hear Cecilia Wiggins on the other end asking what was going on over there at the hospital that had caused Melva Dean Culpepper to show up at her door offering condolences on the passing of her sister, Charlene Teegarten. Last Cecilia had heard was that Charlene had been released from the hospital.

Lydia's eyebrows shot up. "You're exactly right, Mrs. Wiggins. Mrs. Teegarten seemed in fine spirits after getting a good night's rest in the hospital and was taken back down to the nursing home just half an hour ago."

"Melva Dean said she talked to the black nurse."

Lydia looked over her shoulder at Maybelline and gestured to the phone, mouthing that it was Mrs. Wiggins on the phone. "Yes, she's right here, Mrs. Wiggins. Hold on and let me ask her."

Lydia placed her hand on the phone and lowered it to her lap. "Did Melva Dean come in here asking about Mrs. Teegarten?"

"Mm hmm," Maybelline said, writing on her report. "She asked to see her and I told her she was no longer with us." Maybelline sensed Lydia casting a look of consternation her way, and she looked up to see that she indeed was.

"No longer with us?" Lydia questioned. "Mrs. Wiggins is saying that Melva Dean expressed her condolences for her sister's passing."

Maybelline looked to the ceiling then started nodding. "Oh, my. I can see now why what I said would make her think that. I'll call Melva Dean right away and straighten it out."

Lydia couldn't help letting out a soft chuckle. "Good grief. What a small town we live in." Then she spoke back into the phone, letting Mrs. Wiggins know that her sister was fine and that they'd call Melva Dean and clear things up.

"See that you do. News is spreading like wildfire. My neighbor, Lula has already stopped by with a chocolate cake as a sympathy offering."

Lydia could hear Mr. Wiggins in the background saying something about no need to shut it down so quickly, because if they were lucky, they might get a ham out of it.

Lydia hung up the phone with a shake of her head. It had been quite a morning what with Ray down the hall, bringing Ollie Bellamy in and sending Mrs. Teegarten back to the nursing home. She hadn't even noticed that Melva Dean had come into the hospital. She got up and headed down the hall to Ollie's room, passing by Maybelline to hear her on the phone explaining to Melva Dean that Mrs. Teegarten had in fact not died and she was sorry for the miscommunication.

To be honest, Melva Dean didn't really care all that much about Mrs. Teegarten. She had used her for an excuse to get in the hospital. Melva Dean was really there because she had heard that Ray Bellamy was back in town and she was trying to figure out a way she could get to him and ask questions about the day her husband, Westley had disappeared. Ray had been gone several years by the time Westley seemed to drop off the face of the earth, but it was well accepted around town that Westley had it out for Ray, and it was also accepted that Westley was most likely one of the reasons Ray had left town. So it only stood to reason, at least in Melva Dean's mind, that Ray might have had something to do with his disappearance.

Melva Dean remembered that day well. Wes had thankfully left the house early that morning, leaving her and her boys some peace. He had gained more weight in the last couple of years and was like a lumbering bull in a china shop. Nothing was ever quiet or soft with him. As she heard the door shut behind him, she rolled over in bed, pulled the covers up and happily went back to sleep.

She had gotten up a little later, and was feeding the boys breakfast when Phyllis, her sister-in-law drove up. They sat at the table and enjoyed small-town talk and a cup of coffee, something they did every now and then. As Phyllis was leaving, she mentioned that she had noticed Westley's car out on the side of the road out on Route K while driving to Poplar Bluff earlier in the morning, and it was still there when she'd come back into town.

Later that day, after Phyllis had left, Melva Dean called up to Earl's to ask if somebody could go bring the car back to her house. She supposed she could have left it there, but something didn't sit right. She had remembered the day before walking out of Lee's Grocery store and seeing someone drive by that she could have sworn was Ray Bellamy. When she'd asked Phyllis that next morning in her kitchen if she knew Ray had been in town, Phyllis said she hadn't known that nor had she seen him. The whole thing left her feeling a little watchful. Living with Westley had always caused her to feel on edge; no telling when he'd blow up or take a swing at her. Now, living without him and not knowing where he'd gone or when—or if—he'd ever show back up made her every bit as edgy.

Hearing the crunch of tires, Melva Dean went to the screen door and squinted at the car being pulled into her driveway. She took a long drag on her cigarette, told the boys to stay in the house, then walked out on the porch to sign the delivery receipt Mac had waiting for her. Mac handed her the keys and asked her what was up.

Melva Dean shrugged and swatted at a fly that flew in her face. "That man's been out cattin' around ever since we been married. Maybe he left his car, got in some lady's car and they've drove off into the sunset."

Mac studied her. "Wouldn't be such a bad thing, eh?"

Melva Dean eyed Mac and decided it was best to give a non-committal half-laugh.

Mac looked down at his clipboard with a frown. "Says here you called it in. So you saw the car out there?"

She held her cigarette out and nervously flicked at her nails. She looked Mac straight in the eye, and without batting her own, said, "I didn't see it. Let's just say . . . I had a hunch."

Now, years later, Melva Dean hung up the phone from Maybelline, only half processing the fact that Mrs. Teegarten was in fact not dead. It was Ray that was more on her mind. Or more importantly what he knew about Westley. She'd have to try to catch up with him later. But then . . . she sat down, took out a Virginia Slim and as she tapped it on the pack, she began to think.

She had been watching the door every day since Wes had left. It had been so long now. Did she finally accept this? Would asking Ray what he knew make any difference? She took a deep breath and laid the cigarette and pack back on the table. She stood, deciding that this would be a new day for her and then walked out her front door. She needed to go over to her neighbor Skip and Edna's house and tell them that she had been wrong, that Mrs. Teegarten had not died after all.

Ray was aware of the goings-on in the room next to his where Ollie was. He was aware that Lydia was in that room too. He heard her voice, soft yet competent, discussing with Maybelline as they made sure Ollie was comfortable and watched his vitals. Ray leaned his head back on his pillow, trying to make sense of everything.

He looked about the small hospital room and realized that everything he thought he knew wasn't the way it really was. He had assumed all this time that Lydia still loved him. In his imagination, she still pined for him but had to accept that he couldn't stay around and be the victim of her betrayal. He had gone on to bigger and better things. And she had taken Shane in his place.

But now, he wasn't sure of anything.

His eyes squinted as he thought back to those days with Lydia, kissing and hugging in his car, under the bleachers in the gymnasium, in the movie theater. Things had definitely gotten hot and heavy. Could he have gotten her pregnant? A dizzying rush flooded his entire body as this question came to mind. He had never thought to ask it until just now. His heart beat frantically, beads of sweat popped out on his forehead. There was that one time when they'd both been practically naked and he'd been kissing all over her. He shook his head. Lydia had always put a stop to things before they went too far. Ray rubbed at his forehead. He had felt certain that Shane was the father. After he had seen them together out at the fair, both of them acted so awkward, barely speaking to him. And he knew, he *knew* that Shane liked Lydia too. Shane being the father was the only thing that made sense. But if it wasn't Shane's . . .

Ray looked out the window and put a hand to his mouth. What had he done?

It was then he felt a presence in the room. He turned to see Lydia standing there, and he suddenly felt off-kilter.

"Hello," he finally said.

"Hello," she said back and walked over to his bed. She was strictly professional as she began to inspect his bandage. "How are you feeling?"

He gave a derisive laugh, hiding the turmoil inside him. He resorted to his standard coping mechanism of offering up his charm. "Well, not so good." He looked up at her as she worked. She was not the teenage girl he remembered; instead he saw a competent, confident, and quite lovely woman.

"Am I hallucinating from the drugs or something? I could have sworn Shane told me you and Sam are married."

"Yes, we are," Lydia said and picked up his wrist and looked at her wristwatch. After a moment she looked over at him. "Your pulse is fast."

Ray's grin grew wide and he tipped his head. "I should think so. I have been the victim of a shooting by a madman."

Lydia didn't do too well in suppressing a small smile. "Stop your bellyaching, you're going to be just fine."

"I need to talk to the management about your bedside manner."

"I am the management," she said and punched and fluffed at his pillows behind his head.

"Is that so?"

"Yes, and soon to be a doctor."

Ray sat up a bit. "A lady doctor?"

Lydia pushed him back against his pillows. "There is such a thing. I start med school in the fall. I've wanted to do it for a while. Dr. Scott, Sam, and Mom have all been very supportive."

Ray studied her and felt long-dead butterflies rise up within his belly. "Tell me more," he said.

Lydia turned to him, his soft words landing like a velvet lasso upon her heart. Then she remembered that he'd left her eighteen years ago right when she needed him most. But could she really blame him if she had never explained what had happened? Before her mind got jumbled up more, she cleared her throat and said, "I think . . . there'll be time for that later. Dr. Scott will see you in a little bit. Stitches are looking good. Vitals are good. You should be good to go. I'm assuming you're here for Mrs. Meeks's funeral? You have a place to stay?"

"Yes," Ray said. "Staying with Jackson out at Viola's house."

"Ollie's fine, not that you need to care, and I don't blame you."

"Shane says you kind of take care of him. That's a little perplexing. I've got questions. Seems a lot of things have gone on since I've been gone."

"Shane talks too much. Okay then, any pain? Can I get you anything?"

Ray shook his head. "No, thanks."

Then he watched her turn and leave, and he lay there thinking. Lydia looked damn good, and such a professional. He always knew she'd been smart, but now she was going to be a doctor, and good lord above, she was married to Sam. He turned his head and looked out the window and wondered just what in the hell had happened eighteen years ago. How had he gotten everything so wrong, and why, after all these years, was he feeling a great upheaval rising in his heart?

Chapter 25

1975

Viola's funeral took place in the church on top of the hill just outside of her neighborhood. Large oaks stood tall, slightly swaying in the breeze, offering shade and a certain bowing of their heads in honor of Viola Ruth Meeks. Pastor James Freeman, father of Zeb Freeman, the hospital orderly, led the sermon. Viola's casket, silvery blue, sat closed at the front of the church; a display of white roses and blue and pink hydrangeas lay atop it. Roses and hydrangeas were in every corner of the church, across the pulpit, and lying across the windowsills. They had all been provided by Ray.

Her family and friends gathered in and the pews quickly filled, ladies in their Sunday best and matching hats, men and children pulling at the necks of their too-tight suits and dress collars. Everyone there was very much there out of love, honor, and adoration for Viola Meeks. There were a few white people taking their place at the back of the church, except for Ray, who sat up in the front pew next to Jackson, Jackson's wife, Olivia, and their three daughters—Dorothy, Clarice, and Kayla—as well as

Kayla's husband, Carlous, and their daughter, Helen. Viola's one remaining sister, several nieces and nephews, and great nieces and nephews also sat in the front pews.

Pastor Freeman preached a wonderfully soothing sermon for sister Viola, calling upon the congregation to join him in thanking God for blessing their lives with such a fine and loving lady, and to thank the heavens for welcoming her, now in peace with her loving God, Jesus, and her faithful husband, Sullivan Meeks.

Pastor Freeman's rich baritone voice rose and fell in comforting cadence as he thanked the lord for the gift of Viola here on earth. "We know that Heaven has always been such a beautiful place, but we now know that it is even more dazzling and delightful, not only because of Viola's beautiful presence, but because it is now adorned with her sweet, sweet roses and buttercups and hyacinths and hydrangeas." Pastor Freeman's words were met with amens and the soft flapping of cardboard fans.

Eula Glover played the piano and Viola's three granddaughters stood in the front of the church singing "Amazing Grace," which brought everyone to tears. Then Jackson spoke of his loving mother and how he was the luckiest son in the world.

"My mother was the strongest person I knew. My father did well in raising me, and I loved him and still love him to this day, even though he has been long gone. But I am the man I am today because of Viola Meeks." He shook his head and looked down, a short pause to gather his emotions and to try not to cry.

"My mother made sure that I studied hard and went to college, and after I got that degree, she made sure I didn't sit on it but searched out a job and got to work. I started out as a high school history teacher, and my mother told me every time she saw me how proud of me she was. But, despite how proud she was of me, she always said that I shouldn't get a big head and I wasn't done." This drew soft chuckles from the congregation. "Because of this, I am now principal of that high school. I continue to stand proud; I will continue to forge forward because I know Mamma is up there telling me, 'Son, you're still not done.'" Another chorus of amens followed his words.

Jackson took a deep breath. "I look out on all of you today and wonder at how many lives have been truly blessed because of my mother and her gentle and wise touch."

Jackson could now see the white folks in the back of the church—Lydia and Sam Cooper, Shane Cooper and his wife Lorna. There was Birdie Tyler, Melva Dean Culpepper, Judy Grant, and half a dozen or so other ladies that Jackson knew had come to his mother for medical advice and assistance. "Yes," Jackson concluded, holding them strongly in his gaze. "I'm sure you all know how blessed you are to have had my mother in your life."

Jackson paused after finishing his eulogy, waiting for the refrain of amens to subside. "Now, as some of you may know," he continued, "my mother, who had the biggest heart in the world, had a sort of adopted son—Ray Bellamy." Jackson looked over at Ray. "He wanted to say a few words."

Ray got up, adjusting his sling, and placed a piece of paper on the pulpit. "Thank you, Jackson, and thank you to all of Viola's friends and family." He took a deep breath. "I will forever be beholden to Viola for helping me. She didn't have to help me, she could just as well have turned her back on me. I was, after all, a smart-alecky kid who decided to tear up her flowers one hot summer night when I was bored and full of myself. I know my stupid actions caused her to cry. What you all might not know is I cried too."

Here Ray had to pause to keep himself from breaking down. He steadied himself and continued. "I was ashamed and lost and so very, very sorry for what I'd done. I deserved any punishment she would have given me, but instead, she took me into her heart and taught me so much, and gave me time and attention. I will be forever grateful. I will forever love her. She is the mother I never had, and I will miss her terribly." Ray drew in a choked breath and paused. "I'm so sorry she's gone. Pastor Freeman, you are right, Heaven is certainly rejoicing now."

As Ray spoke, his entire being was a jumble of befuddled emotions. He looked at the back of the room and saw Lydia and Sam sitting there. Before the funeral, Ray had stood inside the church looking out the window. He'd watched them both arrive, pulling up in a turquoise Chevy pickup truck. He'd watched as Sam got out and stood beside the truck. Tanned and strong, Sam was tall, taller than Ray now. Ray saw something he'd never seen before, or had it been there all along? He saw the poise of a man who knew himself and his place in the world. He exuded goodness and fairness, success and respectability. The place Sam stood in was a fine one.

He had continued to watch as Sam walked around to the other side of the truck and offered his arm as Lydia got out. They walked, a handsome couple, up to the church. At one point Lydia said something, and Sam dipped his head toward her. Then Sam placed a hand on the small of her back as they stopped to talk to someone in the church yard. Ray watched them standing together under the shade of the oak trees and saw the camaraderie, the partnership, the intimacy. Ray pressed his forehead to the window glass. The loss, the aloneness that he'd been outrunning all his life, swooped up large and vexing, threatening to suffocate him. He loved her still, though he'd been denying it for so long.

After the funeral service, folks gathered out in the church yard under the trees. Platters and bowls filled the picnic tables next to the church, offering ham, fried chicken, barbecued pork, macaroni and cheese, slaw, corn on the cob, green beans, navy beans, brown beans, deviled eggs, cornbread and biscuits, cakes and pies. People went through the lines and filled their plates, and it was with a mixture of relief and dread that Ray saw Lydia gesturing to him to come and sit with them—her and Sam and Shane and Lorna.

Ray switched his plate to his left hand held in the sling as he saw Sam walking up to him, holding out a hand to shake. Ray took his hand and then felt himself being pulled into an embrace as Sam hugged him. The hug held for two, then three, then four seconds. And for a brief moment, Ray felt eighteen again, and it was a time when he and his friends still loved each other.

"Good to see you," Sam said as he drew apart, and he meant it. He looked at Ray and took a deep breath. "Damn good to see you."

Ray looked at his friend and knew that, just as he'd never stopped loving Lydia, he'd never stopped loving Sam or Shane. For years he would have claimed to the whole universe that it wasn't true. But it was. And he stood there, not knowing what to do with this realization. Finally he gave a cautious smile. "Good to see you too, Sam."

They sat and ate, first in careful conversation that stayed on the surface, commenting on Viola's beautiful service, how they would miss her, how they still loved her flowers.

"I've actually, well, continued her flower growing," Ray offered quietly. The group looked up at him, waiting for what they had been wondering for eighteen years: Where had Ray gone and what had he been doing?

"I've developed gardens in Kentucky where I live. I have greenhouses providing plants to farms and businesses, and the gardens are for tourists. It's called Vail Dolyia Gardens."

They all sat silent for a moment, corn cob held in mid-bite, fork full of potato salad held halfway above the plate, mouthful of cornbread stopped in mid-chew as they stared at Ray. Finally, something. Something. Still a small piece, but something that he was sharing of himself, and they all held the moment in delicate silence, urging him to go on. They desired it like a thirsty man desired a drink of water.

Finally Lydia said, "I've heard of Vail Dolyia Gardens. I've heard it's lovely. My gosh, Ray, that's you! I heard it's a piece of art. A state treasure."

"Oh, well, I wouldn't go as far as that," Ray said. "But I'm mighty proud of it. Got ten greenhouses for vegetables and flower seedlings. They produce all year round. The gardens, about thirty-five acres of rolling hills, a natural-running creek, a couple of ponds. Viola had a friend who helped me design it. It's still a work in progress; we add to it and change things every year. Got great footpaths all around it and some real sweet foot bridges, fountains, benches, and gazebos. And trees, lots of them ornamental, and flowers and flowers for as far as the eye can see."

"Sounds absolutely . . ." Lydia started as she studied Ray. "That's just wonderful."

Shane swallowed his mouthful of cornbread. "Yeah, that's just great to hear. I've wondered, ya know, what you been up to. Don't blame you for never coming back to Westfall, I guess, if you've got something like that to your name."

"Oh, I came back. Once."

They all looked at him and waited.

"It was in 1964, I believe. A while back. Came in for just a day. Came out here to meet with Viola. That's when I talked with her friend Jasper Coats about the landscaping for the gardens."

"It was 1964?" Shane asked.

Ray nodded. "I went into town and looked for Dad, but he wasn't around. Which was fine because I . . . well I wasn't up for visiting."

"So you were mostly out here at Viola's then. Did you go up to the river?"

Ray took a bite off his corn cob and chewed, slowly looking across the table at Shane. He swallowed. "Maybe." He wiped his mouth with his paper napkin. "Probably did. I can't imagine visiting without taking a look at the river. It's in our veins, you know."

"Yeah," Shane said. "That's what they say."

Sam cast a side-eye at Lydia, who returned one back at him. Then they looked from Ray to Shane.

"I was here in 1964," Lydia said. "Came home to visit Mom for her birthday in March."

Ray nodded. "We just missed each other, then. I was here in late April."

"And speaking of Mom," Lydia said, gesturing behind Ray. He turned to see Phyllis walking up to them with a small blonde-haired boy holding her hand.

"He was hoping to get a piece of cherry pie, so I brought him out here. Did the services go well?" Phyllis asked as she walked up to them.

Lydia got up and went over to them, bending down and giving her son Cody a kiss on top of his head. "Mom, you remember Ray?" She nodded over to the table.

Ray stood up and shook her hand. "Mrs. Culpepper, nice to see you."

Phyllis patted the hand that shook hers. "I'd heard you were in town, Ray. Good to see you too. I heard you got yourself in a bit of a scuffle with your dad."

Ray couldn't keep his eyes off the boy. He was the cutest thing he'd ever seen. The boy rounded the table and stood by Sam, who pulled him up on his lap. "Yeah," Ray said, patting his sling. "Guess some things never change."

Phyllis smiled. "Oh, you might be surprised. Although Ollie, now, I'd say he is pretty set in his ways. Sorry he shot you though!"

Ray gave his head a tilt. "Comes with the territory, I guess. I came to collect on a debt. He stole some money from me a long time ago. Danged if I know why I figured he'd have the money. He didn't like me coming back and asking for the money, so he shot me."

Lydia studied Ray as he said this. "Stole money from you?"

"Yeah, it's nothing now. It was right before I left." Ray paused and looked at Lydia, something he hadn't thought of until now starting to itch at the back of his mind. Unable to make total sense of it, he shrugged. "Don't need the money, of course. Just wanted to let him know I was still mad at him about it. Fat lot of good it did." He smiled. "He's still mad at me, so I guess I'd call that even." He looked over at Lydia. "I hear you kind of take care of him."

Lydia took a deep breath and nodded. "Yes. He . . . uh, he did a favor for me once. A long time ago. Helped me out and I appreciated it. Anyway, I check in on him. Bring him food. Sometimes we sit and talk."

Ray's brows raised. "Phyllis, I believe you're right. There seems to be a great deal that has changed. Guess I just hadn't seen it coming." He looked at Lydia, then took a quick glance at Sam, who was gently bouncing the knee his son sat on. Sam looked up at him then ducked as Cody flipped a fork at him.

"Mamma, Ray's been telling us about his gardens in Kentucky. You've heard of Vail Dolyia Gardens? That's Ray!"

Phyllis smiled at Ray. "Oh my. Yes! I have heard of Vail Dolyia Gardens. Well, I'll be."

"You'll have to come out and see them," Ray heard himself say. He'd had no intention whatsoever of revealing any of this to them, but the words just seemed to come out as easily as if he was slipping into the river for a swim. And he'd had no intention of inviting them out to his place. But again, it came easy. He wanted them to see what he'd done. He was proud of it and now, well, now he wanted to share it with them. He was surprised at how quickly the noble mountain he'd been sitting on, the angst and bitterness of the past eighteen years, had begun to melt away. He still had so many questions, but he couldn't deny that sitting here with his friends felt good.

"It's a date," Phyllis said. "Now tell me, what else have you been up to? Got a wife and kids?"

Ray shook his head as he saw Lydia let out an irritated sigh toward her mother. "No, I've been too busy playing the field, and playing in it, literally." He raised his brows and gave a playful smile. Everyone laughed, and there was an ever-so-slight relaxing of the tension as they saw a glimmer of the funny and charming Ray they remembered.

The funeral services over, Ray now found himself in Viola's house along with Jackson and his family. They had gathered there to discuss the will, and Ray offered his dismay at Viola having left him her house.

Jackson cast warm dark eyes upon him and smiled a knowing smile. "Mamma didn't care who got her house. She just wanted some way to get you back to Westfall."

Ray squinted in thought. "What? I came back here. That once."

"Yes, that once, and that was over ten years ago. And it wasn't just coming back. Mamma knew you still had friends here and you should stay in touch with them. I know she's asked you about them and you always gave her some nondescript answer. Anyway, looks like it worked, because here you are."

Ray looked around the room and saw the smiling faces of a family who were in on the joke. "Did you all know about this?"

Clarice, one of Viola's granddaughters, grinned. "Oh, yes. She was bound and determined to get you back here. I can just imagine Grandma standing here, right now, and I believe she is, hovering over everything and smiling that big smile of hers, so tickled that what she did worked."

Ray took a deep breath. "All of y'all are schemers, every one of you." They all chuckled. "But . . . I don't mean to be disrespectful, but what am I going to do with her house?"

Jackson cleared his throat. "Look, Ray, you've done real well with your place in Kentucky. We've loved visiting you. Mamma was right proud of you, but she told me a time or two that you seemed lonely. She wanted more for you, and she knew reconnecting with your old friends would help. It was more than just getting you to town. It was more than just the house."

"Well if you must know, I invited all my friends out to my place in Kentucky."

"There, ya see, Mamma's already done good."

"Please tell me what I can do with this house that is respectful and in honor of Viola's memory."

"Well, seems like you've already done a great honor to Mamma with your Vail Dolyia Gardens. Naming it after her, so to speak. She has told everybody and their cousin and then some about what a beautiful place it is. I don't believe you need much in the way of marketing because her talk sure brought tourists from miles around. She loved going there. Don't you worry, Ray. You've done good by her."

Ray nodded at Jackson then looked around the room. "So, am I to live here, travel back and forth? I . . . just don't know."

Jackson went over and stood by Boyd, Viola's great-nephew, placing a hand on Boyd's shoulder. "As you might know, Boyd here just got married six months ago and now has a baby on the way. We all think, and if you agree, Ray, that it would be nice for Boyd and his lovely bride and child to live here. What do you think?"

Ray looked over at Boyd. "I don't know." He leaned forward, bracing his forearms on his thighs and rubbing his hands together, trying to hold a serious expression, but he couldn't hide his smile.

"What kind of flower-tending skills do you have, Boyd?"

Boyd smiled back. "Nothing like you or Great-Aunt Viola. But if you wouldn't mind, I would certainly heed your advice and help."

"Jasper can certainly help too, but I will gladly help you make sure all of Viola's gardens are tended well."

Jackson gave Ray a sly smile. "Does that mean you might be coming back more often than you have been?"

Ray shook his head and stood and pointed with a friendly finger at all of those in the house. "I've been bamboozled by all of you all."

Then he went over to Boyd. "You got a dollar in your pocket?"

Boyd stood up and pulled his wallet from his back pocket. He took out a one-dollar bill and handed it to Ray. Ray took it and held it up.

"Consider the sale of this house final and paid in full."

Everyone grinned and clapped, and Ray looked around the room and loved what he saw. Tears came to his eyes, and he drew in a deep breath.

Jackson shook his hand. "Mamma would be pleased."

Ray nodded. "She was smarter than any of us are, that's for sure."

Jackson nodded. "You'll be staying in this bedroom off the back screened porch. But before you settle in, I think I heard Mrs. Culpepper invite you over to her house for coffee this evening." Jackson sent him a level gaze. "You best go. Now that you've found your friends again, you don't want to lose them."

Ray drove out of the neighborhood and down Route K toward town. It was about twenty-four hours ago that he'd come to Westfall, and his head spun with all that had happened. He was a tilt-a-whirl of feelings from getting shot by Ollie, seeing Lydia at the hospital, hearing that Lydia had married Sam, seeing Lydia and Sam's beautiful little boy, saying goodbye to Viola at her funeral, and ending with the warm knowledge that Viola had always been looking out for him. Not that he ever doubted it; it was just a wonderful thing to see it in action.

And then, without notice, he started crying again and had to pull over. He found himself in the parking lot of the river park and boat ramp, the same area where he used to live with his father in the house by the river. He pulled into the park and over to the asphalt that slanted down into the river where people now launched their boats, a nice addition brought about a few years ago by Mayor Saunders. The river gently traversed a bend here, and the water ran deep, cold, and blue-green. In the dimming light, the sun barely visible through the dark trees, lavender and orange clouds drifted above, giving the whole scene the look of a watercolor.

He could barely make out the place where his and his dad's house had sat. He looked now, as if spying into a window, and saw himself as a young boy, Ollie yelling and shaking an empty coffee can at him, explaining that he didn't know where the hell they'd be getting money for food. And then his father's hand reaching out and slapping him across the back of the head, knocking him out of his chair. He saw the little boy pick up a glass of water and throw it into Ollie's face, and then they were both yelling at each other and then here came little Ray, blasting out of the front door and running toward the river. He looked again and saw Ollie frying him an egg and putting it on his plate. He watched as Ollie sat down beside him and pointed and talked about things in the paper. He saw Ollie tossing a flyer about the state extension services master gardener program on the table. He watched another scene—they were older now—high school Ray half-carrying Ollie into the house and shoving him onto his bed after bringing him home from the Catfish Grill on prom night.

Ray leaned his forehead against the steering wheel. Like those scenes from his old house, his whole life had become a jumble of good and bad things, and he didn't know what was good or bad anymore. Had he wasted eighteen years thinking how right he was and how wrong everyone else had been? He took the sling off his arm, pulling it over his head and tossing it into the passenger seat. It had been confining him just as much as his faulty presumptions, and he was tired of it.

He sat up straight and shook his head, wiped at his eyes and nose, put the car in drive, and drove over to Phyllis and Russell Culpepper's house. They were waiting for him on the porch, Lydia and Sam and Shane, almost as if they'd never been apart. Almost. In the darkening shadows, the last of the golden light from the sun cast a dim glow out on the porch. He could hear his friends talking. It seemed the most idyllic of scenes. Little did he know that in less than an hour, all hell would break loose.

Chapter 26

1975

Ray walked up the porch steps and leaned back against the railing. A beer was offered, bottlenecks clinked, and talk still stayed a bit on the surface as they all delicately stepped around the convolutions of a long-lost friend's return. Another beer was drunk and then another, and it seemed everyone was becoming a bit drunk, welcoming the support of the known confidence-booster of beer.

Lorna, Shane's wife, was also there, and the conversation at first focused on getting to know her—she was a fifth-grade teacher at Westfall Grade School. She and Shane had two children—a daughter, eight, and a son, seven. They were both spending the night over at Mr. and Mrs. Cooper's house along with Lydia and Sam's little boy.

"So, Shane here is a deputy sheriff, which I still can't believe. Lorna's a teacher, and we know that Lydia is a nurse and soon to become a doctor—always knew she was the smartest one in the bunch—but what is it that you do, Sam?" Ray tried to make his question sound friendly, but he couldn't keep a certain competitive sharpness out of it.

Sam looked over at Shane. "Well, Shane and I own a farm out east of town. It was owned by our cousin, Lorne Cooper. He got pretty old, and about ten years ago we bought it. He lived out in North Carolina then, so we made a trip out there and fashioned up a good sale. It's about five hundred acres."

Ray took a drink of his fourth beer and felt his self-pride begin to slip. Five hundred acres, hmm. "What do you grow?"

"Ever heard of Cooper's potato chips? Well, we grow potatoes and they go into making potato chips."

Shane was grinning. "It was mostly Sam's idea. All I'd heard about potatoes was that they'd caused a heck of a nuisance in Ireland, but we got it up and working. We've got a potato chip factory that we co-own with another cousin, Bobby Cooper. He runs the factory and we run the farm. It's been doing well."

Ray looked from Shane to Sam. "I sell Cooper's potato chips in my concessions in the gardens. They're pretty well known in this tri-state area. I never made the connection."

Sam nodded. "Yes, south Missouri and parts of Arkansas and Kentucky are all good areas for us."

"That isn't all Sam does, though," Shane said. "Go on, Sam, tell him."

"Well, have you ever heard of Cooper Auto and Truck Design?"

Ray shook his head. "Can't say that I have." He was glad of it and then realized how childish he was being.

"I have a garage with four bays. It's down at the corner of Grand and Fourth Street. We do some general mechanic work, but the focus is design work. I specialize in classics, antiques. I do mostly commissioned work. Got a fair amount of clients, and the word is spreading pretty well."

"I noticed that truck you pulled up in at the church. Was that a '53?"

Sam nodded, obviously proud that Ray had noticed.

"That was your work? It was nice. Turquoise, cream top. Looked great."

"You should see the engine."

"Grand and Fourth Street? That's Miller's old Chrysler dealership. It was still Miller's when I was here in '64. When'd you set it up?"

"'Bout three years after that."

"Yeah," Shane said, scooting off his rocking chair and standing near Ray. "You said you'd come back to town back in 1964. That's kind of odd. I mean, did you know Westley Culpepper disappeared that year?"

Ray stared at Shane, then slowly lifted his beer bottle and took a drink. "I heard that. And ... so?"

Sam gave a nervous huff. "That's old news, Shane. You might want to let it go." Sam looked over at Lydia.

It was then that Phyllis made a timely call from inside the house to Lydia. "Lydia, can you come here a sec? Help me with this food."

Lydia excused herself, stood up, and went into the house, frankly glad to be away from any talk about Westley Culpepper. Ray tipped up his beer bottle and emptied it, placed it on the porch railing, said "Excuse me," and followed Lydia into the house.

In the kitchen, he walked up to Lydia, reached down and took her hand, and said, "Can we talk? In private." Seeing Lydia's surprise, he added, "It'll only take a few minutes." He pulled on her hand and nodded toward Phyllis, who was watching the exchange, an open bag of chips held mid-pour above the light-blue Melmac bowl. Still holding her hand, Ray led Lydia out of the kitchen, out the back door, and down the steps into the dark yard. Here in the backyard, away from the western sunset, the air was cooler, lightning bugs starting their yellow blinking in search of mates.

He took a deep breath, which caused a small smile to appear at the corner of Lydia's mouth. "I've never known Ray to be at a loss for words."

Ray looked at her, studied the smile at the corner of her pretty lips, and, for a moment, closed his eyes. Her nearness made his breath catch. "Look," he said, opening his eyes. "I know this isn't the time and place, so, I'm going to be in town for a few more days, and I was hoping we could get together and talk. I've . . . since I've been here, I've realized . . . well I've some questions. If you're up to talking . . ."

"Yes. I want to talk, I've wanted to talk to you . . . I should have told you . . . even back then. I never got a chance. I . . ."

"I've missed you."

Lydia raised her brows. "I've . . ." She looked at him and was aware of a need to move slowly, cautiously. "I've missed you too. But . . ." She held him with a level gaze. "I didn't know where you were, and you always knew where I was, and yet . . ."

"Yeah, I've been pretty stupid for quite a while. There's things . . . that I obviously got wrong. I'm sorry."

Lydia squeezed his hand. They could hear, but just barely, sounds coming from the kitchen—Phyllis moving around, talking to someone. They stood in the dark, their bodies a silhouette against the light coming through the screen door.

"You don't have to apologize. Things . . ." She shook her head. "Things happened. You couldn't have known."

Ray raised his hand that still held hers, laced his fingers through hers, and held it against his chest. "I still love you, Lydia."

He wasn't sure where the words had come from; he wasn't even sure if they were true. Was it more a love for the way things had once been? Was it regret for having left her, and now wanting her back? Was he lying to himself now, or had he been lying to himself these past eighteen years when he'd kept himself so far away?

Lydia's mouth popped open at his proclamation at the same time that the back screen door opened and Sam stuck his head out. "Everything okay out here?"

Their hands came apart, and they each took a step backward. "Everything's fine," Ray said.

Sam stepped down the steps and came up to them. "I don't think it is fine. Not when I just heard you tell my wife that you still love her."

Lydia drew in her breath and looked at Sam then over to Ray.

Ray gave an acquiescing smile, short and abrupt. He studied Sam for a moment, then looked over at Lydia. "I think I'd best be going."

"I think that'd be a good idea," Sam said.

"Sam!" Lydia said to him, and they watched Ray turn and walk into the side yard. Lydia and Sam followed. They were coming around to the front yard when Shane and Lorna were walking down the front steps and walking up to them.

"Ray, wait," Lydia said.

"Everything okay?" Shane asked, picking up on the tension.

"It's nothing," Ray said.

"I don't call it nothing," Sam said. "I don't call you telling my wife that you still love her nothing!"

Shane's eyes went wide.

"What are you gawking at, Shane?" Ray asked. "Of course you're in on this somehow, too."

"In on what?"

Ray gestured in frustration to nothing in particular. "You can't even be truthful with me. I asked you at the hospital, and you could only offer up some pitiful answer that didn't make sense. But I know, I KNOW there was something. Because that's the only thing that does make sense. You're a liar and a loser!"

Perhaps it was the shame that Shane still felt for kissing Lydia eighteen years ago. Perhaps it was an unvoiced anger at Ray for leaving, or maybe anger at himself for being a bad friend. Regardless, something in Shane, led by Ray's insult, bubbled to the top and he took one step toward Ray and hauled off and punched him right in the nose. Ray tripped backward in surprise, then he lunged toward Shane and they tumbled to the ground and rolled sideways, running into Sam's feet and tripping him, causing him to fall on their wrestling bodies and join in the brawl too.

Punches were thrown, grunts and yells of "You're the loser!" and "You ran!" and "You're a liar!" and "Get off me!" emitted from the tangled mess.

Both Lydia and Lorna stepped forward with outstretched hands, dodging the scuffling trio and yelling at them. "Stop it! Stop it right this instant!"

Lydia leaned in just in time to catch a flying arm to the side of her head that knocked her sideways. She stumbled and grabbed at her head, which brought the wrestling match to a sudden stop, and the reprobates looked up in dismay.

"Are you okay?" they all three asked at once. Shane let go of Ray's shirt, Ray unwound his arm from around Sam's arm, Sam untangled both of his legs, one from under his brother, the other from on top of Ray, and they stood up, Sam quickly stepping over beside Lydia.

"I'm fine! Good grief, what is wrong with you all?"

Ray tested his stitched-up shoulder, then wiped at the blood coming from his nose. "Man, I used to be handsome, but with my nose being punched two times in as many days, I'm heading towards ugly." In a different time and situation, it might have been funny, but they all three stood there, heaving in deep breaths.

Ray raised a tired hand. "Many apologies. I never meant . . ." He lowered his hand and shook his head. "I don't know what I meant." He looked around at all of them and tried to say something else, but he couldn't figure out any words that could make this sorry situation any better. So he took a deep breath, waved somewhat haphazardly at no one in particular, turned, walked to his car, and got in. He started it up and drove away, his red tail lights disappearing underneath the street lights.

Shane wiped at his sore nose as he watched the car drive away. "Shit!" he said.

Lydia turned to Sam and held out her hand. "Give me the car keys."

Sam drew back his chin. "What for?"

"I'm going to go after him."

"Why?"

Lydia gave a huff of impatience. "Because I want to talk to him. And I need to check his shoulder."

"Lydia? You can't be serious." But as he talked, Sam withdrew the keys from his pocket.

Lydia snatched them from his hand and ran to the car.

"Let me come with you."

"No!" she called over her shoulder. She got in the car and drove off, leaving Sam standing wide-eyed in the yard, surrounded by Lorna who was standing there with both hands pressed over her mouth, Phyllis who'd come out to the porch holding the now needless bowl of chips, and Shane looking over at his little brother with an anxious expression.

Sam took two steps toward the departing car. "Lydia!" he yelled. Then he turned to the others and pointed a strong-willed finger to the sky. "I will not feel guilty! I will not feel guilty for loving her. For marrying her. He left! He left her!"

"Sam, Sam," Shane tried. "Nobody expects you to. You're right. He left."

"God dammit!" Sam yelled. "Why did she leave? Why did she go after him?"

"Sam, come on. Do you trust Lydia?"

"Yes!" he exclaimed and ran a hand around the back of his neck. "I sure as hell don't trust Ray though! God dammit!"

The heat of the moment suddenly ratcheted down a few ticks as they all turned to the sound of the neighbor's screen door slowly opening up. It was Mrs. Winterowd, grandmother of Lydia's old friends Marjorie and Betsy.

"Everything all right over there, Phyllis?" came Mrs. Winterowd's fragile voice.

"Everything's fine, Mrs. Winterowd. No need to worry. Sorry we woke you up."

"Oh, I wasn't asleep. I was watching *Kojak* and I couldn't tell at first if the ruckus was coming from the TV or from outside. Well …" She squinted into the darkness at the figures on the lawn, not entirely sure that everything was indeed all right. "You all have a good night."

"Good night," the others mumbled, and they sauntered over to the porch, Sam sitting heavily on the bottom step. He took a deep breath and looked back down the road where Lydia had gone, desperately willing her to come back.

Lydia wasn't exactly sure where Ray had gone, but she had a few ideas. She drove over to Miss Lipperton's house where Ollie had a room, but she saw no car there. She drove over to the boat launch where Ray and Ollie's house used to be, but there was no car there either. She drove out on Route K into Viola's neighborhood. There were several cars parked out in front of her house, but not Ray's. So, with the last idea she had, she pulled back out on Route K and headed up to River Leap Park. That's where she found him.

Chapter 27

1975

S am sat on the porch swing and looked at his watch for the hundredth time since Shane had dropped him off at his house. Eleven twenty-two, the watch told him. He looked down the road in front of his house, but no car came into sight. He had tried and failed to settle his churning stomach and heart. He had gone over and over in his head what he would say to Lydia if she came home and told him that she was leaving with Ray. He'd yell and scream and punch a wall. Or he'd pout and cry and fall to the ground. Or it would be a combination of the first two scenarios, but because he loved her so much, he would want her happiness and have to let her go. Sam couldn't stand to think of that. He continued to rock slowly in the swing.

He had seen the love Lydia and Ray had. It had been a strong love, a sight to behold. It shone like the summer sun. No one was more shocked than Sam when Ray left her. It had made no sense. Back then, with his lack of knowledge about sex and pregnancies and abortions, and then rumors about her and Shane, Sam had roughly been able to put a few things together. He had watched as everything fell apart—first Ray left, then Shane, then Lydia. And Sam had done his best to live in a world that was no longer as bright—not only were his friends gone, but Lydia and Ray's love for each other had somehow been extinguished.

He had moved on, grown up, and even though there had been other women, he had never stopped thinking about Lydia. It had been years since Ray had been gone, so it seemed pretty certain Ray had washed his hands of her. He'd heard a story or two about Lydia partying it up in Columbia, and he'd thought, *attagirl*. Everyone seemed to be moving on, and Sam felt a bit bolder. He had hoped, thinking she would never fall in love with him, but he wanted to see her anyway. When she came walking out of the hospital like a ray of sunshine that day in Columbia, and they hugged, he felt something warm and wonderful, and his heart dared to believe.

The longer he was with her, the more he couldn't deny that his boyhood crush had turned to full-on love, which scared the daylights out of him. He might have turned and ran except for Lydia being so wonderful and fun and interesting, and then he began to sense . . . something. A huge smile had spread across his face when she invited him up for the float trip. He couldn't contain his joy, but he also wanted to be careful and not move too fast and mess it all up.

He still sometimes walked around in disbelief that Lydia loved him, that they were married, that they had a son, that they were happy. He'd almost forgotten about Ray.

He looked at his watch again. Eleven twenty-six. He let out a deep sigh.

When Shane and Lorna drove him home, Shane had tried to talk him into coming back to their house, but Sam had said no, he wanted to be at his house if—no, when—Lydia came back. It had been a silent ride, each brother stewing in their own despondent funk. Sam had thanked his brother for the lift, apologized to Lorna for all the craziness, then went into the dark kitchen, opened the fridge, and took out a beer. But he decided he'd had enough of that and put it back. For lack of anything else to do, he settled on taking a shower, and as he stood naked under the warm water, he prayed that the curtain would be drawn back and it would be Lydia, stepping naked into the shower with him, wrapping her arms around him. But no Lydia appeared, and he finally turned off the water, dried, and dressed in clean clothes.

He stood in front of the chest of drawers and studied Lydia's jewelry lying on top. He reached out and gently touched a gold and ruby necklace he had given her. Ruby was both her and Cody's birthstone; what a delight it had been when the baby had been born on Lydia's birthday in July. He smiled to himself remembering that day and all the times they had celebrated both his son's and his wife's birthday.

He walked down the hall into Cody's room and turned on the little light beside his bed. It had a Cardinals baseball lampshade that went with the Cardinals baseball bedspread. The same ball that Sam had caught so many years ago at a Cardinals game now sat on a shelf in his son's room. He sat down on the bed, ran his hand across the bedspread.

He got up, aimlessly walking, and went across the hall to the guest bedroom. They had cousins in North Carolina, Arkansas, and Texas, and they had stayed in this room when visiting. Good times. He cherished his family. By the light from Cody's room, he spied a book lying on the seat of the wingback chair. He went over and picked it up and saw that it was Lydia's Westfall Warriors 1957 yearbook. He turned the table light on and flipped the book open, several loose-leaf items falling out.

He picked up the flyer that advertised the 1957 Riley County Fair. He frowned at it, wondering why in the world this was in the yearbook. That had not been a good night, and his heart lurched as it always did when he thought about what Westley had done to Lydia. He picked up a black-and-white photo and saw a picture of all of them leaning against a car, the Current River in the background, flowing serenely yet powerfully by. Lydia was standing in between Ray and Shane. She was smiling, almost laughing, and her head was tipped over onto Ray's shoulder. And there he was kneeling in front of them, little Sam, a skinny little boy and so much out of his league, and he didn't even know it. How in the world had he ever thought he'd have a chance with her?

Sam continued to study the picture, and he sat down in the chair. A pressed carnation, now dry and brown, fell out of the book into his lap. He delicately picked it up, afraid it would crumble. He looked at it. The quiet of the house began to fold in on him. He could hear the ticking of the grandfather clock out in the hall. It was the carnation Lydia had given Ray at the prom. So long ago. A lifetime ago.

He dropped the flower and the photo back onto the book and closed it and sat in silence. He didn't like the house so quiet, so empty. He felt like he weighed eight hundred pounds. With his heart so heavy, it was an effort to even move. Finally he stood, feeling slow and off-balance, laid the yearbook back on the seat of the chair, and walked back up the hall. That's when he went out to the porch and sat there. And waited. He'd been sitting out here ever since, the black-and-white photo, the dried carnation rolling over and over in his mind.

Lydia parked in the River Leap parking lot, the same place where Marjorie had parked her grandmother's car that first time she had gone to the river. Now the river, with its mighty current, seemed like an old friend, being both a gentle source of comfort as well as a powerful observer of all those who came and went, and stayed.

She walked up the gravelly path to the cliffs. The moon shone high and bright in the clear sky, causing mottled shadows to dance down along the path in between the thick branches of the oak trees. Tree frogs were chirping loudly, but she could still hear the soft rush of the current below.

"Ray?" she called softly. She thought she saw him sitting on one of the flat boulders.

"Over here," came his choked response.

She walked up to him. He sat with his back against a rock wall, arms resting on raised knees, and was fiddling with a stick. His face shone silvery in the moonlight as he looked up at her. "Well, that was about the most idiotic thing ever," he said.

Lydia sat down next to him and took in a deep breath. "Oh, I don't know. I remember all three of you finding a rope and trying to tie it on—" She leaned out and squinted over to some overhanging trees. "Was it that tree limb over there? And you all started arguing what was the best way to do it, and Sam grabbed on to it before it was tied and he pulled it down, and then all three of you started yelling at each other and you jumped in and started pummeling on Sam, but he managed to grab the rope and climb back up the hill and you all chased after him."

She looked over at him with raised eyebrows. "And there was that time the three of you *accidentally* caught the high school baseball dugout on fire when y'all were lighting firecrackers that one—"

"Okay, okay," he said, reluctantly releasing a smile. "I get it, we're a bunch of idiots. Always have been. Always will be."

"A bunch of idiots who love each other."

They were silent for a long moment.

He concentrated on the stick for a while then said, "I thought when I left, it was the right thing to do. I was so cock-sure about what I thought was a big old heap of cheating and betrayal. And every time I woke up, every day, *every day*, I thought of you all. I tried to tell myself it didn't matter."

"Ray, can I ask you to stop beating yourself up about this? It was sad and hard when you left, but you know, I guess it's been okay. You've got this great business, which I can't wait to see, by the way. You were too much for this town. You had to leave. And I see now . . . that you had to leave without me."

He turned and looked at her. "That wasn't what I wanted."

She took a deep breath and looked out on the river, sparkling dark silver in the moonlight. "I know. Wasn't what I wanted either. At least back then. But I left eventually too. And then I came back, and it's all good. It's real good. I don't expect you to move back here, of course, but I hope maybe you'll find some good in this little ol' town. Especially in your friends. We all missed you."

"Lydia, it still doesn't make sense. I can't help feeling that somehow I got shafted. I . . . I still don't understand."

Lydia touched her fingertips to her mouth and contemplated. He needed to know of course, but she was afraid and not sure how to tell him. So she started with the easiest part. She turned to him.

"There's a few things you need to know, and I'm going to tell you and I hope it helps. First off . . . Shane and I kissed."

She held her gaze levelly at him and waited, and she was glad when his only reaction was to take a deep breath. She continued, "It was the night of the fair. You weren't wrong about that, you saw it. When you were in jail, I didn't know it and I was getting mad at you because you were late. Shane had snuck some whiskey in and we drank it, and we drank too much and we kissed. And as soon as we did it, we knew it was a mistake. We felt shame and remorse and it was just not good at all. I thought about telling you, but there were some other things . . . that happened. Anyway, Shane felt horrible about it for such a long time. I think he still feels bad. Whatever stupid answer you say Shane gave you when you all talked in the hospital, that was what all that was about. The poor guy still walks around trying to do penance."

"So you say he's suffered enough?" Ray asked with a good-natured smirk.

"Yes." Lydia smiled a thoughtful smile. "Shane is good. We all have our . . . well, we all aren't perfect. But I can tell you that Shane is as close to perfect as you'll ever get for a friend." Then she eyed him levelly again. "And I can also tell you that Sam, well, he is perfect."

Ray rubbed his forehead and took a deep breath.

"In every way, Ray, he's perfect. And I know you know this. We saw that goofy little boy follow us around, listen to every stupid thing you all said, and do every stupid thing you all did, and in spite of it all, he grew into a sweet, wise, caring, and strong person. The most clear-headed, loving . . ."

She shook her head in deep thought for a moment. "And most importantly, he's perfect for me. I was as surprised as anyone, but I can't imagine life without him. Sam was always there for me. He has saved me so many times."

Ray's head was now bowed, hanging low, his eyes closed.

"Ray, I loved you once. We'll always have that. You were my first love, and I'll always cherish it. But Sam, he's my last love."

Ray was silent, and Lydia sat with a thundering heart. *Please accept this*, she silently begged. *Please.*

Ray took a deep breath and tossed the stick. He looked over at her, studying her, loving her, and slowly, slowly accepting what she was saying. "I've made a mess of things. I was all ready to ask you to come away with me. I wanted it, Lydia. I didn't think I did.

I've been telling myself for eighteen years that I didn't want it. But then I wanted it even more when I found out you and Sam were married. Stupid, I know. But then . . . I saw you two together." He reached out and took her hand. "I do love you. I freely and openly admit it. And I will always love you. But I see. I see it—you and Sam. You guys look great together. And your little boy. It was meant to be." He gave a soft chuckle. "Who'd a thought?"

She held him in a loving gaze. "It warms my heart to hear you say that."

He loved her enough to be happy that her heart was good. He let himself get lost in her eyes, and he felt something give. It was a slow and sad give, but also freeing.

He reached up to gently touch a strand of her hair then let his hand drop back to his lap. "I left, very stupidly, but . . . I always . . . wondered. If . . . if all you and Shane did was kiss . . . then . . .?" He couldn't finish the sentence. Couldn't articulate his question because he couldn't for the life of him figure out what the answer could be, and he wasn't altogether certain he really wanted to know.

Lydia nodded. "I need to tell you something else Ray. It will explain a lot. But before I do, I need you to know . . . I need you to know that I'm all right."

He frowned at her.

Lydia took a deep breath. "Something horrible happened. And I wanted to tell you way back then, but I couldn't. And I need you to listen now, and I need you to try to not be mad or sad or . . . I need you to just listen."

And then she began her story. The same story she'd told Phyllis back in 1964. The same story she told Sam three years after they were married. No one had told Shane, and that was just as well. Now Ray listened, his dark-blue eyes meeting hers, darting back and forth, his breath nearly stopping.

As Lydia laid out the story, telling him in a hushed tone about that night after she had come home from the fair, a shrill whistle began screaming inside of his head, growing louder and louder and louder. He gulped at the air, trying to get his breath, he grew cold and began to shiver, his throat constricted and tears rolled down his face. He clutched at Lydia's hand, and the whistle became a deafening roar, threatening to crack him into a million intractable pieces.

"I couldn't tell you," he heard her say. "He said he would bring it back on you. And I knew he would. I had to keep quiet." Her face rose up blurry and dreamlike in the moonlight. "And I couldn't tell you because you didn't need one more reason to kill him, because I knew you would. Yes, there was that. He needed to be killed."

All he could think was, *I left her. I left her. Right when she needed me the most, I left her.*

And he agreed. Westley Culpepper had needed to be killed.

Sam looked at his watch again. Eleven thirty-two. He took another deep breath, trying to calm his heart, and looked out onto the dark road. He rocked. He listened to the crickets and the tree frogs. He ran a hand across his face. He looked down at his lap and then back out at the dark road again. A lone lamp inside the hall cast a glow out onto the porch. Then he saw her. The car drove up the road, its headlights arcing toward him as she turned from the street and pulled into the driveway. She turned off the car, the lights went dark, and he watched her get out and walk toward him. The fluttering in his heart threatened to make him sick.

Then he saw her face and could see her sweet eyes upon him and he knew, and he let out a breath he hadn't realized he'd been holding, and it all settled down, like a comforting cloak covering him, warm and reassuring. She walked up to him and sat down beside him, silently laying her head on his shoulder with a deep sigh.

They rocked a few moments in the swing. "You okay?" he asked.

"Yes," she said. "Are you okay?"

He raised his arm up over her head and brought it back down across her shoulders, kissed the top of her head, and laid his cheek against her hair. "I am now."

They continued to slowly rock back and forth. "Is . . . is Ray okay?"

She took a deep breath. "He'll be fine. He understands things now."

Then she turned to him. "I love you, Sam Cooper. And thank you for loving me." She kissed him then, a full luscious kiss, the kind they still shared even after ten years of marriage and a baby, and morning bad breath, and yelling at each other about her not liking how he never picked up his dirty clothes, and about him not liking how she drove the riding mower too damn fast.

He kissed her back, and he felt his heart would burst. He sent a silent salute to the skinny little boy in the photo. *Everything will be all right*, he wanted to tell him. This here, him and her, was meant to be, and if he'd ever doubted it before, he would never doubt it again. Then he picked her up and carried her into their bedroom.

Ray drove back from River Leap in stunned silence after what Lydia had told him. He was trying his best to do what she'd asked him, to know that she was all right. But he couldn't help gripping the steering wheel and cursing every side of Westley Culpepper. He heard Lydia's words begging him again, and he took a deep breath now and gave a scornful sneer, knowing that Culpepper was long gone. She was all right, she had told him. She was all right.

But he wasn't sure if he would be. He had gotten it all so terribly, horribly wrong. He wasn't sure how, or if, he would ever get over it. He had hated her in his mind for so long after he left. And now, he hated himself. How different his life would have been if he'd just stayed and waited and asked her.

He drew in a short sob and shook his head. He had said out in Phyllis's yard tonight that he loved her, and he did. But what kind of person who really loves someone leaves them?

He slowed the car as he came up on Viola's neighborhood, but he knew he wouldn't be able to sleep, so he drove on into town and pulled up in front of Miss Lipperton's house where his dad rented a room. He parked and walked around to the back of the house and up a set of stairs. Through a second-story window he could see his dad sitting in a chair reading *Time* magazine, the table lamp casting amber shadows on the rust-colored furniture.

As with most houses in small towns, the door was unlocked, so Ray quietly let himself in, walked into the little living room, and sat down on the couch. Ollie gave him a nod, seemingly unsurprised to see the son he'd shot in the shoulder a day ago after not seeing him for eighteen years now sitting across from him.

Ray pulled a gold and harvest-green plaid pillow into his lap and looked over at his dad. "You feeling all right?"

Ollie nodded. "Got some pills or some such to take when I left the hospital. Try to keep the ol' ticker from getting so wound up." He turned a page in his magazine. "*You* feeling all right?"

Ray tested his shoulder. "I guess. Think I might've popped a couple of stitches. I got in a fight with Shane and Sam."

Ollie shook his head. "Ain't that a sight. You been gone for so long and the first thing you do when you come back is start punchin' on them."

Ray cast his dad a sardonic look. "Noooo, the first thing that happened when I came back was I got shot by my dad."

Ollie huffed. "Well, you had no cause to come by all cocky asking for that money. I gave that money to Lydia a long time ago. She come up to the house that day and she was in trouble. I knew that for sure. She needed help, so I found your money and gave it to her. I figured you were probably the cause of it anyway."

Ray hugged the pillow to his chest and let out a deep sigh in wonderment. "So, I guess that's why Lydia has been so nice to you all these years."

Ollie shrugged. "Ain't any nicer to me than any of the other ladies here in town. Don't get me wrong, Lydia's a fine gal. I'm sorry that things with you and her went south, but there's other gals for you. But Maggie down at the Catfish Grill is nice to me. And Miss Lipperton's nice to me. She was nice enough to rent me this here room. She brings me books and magazines from the library. We have supper together every once in a while. Play cards. She's a smart lady. Lula's right nice."

Ray studied his dad with a bit of mirthful surprise. "Lula?"

Ollie waved his hand at him. "Pshaw. Nothing there. As a matter of fact, she's always on me to stop drinking. Nothing but an interfering woman." And to prove his point, he reached over and grabbed the beer bottle sitting on the side table and took a sanctimonious swig.

Ray looked around the room and sighed. "So . . . you gave Lydia the money?"

"She was in a bad way. She asked for you, but you weren't around. Went on up to Mrs. Meeks."

Cradling the pillow to his chest, Ray sat with this for several moments. And then, in an attempt to understand his thinking, his heart, his life, Ray asked a desperate question to the one man who was both too stupid to know how to love right and too smart not to know the answer. "Dad, why did I leave? I loved her. But something in me . . ." He shook his head. "It's like I didn't think. I just left. Like I just jumped in the river and let the current take me."

Ollie lowered his magazine and put his bottle back over on the table. He thought for a long moment, the ticking of the clock on the wall the only sound. Finally he said, "Son, I've done wrong by you, I know that. I know a thing or two about leaving. My mamma left when I was young, and my daddy wasn't around much neither, and when he was, he wasn't a nice person. I was raised partly by an aunt and uncle. They were okay to me, I guess, although he could sometimes be a bastard to me. And then there was me getting shipped off to live with another aunt. I was about twelve, thirteen I guess. She needed help and was pretty sick, and I did a lot of tending to her." Ollie looked off into the distance, not sure if he liked bringing up these old memories. "A couple of years after living with her, she died. Next thing I know, I left there, lied about my age, and joined up in the army.

"Anyway, I didn't know anything else. And you here, you were raised in a place where your mamma left you too. I didn't leave but I, well maybe I still wasn't there. Not in the right way, I s'pect. You didn't know anything else either. Maybe it was the only thing you did know." He gave a few decisive nods. "You leaving was what you knew. Don't excuse it none, but it kinda makes sense. I guess you've done a sight better than the rest of us maybe, because it looks like you came back a better man. It's not all lost."

Ray blinked slowly, the thickness of the night beginning to weigh him down, the dim light of the room closing in on him, and the heaviness of Ollie's words seeping into him like molasses. Brown, syrupy, sweet molasses. He looked over at his dad and saw someone who was two parts mean, one part smart, and one part trying to do the best he could. Ray brought his hand up to his mouth and said, "Hmm," and felt something between reluctant acceptance and precarious affirmation begin to relax his face, then his neck, then his shoulders. "Since when have you become such a philosopher?"

Ollie harrumphed and tapped the magazine in his lap. "I know a thing or two. This here magazine's got an article about it, and I'm reading it right now. About psychology and some such. Gonna ask Lula about it next time I see her. It says here . . ."

Ray felt himself lean sideways down on the couch. He drew his legs up and scrunched the pillow up under his head and lay there listening to his father tell of some psychological research about relationships. He heard him read something about how people will have different perspectives based on what they experience, and that a perspective can be a person's reality and influence their choices. He listened long into the night, Ollie going on and on, until finally he fell asleep.

Chapter 28

1975

The next morning, Ray walked out of Miss Lipperton's house to see Lydia, Sam, and Shane standing on the front walk, obviously waiting for him to appear. Ray slowed his walk and took cautious measure of them with squinty-eyed interest.

"Don't you all have jobs or something to go to?" he asked, but there was a hint of a smile.

"We wanted to see if you were all right," Lydia said.

Ray walked up to them and took in each one of them. He had made friends over the years. He had several good partners in his business. But he could not deny the fact that these people standing in front of him were the best treasures of his life. The fact that he'd taken so long to realize that would be a thing he would ponder for the rest of his life. The fact that he'd finally figured it out would be one of his saving graces.

"Except for that punch to my nose and a kink in my neck from sleeping on Dad's couch, yeah, I'm fine. Thanks for asking." He studied them for a second. "Y'all alright?"

They nodded. "We're fine," Lydia said.

"We wanted to ask you something," Sam said. "We were hoping that you were serious about your offer for us to come out and see your place in Kentucky. If the invitation is still out there, would it be okay for us to come?"

Ray looked at him and then let the hint of the smile grow bigger. The fight last night would be brought up later, laughed at, and go down in the annals of the good ol' days. Sometimes nothing clears the air like a good knock-down drag-out.

"I'd be honored," Ray said, feeling an almost overwhelming sense of reprieve. "How soon can we plan it?"

Three weeks later, they all came, driving in one car filled with ham sandwiches, Cooper's potato chips, and a jug of ice water with four Dixie cups. After a four-and-half-hour drive, they were met by a smiling and proud Ray ready to show off his years of hard work. They were in awe of the beauty and artistry as they took a tour of the gardens and walked over hills of picturesque beauty, trees and flowers in a thousand shades of color. They had lunch in one of the on-site restaurants, asking questions about that pond and that creek, about that little waterfall, the fountains, the footpaths, the maze made of boxwood, the tree that had purple flowers on it. They praised Ray over and over until he finally told them to stop, but they didn't, and Ray loved it.

He took them to the greenhouses and had them pick out a few plants to take home. Then he took them up to his house, a large two-story, five-bedroom Tudor cottage tucked against a hill and overlooking the lake. Beautiful mature oaks, elms, and weeping willows offered lush shade; flowering bushes and, of course, hydrangeas bordered the stately structure.

They all pitched in to cook, Ray grilling steaks on the large deck, Lydia and Lorna chopping vegetables for the salad, Sam slicing and buttering garlic bread, Shane being the bartender and having fun with Ray's abundant bar. They sat in warm and cheerful companionship, enjoyed their food, and shared stories.

Shane raised his glass. "To Vail Dolyia."

They all raised their glasses and drank a toast.

"I love that name," Lydia said.

Ray lowered his drink. "Well, I'm glad to hear that. It's named after you."

Everyone went silent and looked from Ray to Lydia.

"Oh?" said Lydia.

"Well, it's named after both you and Viola, actually. I took all the letters of both your names, jumbled them up, smushed them together, and came up with Vail Dolyia." Ray looked over at Sam and Lydia. "I hope . . . that's okay."

"I think," Sam said, "that's about the coolest thing I ever heard."

Lydia's face broke into an appreciative smile. "Thank you."

Ray smiled. "Viola sure was tickled about it."

They finished their meal, cleaned up, and wandered back out to the deck and leaned on the railing to watch the sunset over the lake.

"Almost as pretty as the Current River," Shane murmured, looking out on the view.

They all nodded. "Best river ever," Sam said.

"The best," Ray agreed. "So many good days spent on that river."

"It's like it runs in our veins, you know?" Lydia said. "The Current is part of us."

"You all talk so warmly about the river and all of it," Lorna said. "I love to hear all the fun stories."

"It was mostly all good," Shane said and looked down into his drink. "Except for this particular dumb-ass deputy."

"Whatever happened to him?" Lorna asked.

"I don't know, but we all wanted to kill him," Shane said.

Ray and Shane and Sam and Lydia looked at one another.

"No one knows," Sam finally said.

"Just disappeared one day," Lydia said. "So I'm told."

"It's been a long time. Surely he's dead," Sam said.

"Surely," Ray said.

Shane studied the group, not exactly sure that everyone was telling the truth, but seeing Sam's level gaze upon him, he let it go. "I guess we'll never know," he said.

They looked out to see the last pink and peach-colored sun rays just above the horizon, casting their group in a warm glow. The day would end, but it wouldn't be the end of their days together. It had been a long road for all of them, but here and now in this moment on Ray's deck with all of them together, they knew nothing would ever draw them apart again.

Chapter 29

1964

Ray and Sam and Lydia and Shane never found out what had happened to Westley Culpepper. They only knew he was gone, and they were hopeful he would stay away for good.

He would.

Perhaps it was best that the killing, such as it was, had gone to Phyllis. The younger ones' souls were protected that way, not having to carry around the weight of such a thing into their older years. At her age, Phyllis was old enough and strong enough to carry the weight and, in fact, did not mind it at all. She had no qualms about taking advantage of an opportunity presented so conveniently before her. Indeed, it had quite literally been laid at her feet. As for Phyllis's soul, it would be just fine.

Phyllis came up to the top ledge of the cliffs several weeks after Lydia had told her what Westley had done. River Leap had, after all, been part of Lydia's story, and here she sat and tried to clear her head and think of what to do, because of course something had to be done. She had never even been to the top of River Leap before that fateful day. She went up there early that morning, the sun not yet up but teasing a gray flinty blush along the horizon. A still, unmoving veil of fog lay low on the river. She heard the soft, peaceful rustle of the water, the current rippling over stones on the far side of the shore, seeming to whisper to her that she was right where she needed to be. She heard right below her the almost imperceptible gurgle of the cold green water sucking into small whirlpools above the dark boulder maze beneath the water.

For the first few days after Lydia had shared what Westley had done to her, Phyllis had burned with rage. She could have easily killed him in the heat of her fury, a butcher knife lying at easy reach on the kitchen counter as she stood in Melva Dean's kitchen when Westley had come into the house. She had come to talk with Melva Dean a few days after Lydia had gone back to Columbia, not sure what she would say, but she needed to do some kind of covert research to try to learn what Melva Dean knew. She found not exactly what she was looking for, but supportive evidence just the same, when she spied a black eye that Melva Dean had camouflaged with makeup. It was as plain as Melva Dean's face that Westley's bullying ran deep.

Phyllis had let the butcher knife lie untouched. She had cooled herself standing there in the kitchen, spoken to Westley through gritted teeth, and somehow gotten herself out of the house. She had later thought about running him down with her car, the red-and-white Bel Air being an easy weapon to take down the lowly deputy right there on Main Street, but reason prevailed. And soon, although the rage still burned furiously, something within her cooled to an icy bastion. It fortified her and made her stronger in her mission. There would be a time, she knew, and she would watch and wait.

She knew now why Lydia had not wanted to go to the Sunday dinners at the step-grandparents' house. Phyllis was now the one who sat at those dinners barely able to chew her food. She watched as Westley shoveled food into his mouth, told his stupid jokes, and posed as God's gift to the town. It made her sick. She wondered who else out there were his victims, because she knew there were more. A bully was a bully until he was stopped. And he needed to be stopped.

Her chance came a few months after Lydia's visit, when Westley appeared before her in the dim light of that morning as she sat on the top ledge of River Leap. They were both equally surprised, Westley taking a step sideways as she came into view.

"What in tarnation, Phyllis! What the hell you doing up here?"

"What are you doing up here?" she countered.

Westley looked over his shoulder, then back at her. "I come up here occasionally, doing rounds. I park my car out on Route K and walk in. I'm quiet that way and can sneak up on anybody out here doing what they're not supposed to do. This place can be a pit of sin and bedlam, ya know. Caught the Wallace boys out here early one morning, skinning a deer they'd caught out of season. That was a nice find." He chuckled.

She gazed at him with a controlled assessment that surprised even her. The fact that she didn't jump up and slap him full on the face was a testament to her strength. She gave a small smile that anyone—mainly Westley if he'd taken time to study—would have seen was a sneer swimming in a lethal concoction of composure and mania.

Whether he saw or not will never be known. He stepped closer to Phyllis and placed one foot up next to her on the rock where she sat. He hunkered down closer to her and rested his forearm on his thigh.

"My dear little sister-in-law, you aren't up here doing anything you're not supposed to be doing, are ya?"

She sat very still. "And what would that be?" she asked.

Westley shrugged. "Smoking dope. Skinning a deer. Meeting a lover." He gave a chuckle at what he thought was his cleverness.

"You raped my daughter."

Westley froze. A barred owl from across the river called out a morning song—*Who cooks for you? Who cooks for you?* The current below continued its soft rustle over the river stones.

In one smooth motion, Phyllis stood. Who's to say whether it was more Westley tripping or more Phyllis pushing? In any case, as Westley tried to stand straight, he took a step backward onto the edge of the rock ledge, teetering for a second, then losing his balance. Sensing in a split second the horror of his unmistakable trajectory, his arms flung out, his eyes went wide, and he tumbled over backward off of the cliff. He crashed into the river with a heavy splash, but not before cracking his head on a rock that was just above the water. Knocked out cold, he sank into the river, folding backward over himself into the crevice of the underwater boulders.

Phyllis brought her hand up to her lips with a mixture of alarm and dismay. For the next few moments she stood at the top of the cliff and watched and waited. Had anybody else seen this? Her eyes cast out across the river, then down along both sides of the riverbanks. She could swear the thundering of her heart could be heard clear up and down the river valley. She waited in silence. Looking, waiting, looking. She saw no one.

She also did not see a body resurface. She craned her neck outward to look at the spot where he'd gone in, and down along the river. Nothing. Now even the ripples caused when Westley's body had hit the river were starting to smooth out, blending with the normal river current. Nothing.

She would wonder later: Had it indeed been a killing, or simply a fall?

The sun was now starting to shine in the dim morning, yellow rays streaming horizontally through the trees and beginning to burn off the thin layer of fog. More birds could be heard chirping their early morning songs. There were no whispers to her from the river now, but as it continued to flow down the valley in contented repose, its clean, cool current offered up a blessing of sorts. Watching it, Phyllis slowly allowed her shoulders and neck to relax.

Looking once more out across the beautiful Current River, its shimmers now beginning to sparkle in the new day's sunlight, her heart slowed to a manageable pace. Phyllis turned, took hold of a craggy bush to maintain her foothold, stepped across the flat rock ledges on trembling knees, and walked back down to her car. She got in, put both hands over her mouth for a moment, drawing in deep breaths, then reached down and turned her key and put it in drive. With hands gripping the red steering wheel, she drove out of the park, down Route K, past Deputy Culpepper's car parked alongside the road, past the houses where Viola and her friends lived.

She drove with a tremor in her body. Had she just played God? Had she just done to Westley what she hated him for doing to others? She didn't know how to answer. Perhaps the question didn't need to be asked.

She drove into town and went over to Melva Dean's house where they sat and had a cup of coffee, two sisters-in-law enjoying a morning chat. She happened to mention that she saw Westley's car parked out on Route K. Melva Dean said she'd call it in. Upon leaving, Phyllis told Melva Dean that any time she needed help watching her boys, to let her know. Then she drove to her house, walked into the living room where her husband sat, her sweet Russell, and gave him a loving peck on the cheek.

She would fix him bacon and eggs for breakfast, and also later fry some chicken, heating the Crisco in the cast-iron skillet and peppering it just the way he liked it. He was a good man, and she was thankful he was in her life.

Later, they might go out for a drive, they might meet some friends up at River Leap to eat cold fried chicken and sliced cantaloupe. They would tip their toes in the cool river water and laugh and splash and enjoy the day.

Phyllis would carry on with life because that's what you do. Later the next year, she would be happy when Lydia would tell her she and Sam were engaged. She would be even happier when Lydia would tell her they were moving back to Westfall. A few years after that, she would delight in her new grandson, Cody Cooper. There was a lot more living for Phyllis to do, and knowing that her daughter was safe and loved, she would indeed take delight in all of it.

The Current River would continue to be the site of fun and memories to families visiting River Leap Park to picnic and swim, splashing and embracing the cool relief from hot summer days. When Ray would come back to town, he and Shane and Sam would go up to the tall rocks and look out across the beautiful scene, and though it wouldn't be quite the same, it was very close to a time when three boys loved and trusted one another. The river current would continue to run strong and powerful, clear in the shallow parts, green and ghostly in the deep parts, hiding all manner of secrets.

About the Author

M. Lee Martin was born in Missouri and has been writing since third grade when she made high marks for book reports that were actually of stories she wrote herself. She earned her bachelors and obtained a graduate certification in Positive Psychology at University of Missouri, Columbia.

Ms. Martin developed a deep love and connection with the beautiful Missouri Ozarks—especially the Current River. *River Current* is her first published novel, with more entertaining stories already in progress. In addition to writing, the author relishes time spent with family and friends, without which there would be no stories.